My Long List of Impossible Things

MICHELLE BARKER

annick press
toronto · berkeley

Annick Press Ltd.

We acknowledge the support of the Canada Council for the Arts and the Ontario
Arts Council, and the participation of the Government of Canada/la participation du
gouvernement du Canada for our publishing activities.

Library and Archives Canada Cataloguing in Publication

Title: My long list of impossible things / Michelle Barker
Names: Barker, Michelle, 1964- author.
Identifiers: Canadiana (print) 20190185368 | Canadiana (ebook)
20190185376 | ISBN 9781773213651
   (hardcover) | ISBN 9781773213644 (softcover) | ISBN
9781773213682 (PDF) | ISBN 9781773213668
   (EPUB) | ISBN 9781773213675 (Kindle)Classification: LCC
PS8603.A73557 M92 2020 | DDC jC813/.6—dc23

Published in the U.S.A. by Annick Press (U.S.) Ltd.
Distributed in Canada by University of Toronto Press.
Distributed in the U.S.A. by Publishers Group West.

Printed in Canada

annickpress.com
michellebarker.ca

Also available as an e-book. Please visit annickpress.com/ebooks for more details.

"*If only it were all so simple! If only there were evil people somewhere insidiously committing evil deeds, and it were necessary only to separate them from the rest of us and destroy them. But the line dividing good and evil cuts through the heart of every human being. And who is willing to destroy a piece of his own heart?*"

—Aleksandr Solzhenitsyn

"*I love those who yearn for the impossible.*"

—Johann Wolfgang von Goethe

For my mother,
and in memory of her mother and sisters—
an incredible group of women.

This is not their story, but it could have been.

GERMANY,
1945

CHAPTER ONE

EVERYTHING IS TO REMAIN AS IT IS

It was early March, drizzle-cold, and the world outside our window was noisy. Military vehicles rumbled down the road, and refugees and displaced Germans created a constant traffic from the east, their wagons overloaded with pots and blankets.

My older sister, Hilde, burst into the house trailing a conversation behind her like an unraveling scarf. "They say Ivan is getting closer. They say—"

"That's enough." Mutti was in the kitchen taking bread out of the oven. "And you will please lower your voice. Katja is practicing."

But I'd heard. Ivan was the Soviets. That was what everyone called them—as if they were one man, the size of an entire army, wearing giant *kirza* boots.

Hilde wandered into the sitting room. "Don't you have anything better to do?"

"Who told you that?" I asked quietly. "About Ivan?"

"A girl. I don't know. I don't ask their names anymore."

Right. It was like naming barn cats. You called them Cat or Mouser, and then your heart didn't get broken every time they moved on. But I always asked their names. A name could be held on your tongue, like chocolate.

A name can dissolve. I didn't want to think about that, but sitting at my piano working on the *Moonlight* Sonata, it was difficult not to.

I persisted. "What did she say?"

"Nothing," Hilde said. "It's nothing to worry about."

"Stop treating me like a baby." I was sixteen—old enough, I felt, to know the truth about what was going on.

That morning I'd heard the radio, before Mutti had shut it off. "Everything is to remain as it is," the Nazi *Gauleiter* announced. "The German population is in no immediate danger." I wanted to believe him, but his voice was full of forced calm—like we were panicked horses a startle away from bolting. Even I could tell the people from the east were fleeing their homes. Was the danger like typhus? Would it spread?

Hilde went back to lingering by the side door, waiting for the postman—these days we never knew when he'd show up— while I practiced the opening arpeggios of the *Moonlight's* third movement in the right hand. The first bars were charged with fury, hard to play without my fingers getting tangled. It took up enough of my attention that I could ignore my sister's smug look: *I'm waiting for a love letter. All you can do is play that stupid piano.*

Hilde was like a planet; the force of gravity around her drew men in. She was taller than I was, and prettier, and had nicer hair.

Even the postman was in love with her, and he was at least sixty years old. I'd never had a boyfriend. But what did I care? A piano didn't run off to war hoping for a fancy belt buckle that said *Gott mit uns*—God with us—like Hilde's boyfriend did.

"Beethoven wasn't pleased with this sonata," Herr Goldstein had told me during one of our lessons. It was winter and the cellar was especially cold. He'd brought down a mug of warm water for my hands, and we both kept our coats on. A yellow Star of David was sewn conspicuously across his. "He considered it inferior to his other pieces for piano."

"How could he think that?" I said. "It's the best sonata he ever wrote."

"I agree." My piano teacher gave one of his theatrical shrugs. "But an artist is rarely satisfied with his own work. Look at you, how hard you are on yourself."

The memory was even sweeter than the smell of Mutti's bread. He had called me an artist.

But I was an artist with small hands. Anything more than an octave reach was too much of a stretch, so Herr Goldstein had doctored up the sonata, crossing off nonessential notes to make the bigger chords manageable.

"For God's sake, stop playing the same bits over and over," Hilde shouted from the door. "You'll make us all crazy."

"It's called practicing," I said. "It's how you get better."

When the postman arrived, she stepped outside and asked, "Anything for me?"

"No, my dear. I'm sorry," he said in a softened voice.

I didn't know why she bothered waiting for mail anymore. There hadn't been a letter from her boyfriend, Paul, in months.

These days most mail arrived in black-bordered envelopes, like the news of Papi's death. The postman had the worst job, handing over those envelopes and watching people's faces crumple. Papi's farm jacket still hung in the closet—smelling like the hay fields, expecting his return.

Hilde's skinny, pimpled boyfriend, Paul: if he was all that stood between us and the Soviets, we were in trouble.

Mutti darkened the doorway between the kitchen and sitting room. "The bedsheets should be ready for scrubbing now."

I groaned. Washing bedsheets was a three-day chore. They'd been soaking in soapy water since yesterday, in gigantic pots in the pig kitchen.

Hilde glared at me. "Today you're helping."

"Herr Goldstein said it's not good for my hands," I said.

"Herr Goldstein isn't your teacher anymore."

"Hilde." Mutti gave her a pointed look. Herr Goldstein was one of those names that silenced a room and made everyone pretend to be busy.

"And I don't care about your *delicate* hands." Hilde flicked her long hair back. "You didn't make her help yesterday," she said to Mutti. "It's not fair."

Hilde was eighteen, but my piano playing reduced her to a whiny five-year-old.

"All you did yesterday was boil the water," I said. "You didn't need my help."

"All you did was play the same notes you're playing today," Hilde said. "You're not even getting any better."

"Shut up. That's not true."

"Girls." The dirty washrag was in Mutti's hand. One of us

would get it in a second. "You will help this morning, Katja. The piano isn't going anywhere."

I wanted to work on putting the right and left hands together in the opening bars, but I would have to do it later. I rose reluctantly, exchanged my house shoes for wooden clogs, and went outside. The winter snow had melted and the ground was thawing, but the world was in that in-between stage where everything looked brown and bare and smelled like sour chicken shit. The mud sucked at my clogs as I crossed the small yard to our barn.

The pig kitchen was dim and cold and smelled of the boiled potatoes we cooked for the pigs. A hint of manure lingered from the other side of the barn, even with the door closed. Three large buckets in the middle of the room held the soaking bedsheets. In a corner sat a basket of potatoes from last year's harvest.

Mutti brought out the washboards and we began scrubbing. The bedsheets were heavy when they were wet. After ten minutes my arms ached. Mutti used to sing when she worked, but that was before Papi had been killed. Now she just worked, hair pulled tight into a bun, face pulled tighter with determination. The back-and-forth scrubbing reminded me of the dull noise of marching soldiers.

"Ach, Katarina, do a better job," Mutti said. "It's all for nothing if they don't come out clean."

Hilde gave me one of her looks. "I'm not redoing the sheets because of you."

There was a blur of sound in the background, as if the crowd on the road had swelled. I heard it, then set it aside, more concerned about how I would practice the piece I was preparing for Mutti's birthday without her finding out. It was by Schumann, her favorite composer, from a collection of *Lieder* Herr Goldstein had given me.

Suddenly the blurred sound clarified into shouts and shooting. Panic rose like fire on Mutti's face. "Stop. Stop the washing."

We crowded around the small window. Soldiers with rifles ran across the field, noise exploding everywhere. Our neighbor stood beside his cows with his hands in the air.

My whole body prickled. "But the *Gauleiter* said . . ." Everything was to remain as it was. Wasn't that why we were washing the sheets?

Mutti rushed us across the soggy yard and into the still-warm kitchen without even changing her shoes. She pulled the portrait of Hitler off the wall and threw it behind the compost pot. Supporting Hitler was one of those things we'd been pretending about for years. You pretended, or you got in trouble.

"Into the attic." She was shoving us out of the kitchen when three soldiers burst through the front door—the door reserved for guests. They wore long coats, heavy boots, and helmets. Eyes wild, breathing hard, they pointed their rifles at us and my heart thudded into my knees.

Mutti grabbed a cookie sheet and held it in front of us like a shield.

"*Nemetski?*" one soldier asked.

Mutti looked confused. "We are German."

The soldiers stomped through the house in their muddy boots, opening closets and cupboards, rattling the cups and saucers of Mutti's coffee sets—the ones with a man and woman having a picnic under a willow tree. One of them found the piano and leaned on an octave of bass notes with his forearm.

Another pointed at me. "Papa here?"

"*Nee*," I said.

Beside me Mutti stiffened. *Don't speak out.* It was one of her wartime rules. But surely the soldiers would figure it out. There were no men left in the village anymore except grandfathers and young boys.

"My husband will be back soon," Mutti said in a confident voice.

When a soldier put out his cigarette on the floor, I grimaced. *Savages.*

The men found a bottle of Papi's schnapps, cheered, and took it outside. We watched from the window as they opened the barn doors and fence gates, and our cows, pigs, and chickens filed out onto the road. There went our milk, meat, eggs—and not just ours. Mutti sold food at the market in town.

"If Ivan is here, that means the war is almost over, doesn't it?" Hilde asked in a quiet voice.

"Almost over," Mutti said. "And just beginning."

A wave of unease rose inside me. I waited for her to tell us it was time to go back to the bedsheets. I was chilled, my sleeves still damp from the washing. The fire in the grate had gone cold.

The door burst open again. "Out," said a soldier. He tapped the gold ladies' watch on his arm and held up ten fingers. Then he left.

"What does he mean, out?" I said.

But Mutti was already on her way to the kitchen. "We have ten minutes. Take only what you can carry, and only the important things. Clothes, food. Nothing frivolous. Hurry."

"But why are they making us leave?" I said.

"They have guns," Mutti said. "They don't need a reason."

I felt dizzy. Out meant out. "We can't walk away and leave

everything behind." I'd never lived anywhere except in this house. I knew all its bumps and corners by heart.

Hilde glanced at Mutti. "We'll be back soon. Right?"

"It's only temporary," Mutti said.

Outside our window people passed with their horses and wagons, the women riding with the children, the men walking alongside waving long sticks to keep the horses moving. Only temporary? Their wagons were so stuffed it was a wonder they didn't topple over.

Mutti rushed around gathering food. I was surprised to see she already had a bag packed with photographs and clothes—things she must have prepared in advance.

"Where will we go?" I asked.

"I'm sure Aunt Ilse and Uncle Otto will take us in until this blows over," she said. Like a storm, or the smell from the fields when the manure had been spread. She handed us each a bowl and cup, a fork, a shawl. She wrapped up the bread she'd made that morning, and packed all the salami.

I ran to the piano and grabbed my book of Beethoven sonatas, and the book of Schumann's *Lieder* Herr Goldstein had entrusted to me before he'd gone away. *You'll take care of it for me*, he'd said.

"No, Katja, they're too heavy," Mutti said. "You'll have to choose one."

My heart argued with me back and forth. It was like choosing which kitten to save.

Hilde stood there with her hands on her hips. "What will you do with piano music but no piano?" She always said she was the one God had given all the common sense to.

No piano. I had stepped away from it so easily that morning.

You never knew when something would happen for the last time. If you did, you'd cling to every precious second. I stuffed Herr Goldstein's book into my bag and then eyed the piano—the most immovable instrument of all time—as if there were some way of bringing it. How did you fit a lifetime onto your back? You folded it and folded it until your life was so small it took up almost no space. Out of impulse, I snatched the doily from on top of the piano and stuffed it into my pocket.

I went to the bedroom Hilde and I shared, put on my second dress and my sweater, and packed socks, underclothes, and a blanket. Then I put on my coat. Out of the corner of my eye I saw Hilde pack a hairbrush and the pictures of fancy city clothes she'd cut out of catalogs and pinned onto our bedroom walls. I suspected Paul's love letters were already in her bag.

Our two beds sat side by side near a tall *Kachelöfen*. During winter we filled it with wood and coal until the ceramic tile radiated heat and made our room as warm as a cave. On the window there were green curtains—beside the ugly blackout curtains—and through it I could see the pond was thawing.

Mutti stood waiting for us at the side door. She fastened a bucket to my rucksack, stuffed our pockets with food, and said, "We have to go."

None of us wanted to take that first step out the door.

"Hold your head up," Mutti said, leading the way. "We'll leave with dignity, if nothing else."

"Who's going to milk the cows while we're gone?" I asked. The cows would come back to the barn when it was time for milking. They would call out, and be upset if no one came to relieve them of all that milk.

But Mutti didn't answer my question.

"The rhododendrons and lilacs will need a layer of compost." Hilde's voice trembled.

We walked past the pond where a willow trailed its branches in the water like hair; past the vegetable garden, the soil not yet turned for spring. I heard Hilde's heart break. It was a delicate sound, the sheen of ice on a puddle shattering and sinking.

I was surprised to hear Mutti singing. "All the birds are already here." It was a song about spring.

I made myself respond, "All the birds, all." When I was younger I used to put my ear to the earth to listen to it wake up. As the thaw began, I swore I could hear the soil stretch with relief. But this year the ground had been shaken awake by soldiers' boots and, farther away, by bombs and tanks.

Papi had planted two pear trees in the front yard for us girls. I wrapped my arms around one of the rough trunks. I wanted to believe we would come back, to know it the way I knew the return of summer.

"Blackbirds, thrushes, finches, and starlings." Mutti's voice cracked. "Come, Katja. You must make yourself brave."

I tightened my grip on the tree. It was Hilde who eased me away, her arms around me, guiding me as Mutti closed the small wooden gate behind us. It shut with a click.

CHAPTER TWO

OVER. AFTER. NEVER.

The *Autobahn* would have been the most direct route to Aunt Ilse and Uncle Otto's place, but it was full of tanks. We took a smaller road, lined with pine trees and jammed full of people like us. I recognized several from our town, including the butcher and his wife. Farmers walked with their cows. Others pushed things in heavy carts that were trussed like Christmas geese. My heart ached at what we had left behind. There hadn't been time to pack up a cart, and Mutti wouldn't have let us anyway.

"Look how they're struggling through the mud," she said to us quietly.

The bucket banged a hundred times against my back. One hundred steps. Or rather, one hundred *more* steps away from home. "The piano will still be there when we're allowed to go back, right?"

Hilde and Mutti exchanged a look.

"The war is almost over," I added. Surely we'd go home again. Even the dogs on the road must have thought so, the way they kept looking behind them.

"Stop making that face," Hilde said. "Of all the things you could be upset about. It's only a piano."

"What do you know about that?" I said. "All you care about is your hair."

All at once the air filled with a sharp scream and Mutti pulled us behind the trees. *Make yourself invisible*: it was another wartime rule. A *Tiefflieger* came out of nowhere, flying barely higher than the trees and shooting at everything. People on the road scattered, ran, fell. I gripped Mutti's hand. The war wasn't on the radio anymore; it didn't echo in empty houses or arrive in black-bordered envelopes. It was right here in front of us.

After that, we chose a narrow path through the fields and forests, sticking together with a group of people—some we knew, many we didn't. The air smelled of smoke and unwashed socks.

When school had still been on, a map of Europe was pinned to our classroom wall showing Germany conquering other countries. The way our teachers had talked about *Lebensraum*, living space, I'd always pictured Germany as a big man flexing his muscles in a small room. The line of pins on the map would advance five centimeters in this direction, and five in that one. Not once did our teachers show the line moving backward, the great German army retreating.

That first night the group of us slept in the hayloft of an abandoned barn. I was slipping off my shoes when the butcher's wife said, "No. Leave them on."

"Why? I don't want to sleep with my shoes on."

"Someone might steal them," Hilde said.

But that night, huddled against my mother and sister in the farthest corner of the loft, we heard gunfire and Russian voices and I understood: you slept with your shoes on in case you needed to run.

After three more days of walking, I couldn't help but ask, "How much farther? Where do Aunt Ilse and Uncle Otto live again?"

"Fahlhoff," Mutti said. She'd brought a letter with the address on it.

It might as well have been China, or the moon—it was farther than I wanted to walk. My feet knew it. Even my shoes were ready to give up.

"I think it's silly to go all the way to Fahlhoff," I said. Especially if we were just waiting for this to blow over. "Why can't we stay somewhere closer?"

"Luckily, no one has asked for your opinion," Mutti said, "so you will please keep it tucked in your pocket where it won't do any harm."

Fine. I didn't want to think about Fahlhoff, some German city in the middle of who-knew-where (I knew where: a place I didn't want to go), or Aunt Ilse, who anyway wasn't even our aunt and didn't know we were coming. Guess how happy she'd be to see us. Three more mouths to feed, and *who are you again?* Distant relatives, which didn't count for much when there was no food anywhere and millions of people were wandering the countryside with nowhere to go. All the Aunt Ilses in the world must have cringed every time there was a knock at their door.

"Ilse will be relieved to know we're alive," Mutti said. "She and I were very close when we were youngsters. We used to play Piggy on the Ladder together in the hayloft."

Mutti with her no-nonsense bun, her lips pursed, scrubbing milk churns or covered in flour—I couldn't imagine her as a little girl playing a game with string. She had talked to us often about Ilse, because Ilse and her husband owned a clothing shop. I was curious to meet someone whose idea of dressing up meant more than taking off her apron.

Hilde wasn't just curious; she was thrilled. "Will Aunt Ilse have Paris fashions? Will she let us borrow them, do you think?"

"Stop making that face," I said. "They're only clothes."

I worried we wouldn't be fancy enough for Ilse, but that was a problem for Tomorrow-Katja. Today-Katja had other things on her mind.

"You know what I really want?" I said.

"Here we go," said Hilde.

"I want a wristwatch." I'd seen them on Soviet soldiers: their serious field uniforms with the fancy shoulder boards, their caps with the Red Star emblem, the rifles and tall black boots—and five ladies' wristwatches lined all the way up one arm.

"You need a wristwatch like a toad needs a waistcoat," Mutti said. "A farmer works by the sun. When it rises, you get out of bed—end of story. A wristwatch is pure silliness."

"That's why I want one." Something dainty, so I could turn my arm and pretend to check the time while admiring the way it looked on my wrist. A farmer didn't wear a watch, but a concert pianist did. Perhaps a pocket watch, with a long gold chain disappearing into my pocket like a secret. It would tick against my chest like a second heartbeat. "Not just one. Two, three wristwatches," I said. "I'd wear them all at once. I'd set one on Berlin time, one for London, and one for New York City."

"*Dummkopf*." Hilde's cheeks went red. "As if you'll ever perform in New York City. Herr Goldstein must have given you that idea."

I was ready to shout at her, but Mutti laughed. "The cows would be grateful. You'd be on time to milk them for a change." She put a hand on my shoulder. "Your sister didn't mean anything by it."

But I saw Hilde's face.

"Anyway," Hilde said, "we don't need to know the time anymore. What time is it? Over. It's after. It's never. You don't need a wristwatch to tell you that. Just look around."

"That's quite enough." Mutti took out the nettles we'd gathered that morning, held them upside down, and removed the stinging hairs with one hand. Then she passed us each a handful of leaves. Hilde portioned hers out, but I ate mine all at once. Even though they tasted like spinach, I imagined they were a big bite of cheese, or bacon, things I hadn't eaten in days.

I reached for Mutti. Hilde mouthed *baby* and walked by herself, but ever since we'd left home I'd been happy to hold Mutti's hand. Her hands were strong from years of churning butter and washing bedsheets and, after Papi was gone to war, mending fences and guiding the horse plow.

We were back on a proper road again, the conversations around us mostly about food. I composed a list in my head of the things I actually wanted:

- my piano, obviously

- to go home again

- a new pair of shoes

- rabbit stew, oh, rabbit stew—the way Mutti made it, turning it into a feast, with sauces and braised this and sautéed that. I imagined us sitting at the dining room table with her favorite Schumann *Lieder* playing on the radio and the midday sun shining right on her pretty coffee set. *Eat your fill, girls,* she would say. We would eat so much we'd have to nap afterward.

- also my own coffee set, but not yet. When I was older and was getting married. To Jacob? Maybe—if I ever found him again.

In the distance, I spied something hanging from a tree branch. I was surprised no one had stolen it. As we drew closer, my skin went cold: it was a body. Closer still, the body of a boy with long thin legs. He couldn't have been any older than I was. I thought of Jacob, and that feeling, the one I'd been fighting ever since we'd left home, came rushing back—as if I'd tripped, but hadn't yet caught myself before falling.

A sign around the boy's neck read, *This is what happens to cowards.*

CHAPTER THREE

MEN WITH KNIVES

The boy wore a black and red armband that marked him as a member of the *Volkssturm*—the young boys and old men who'd been rounded up since October and were ordered to fight, with outdated weapons and no training. People in our town had called it an execution rather than an army.

The breeze made the rope creak like an old floor. Something black stuck out from between the boy's teeth. I realized with disgust that it was the tip of his tongue. His lips were blue, his face pale, and his hands—a dark red—were clenched tight.

"Look away," Mutti said to me, but I couldn't.

"Why did they put that sign on him?"

"He probably tried to desert," she said. "Those boys were so young."

And someone called him a coward? "I'm taking the sign off."

"No, you mustn't touch him," Mutti said. "If anyone sees . . ."

I took out my pocketknife, my grip tighter than it needed to be.

The butcher, Herr Schiffer, limped over with his wife. He had a clubfoot, like Reichsminister Goebbels, so he hadn't fought in the war. I wasn't used to seeing him away from the butcher shop, and without his apron on. *Men with knives.* I put that thought back in its box.

Herr Schiffer eyed my hand. "Tell your daughter to leave the soldier alone," he said to Mutti, even though I was standing right there.

"The sign is disrespectful," I said to him, "and it's wrong."

Mutti looked like she wanted to fling a dirty washrag at me for voicing my opinion. Luckily she'd left it at home.

"Fräulein, we have not had the luxury of deciding right from wrong for some time now." Herr Schiffer's brusque manner had always scared me, the way he'd squint and size things up, in his bloodstained apron. He acted like everything could be chopped into pieces and wrapped in brown paper.

I strode over to the dead boy, avoiding Mutti's arm that tried to stop me, and checking right and left for German soldiers. The smell nearly made me gag. *Don't touch anything.* I cut the twine, pulled the wooden sign off his chest, and threw it as hard as I could into the nearby field.

So many words had been turned upside down over the past six years of war. To me it seemed like the bravest act in the world to refuse to do something if it was wrong. I was a more traditional coward, afraid to kill and skin the rabbits on our farm. Hilde was the one who did that job; she never minded getting bloody. Also, when I was younger, I hadn't liked going to the outhouse alone in the dark, but that was because of Hilde and her stories. *There are men with knives hiding under your bed,* she used to tell me, *and if you hang your legs over the side they'll cut off your feet.* I would jump from my bed as far as I could, hoping the men's weapons were more like bread knives and less like scythes, and I'd run all the way to the outhouse. I wasn't scared anymore, but I still didn't like going in the dark.

Mutti yanked me back toward the road, where Hilde stood with her arms crossed. Behind her was a deep ditch that none of us would look at.

"Stop being so pigheaded," my sister said, "or you'll get us all in trouble." She went to walk with some older girls, but Mutti made me stay behind.

"What have I been telling you all this time?" she asked.

"Don't speak out, don't touch anything, make yourself invisible," I repeated. Silence and invisibility had protected us for the past six years.

"We will survive this war by being lucky," Mutti said, "but luck is something you make." She gathered me in her arms. Normally she smelled like cloves and rosemary, but that was a kitchen scent from home, and we were many smells removed from there. For the last fifty kilometers we'd been at sticky sweat. I wondered if I smelled as bad as she did.

She let go of me and we walked together. *Pretend the ditch isn't there.*

"Does Aunt Ilse have a piano?" I asked.

"If she doesn't, we'll find you one." She patted my hand. "Fahlhoff is much bigger than our town. Someone will have a piano."

"And a teacher?"

"I'm sure there'll be plenty of women in Fahlhoff like Frau Erdmann."

"I didn't mean her," I said. "I meant Herr Goldstein."

Mutti acted as if she hadn't heard me. Frau Erdmann had been my official teacher, but my real piano lessons happened once a week, in secret, at Herr Goldstein's house. His son, Jacob, was always home studying. He wanted to become a doctor. Sometimes when I finished my lesson, I caught Jacob standing outside the cellar—though the room was almost completely soundproof.

But he was two years older than I was. The conversations we had, which had meant everything to me, had probably meant nothing to him. Still, I couldn't think of the piano without thinking of the Goldsteins.

Three years ago they had moved to Poland, and though I wrote to Herr Goldstein, I never heard from him again. Someone else moved into their home. No one spoke about it. Whenever I asked Mutti, she would say she didn't know what had happened to them. But my mother—candid in every other way—wouldn't look at me when she said it. Frau Erdmann wouldn't let me play the Mendelssohn Scherzo that Herr Goldstein and I had been working on. It was better that no one heard it from an open window, she said. So I'd played it at home with the windows closed.

"We'll ask Aunt Ilse about a teacher when we get there," Mutti said finally. "She'll know someone."

The borscht ladies—four round women from a neighboring town who did nothing but talk about how to make the perfect borscht—called Mutti over and she went to walk with them. One carried a cage with a small yellow bird in it that refused to sing. In my head I rehearsed Mendelssohn's Scherzo, a piece that reminded me of approaching rain.

Whatever happened, I swore I would not grow up to be a woman who fixated on soup. I would be a concert pianist, maybe play with orchestras or in a chamber music group. The world I walked through said, *Orchestras? Chamber music? There is no such thing.*

I went over Herr Goldstein's recital rules:

- Memorize the music so well you can start it from any section.

- Stand tall and proud when you walk onstage.

- Tie your hair back so it doesn't fall into your eyes while you're playing.

- Wear shoes that don't give you blisters . . .

. . . unlike the ones I was wearing right now that I wanted to rip off and throw into the deep ditch beside the road. *Don't look.*

I looked. I couldn't help it. The ditch was full of people—all dead. Some of them had their eyes wide open, as if they couldn't believe what had happened to them. Their bodies were puffed up, their skin as purple as the eggplant in our garden last summer. The smell of rot choked me—though *smell* was the wrong word for what it was. It was more like a wall that pressed itself against my nose and mouth until I couldn't breathe.

Less than a week ago, death had been a word received in an envelope bordered in black. Now it had a smell, and a color. Now it had eyes. *This war has turned normal people into savages.* It was a thought I'd had too many times on this journey.

Daffodils bloomed nearby. Even they were pretending they couldn't see what surrounded them.

I couldn't help thinking of Papi, dead now for two years—a hero's death, the letter had told us, as if that made any difference. He'd never wanted any part of the war; he hadn't even voted for Hitler. But he spoke Russian, they needed him, and it wasn't the sort of thing you could say *no* to. Anyway, whether you were a hero or not, dead was dead. We'd never said a proper goodbye to him. Mutti didn't even know where he was buried—or if he was buried.

My aching feet. My empty stomach.

My empty stomach. My aching feet.

Mutti was well into a discussion about whether or not a proper borscht should contain meat, so I caught up to Hilde and the other girls. They weren't paying attention to the ditches. They were talking about the film star Hans Albers. He was dreamy—*no, too fat*—and the controversial Hedy Lamarr who, *shh*, showed her naked body on camera. *Did she really?—Yes, my cousin's aunt's neighbor's friend* saw the film in Hamburg-Munich-Berlin-Some-where.

"Paul and I used to walk to the beach together," Hilde told the girls.

My shoulder grazed a tree branch, which showered me with cold water. "You're not going to talk about him the entire way, are you?"

"Shut up, *Scheisskopf*," Hilde said. It was *Scheisskopf* now instead of *Dummkopf* because Mutti couldn't hear us. "Just because you're too young to have a boyfriend."

"I'm not." I hated when Hilde did this, insisted I was too young for anything that encroached on her territory: and men, boys, boyfriends were definitely her turf.

The girls turned to evaluate me. They were old enough to wear lipstick and see-through stockings, though none of them wore such things now. But they had that older-girl manner about them, the way they huddled together to shield the great secret of life from me. Mutti had insisted on braiding my wispy blond hair to keep it from going wild. They wore theirs loose, and it was long and thick like Hilde's. I imagined them at home spending hours in front of the mirror before a date, curling it just so. Compared to them, I looked like I was in first grade.

I hadn't told Hilde about my crush on Jacob—not because she would have been remotely interested in him, but because she would have spent hours telling me why I couldn't have him. Even though nothing had happened between us, keeping him secret was better. I could add anything I wanted to the secret—a first kiss, Jacob's eyelashes, the scent of lavender from his family's garden—and no one could dispute it.

"Who's Paul?" one of the girls asked Hilde.

Paul was skinny and had a big nose and laughed like a donkey. But he was a real boyfriend. He'd written letters to Hilde from the front, which she'd hidden and wouldn't let me read—but I'd found them and read them all. I'd admired the purple ribbon she'd tied them with, and the rose petals she'd sprinkled on them to make them smell good. And even though I told myself piano was more reliable than a boyfriend, I'd reread the romantic bits, imagining the letters had come from Jacob and were addressed to me.

"When Paul comes back," Hilde said, "he's going to finish his apprenticeship in baking. He'll go to master's school and be a master baker and have his own shop, and I'll work nearby in a greenhouse."

Do you really think he's coming back? I didn't have the heart to say it out loud.

The sky was wrapped in gauze, and only a dull light managed to fight its way through to us. A breeze swirled dust and ash in the air, making my eyes burn.

Hilde pointed. "Look at that guy carrying a table. How dumb do you have to be?"

As dumb as me. I'd wanted to bring our piano. Down the road there were large framed paintings of landscapes, and beautiful antique chairs, things people thought they couldn't live without—until they had to carry them. I wanted to sit on one of the chairs with my legs crossed like a lady and wait for someone to serve me coffee. But when I got closer I saw they'd been shot full of holes.

CHAPTER FOUR

THE THING WORTH TAKING

Afternoon drifted into early evening. We talked about hairstyles, and I told the girls about our rooster that hated me and planned my death every time I entered the coop to collect eggs.

"You're so immature." Hilde rolled her eyes and pulled one of the girls closer, as if my childishness was contagious.

And then, up ahead, Red Army soldiers blocked the road. The mood in our group changed like a lit match on tinder. Even from a distance I could tell this wasn't the usual orderly demand for papers. The men were laughing, unsteady, pushing people around. They were probably drunk.

Mutti marched over to us and made a noise in the back of her throat that usually meant someone, in other words me, had spilled something on her clean kitchen floor. "Do you have your papers?"

I felt for mine in my pocket, though I was pretty sure these soldiers wouldn't care about our identity cards. They were only stopping us to see if we had anything worth taking. Stories of rape and murder had been drifting westward for more than a year now, and I wasn't deaf. If you were a girl, the thing worth taking was you.

Mutti patted my face with dirt, then did the same to Hilde and herself. My stomach twisted into a knot of nerves. Making ourselves ugly was far from foolproof. The Soviet soldiers were unpredictable when they'd been drinking, and they had rifles.

I noticed a church spire jutting above a stand of trees, and pointed to our right. "If we cut across the field, we won't have to pass the soldiers."

Mutti hesitated, looking back and forth from the soldiers to the field. Another group of people was already halfway across.

Hilde tsked. "Just because they're doing it, doesn't mean—"

"Good thinking, Katja," Mutti said. "We'll wait to make sure the soldiers are distracted."

Hilde looked like she wanted to stab me with a stick. "It's a stupid idea. The fields are lumpy and hard to walk on. And it's dangerous. What if the soldiers see us?"

But Mutti ignored her. "When I say go, we go. Quickly, no delays."

We stood behind her, waiting.

"I love how she only listens to you," Hilde said under her breath.

"I love how you're allowed to have opinions, but I'm not," I shot back.

"Now," Mutti said.

It turned out Hilde was right about the field. The ground was uneven and muddy from tank tracks, and stubborn shoots of grass and weeds made the way rough. Running was hopeless, especially in the dimming light. We had to consider each step or risk turning an ankle.

"Keep going," Mutti said. "Don't look back."

When Mutti said not to look at something, it always meant there was a good reason for looking. So I looked. Because we had decided to go, others had followed. It had been a good idea when only a few of us were doing it.

Someone shouted behind us in Russian.

"Get down," Mutti said.

We dropped to the ground, sharp stalks digging into my stomach. I pressed my cheek against the earth. It was cold, but had the rich smell of our garden at home. *Did you know,* I wanted to tell Mutti, *that Mendelssohn wrote all his piano concertos in the minor key because he wanted to be seen as a suffering Romantic?* But according to Herr Goldstein, he was a faker. He'd never experienced any hardship in his life. He'd lived at the right time, Herr Goldstein had said.

Mutti pointed at a copse of bushes to our left. "Start crawling. They might not have seen us. We'll hide."

There were gunshots. Russian shouting drew closer. I pressed my face harder against the ground as I moved sideways. Even with my head turned, I could hear the clink of metal on the soldiers' belts.

We weren't fast enough.

The soldiers waved their rifles to make us stand up. They had a crazed look in their eyes that made me think of horses in a storm. The other Germans who'd been crossing the field with us raised their arms in surrender. Would the soldiers shoot us if our hands were up? My arms shook. I held them as high as I could, as if higher meant *Yes, I surrender even more.*

But shooting was only one thing. I held my breath. Mutti stood on one side of me, solid and unwavering, Hilde on the other, shaking as badly as I was.

"*Chasy, chasy,*" one kept saying. He grabbed our arms to look for wristwatches, using us to hold himself up. I wished I had a wristwatch just to make him go away.

The soldiers took our bags and ripped them open. They threw cups and bowls to the ground. In my bag they found Herr Goldstein's book of Schumann's *Lieder.* They riffled through the pages and then tore them into pieces. In my head it sounded like someone was leaning on fifteen notes at once, making noise instead of music. *I'd promised him.* I opened my mouth to protest, but Mutti edged her foot onto mine and pressed hard.

They opened Mutti's bag. They took the salami she'd been rationing for us, and ripped the family photographs she'd brought. The pieces fell like blossoms, landing in the dirt. Her mouth was tight, her chin trembling.

One soldier took a photograph out of his uniform pocket and pointed at the couple in it, holding the photograph so tightly he was crushing it. Were they his parents? Were they dead?

When the soldiers came to Herr Schiffer, he clasped his bag against his chest.

"Give it to them," his wife said.

"My knives." He wouldn't let go.

The Soviet men laughed; it seemed like they were making fun of Herr Schiffer. One of them tried to take the bag out of his arms, but Herr Schiffer pushed him away and the soldier lost his balance. The men stopped laughing.

I sank my teeth into my bottom lip.

"Don't be—" But Frau Schiffer didn't get a chance to finish. The soldier raised his gun and shot Herr Schiffer in the chest. His wife shrieked and fell to her knees beside his body, but one of the soldiers forced her back up. With his rifle he gestured at us, the girls and women, to form a line.

I knew what that meant. They would choose the ripe ones. I kept my gaze low, something I used to do at school when I didn't want the teacher to call on me. I reached for Mutti and Hilde and held their hands.

There were three other German men in our group, all either old or crippled. They positioned themselves in front of us. "Leave the women," one said. "They haven't done anything."

An explosion of sound stretched from one end of the field to the other. The men, moving and alive one moment, lay crumpled and silent on the muddy field. My ears rang from the gunshots; it was all I could hear.

Nothing protected us now.

A soldier said, "*Frau, komm.*" Woman, come. I looked up. He was pointing at one of the girls Hilde had been walking with, her hair falling in pretty waves around her face, dark circles beneath her eyes. When she didn't move, he grabbed her arm and she fell forward into the dirt. The other men pulled her up and tried to lead her away, but she screamed and leaned back with all her weight. One of them struck her across the face.

"Savages." I didn't realize I'd said it out loud until Mutti crushed my hand in hers.

"Who spoke?" a soldier barked in accented German. He was the one who'd been holding the photograph.

No one responded. My skin went prickly and I stared at my shoes. What had I done?

"Who? Who said it?" He hoisted his rifle and aimed it along the row of us, passing from one to the next.

I glanced at Mutti for guidance. She looked up at the man. There was another explosion of noise and her hand slipped from mine. Her knees buckled, and she fell.

CHAPTER FIVE

BECAUSE YOU SPOKE

The men chose two more women and led them across the field, leaving the rest of us in a slow-moving nightmare. I was trembling so badly I could hardly stand up. The shots had left a smell of gunpowder in the air, and my ears still rang with the sound. Mutti lay motionless, her chest covered in blood, her face softened as though she was sleeping.

Somebody was screaming. It was me.

She's not dead. It didn't happen. But the blood—there was so much of it; even my dress was splattered.

Hilde shook me by both shoulders. "This is your fault," she screamed.

I could hardly breathe. "It's not. I didn't—"

"You did. I told you we shouldn't have crossed this field. I told you it would be dangerous. And why did you have to open your big mouth? If you'd kept quiet, Mutti would still be alive."

The bodies of the four men lay to one side of us like mounds of earth, their wives and daughters bent over them, wailing. My thoughts swirled like flies. *No, no, no. Why Mutti? Why would they shoot her? Because you spoke.*

I knelt next to the woman on the muddy ground, the one who would wake up and go back to being our mother. Her chest was warm and sticky. "Help me stop the bleeding."

Hilde pulled off Mutti's kerchief and we pressed it against her chest, but the blood soaked right through. And now her head would get cold. She always said a cold head led to sickness.

"You're going to be all right." I lifted her left wrist and felt for a pulse, leaving a bloody thumbprint. Her skin was gray, and there was a smell around her that made me realize she'd lost control of her bowels. Dignity, Mutti's most important thing, had been denied to her.

If there was no pulse in her left arm, maybe there would be one in her right. If not in her right, then—

"Forget it," Hilde said in a crushed voice. "She's gone. Can't you see that?" She looked dazed, the way Papi used to look whenever he'd banged his head in the hayloft.

The world had detached from its moorings and was now moving like the ships I used to watch on the Baltic Sea, being battered by the waves. I held Mutti's face in my hands, blurry through my tears. It felt so small and fragile.

Around us were sobs and shattered voices, distant screams, women trying to haul bodies away. The butcher's wife came over to us, holding herself together with her large ham hands. She had a round face and a thick nose, and her dress was covered in blood—the way her apron might have been at the butcher shop.

"You girls shouldn't linger," she said.

I barely heard her. Where were we supposed to go?

The shreds of Herr Goldstein's music book had been ground into the mud. Mutti's identification card lay beside them, spattered with blood. I picked it up, wiped it off on my dress, and slipped it into my bag. Panic made my pulse race. I felt like our horses that clamored and whinnied to leave the barn, until they were actually out—and then all they wanted to do was go home. Who would take care of us?

My usual hunger pains were gone. I felt nauseous.

Hilde sat a few feet away, staring at the ground.

"Come here," I said. "Please."

At first she ignored me. But finally she came over and sat down beside me. I leaned against her. For a little while she stared at Mutti, but then she reached over and stroked my hair. Sometimes she did that, made a sudden and complete transformation from sister to human being, as if a secret Hilde hid inside the prickly person I knew, like a nesting doll. There was dried blood beneath her fingernails. The thicker patches of it on her hands were cracking.

In the western sky, the sun had left a burning haze of red. Hilde gathered the scraps of Mutti's photographs and stored them in her dress pocket. Nearby, trucks rumbled down the road and men shouted at each other in Russian. Somebody laughed.

The butcher's wife returned with a bag on each shoulder. "There will be more soldiers," she said. "Your mother wouldn't want you to put yourselves in danger."

Hilde rose to her feet, but I didn't move. "We're not leaving Mutti here."

"Where do you think you can take her?" said the butcher's wife. "Come with us. It will be safer in the village."

Mutti's skin was turning purple, like the people we'd seen in the ditches. "We should bury her," I said. It was one way to give her back her dignity. Even though burying Mutti meant she was really dead, it was worse to think of her lying out in the open like this.

The butcher's wife shook her head at us and walked away.

All I had to dig with was a spoon. As soon as I stuck it into the ground, it bent in half. I used my hands, scraping at the dirt with my fingernails.

Hilde pulled up weeds and threw them at my feet. "This field is ruined," she muttered. "Next winter will be hard if all the fields look like this."

You mustn't be defeatist, Mutti liked to say. I dug my fingers into the dirt twice as hard. But after several minutes of futile digging, I had to admit it: "This isn't working."

"We have to move her," Hilde said. "You take her shoulders. I'll take her legs."

Mutti was a small, slim woman, but her body was the heaviest burden I'd ever borne. I wanted to cradle her, like a bird, but her head lolled and I had to grip her shoulders hard to make sure I didn't drop her. I walked backward, moving her as if she was a piece of furniture, stumbling on the uneven ground in the gathering darkness.

We found a flat, soft place behind the bushes and set her down, and then I went back for her bag. I hated the bushes. We might have hidden there, if we'd been faster. The bushes could have saved Mutti.

We straightened her dress, so soiled, and covered her with leaves and branches, making her even dirtier. She wouldn't have liked it. She'd never had patience for mess or disorder.

When we were done I could barely look at the mound of dry leaves. *Look away.* That was what Mutti would have told me to do. But it didn't matter where I looked. Even in the night sky I could see houses, like constellations, with mothers in them and tables set for supper.

We hadn't been there to bury Papi—to say the important things or leave a memento. *It wasn't done properly,* Mutti had said over and over, staring at the wood grain of our kitchen table with the black-bordered envelope in her hands.

I took out the doily I'd brought. Mutti's crocheted doilies had adorned every surface in our home. I loved their delicate patterns, and the way the empty spaces were as important as the lace. When I closed my eyes and traced it with my fingertips, it was like reading home through the patterns and pauses.

My bottom lip trembled. "There's no headstone. And what if animals find her, or soldiers? We need to mark it somehow, so we can visit and keep her gravesite tidy." We'd always tended the family plot in our town, where Oma and Opa were buried.

Hilde found two sticks, one longer and one shorter. "We'll make a cross."

"But how will we attach them?" Every little thing felt huge and insurmountable.

Just as Hilde was searching in her bag for something that might help, a gunshot rang out in the darkness. Too close, a drunken voice shouted, "*Frau, komm,*" with a Russian accent.

Hilde placed a hand on my arm. Neither of us spoke. I hoisted my bag onto my back and held Mutti's against my chest. I couldn't bear to leave it behind.

I wanted to say goodbye again and again, but no amount of goodbyes would have been enough. The crunch of our footsteps on dead branches was the sound of us leaving Mutti forever.

CHAPTER SIX

BOMBPROOF

We spent the night in a collapsed shed. I was so tired, but as soon as I closed my eyes all I could see was that Soviet soldier lifting his gun. So close to us he hadn't narrowed his eye to aim. So close I had noticed the mole on his cheek, and a twitch at his mouth. Mutti's chin had trembled. Right at the end, she'd been afraid. How would I ever shut my eyes and not see these things?

They *were* savages. I wasn't wrong. But I shouldn't have said it out loud.

Before I knew it, sunlight came through the cracks in the wood in thin jittery lines. The air held an early morning chill. The day was waking up and it rumbled like a giant bear. Everything shook: the ground, even the bones in our bodies. I knew what that sound was: tanks. There must have been hundreds of them.

We couldn't stay.

"Do you know the way to Aunt Ilse's place?" I asked my sister.

"Stop calling her that. And no, of course I don't."

I dug around in Mutti's bag until I found the letter from Ilse. I was about to open it when Hilde snatched it out of my hand.

"That's important," she said. "It has the address on it." She slipped it into her bag.

Anger sparked behind my eyes. "Don't treat me like a baby."

"It doesn't belong to you."

"I'm not going to read it," I said.

"Aren't you?" She fastened her bag and pulled the straps tight. "You think I don't know you read Paul's letters?"

My face heated up. I'd been so careful with the ribbons and petals.

She brushed dirt off her dress.

"How will we know the way?" I asked.

Hilde didn't answer.

"What if Ilse and Otto don't want us? What if they're awful?"

"They won't be. Mutti wouldn't have wanted to go there if they were."

What if they're dead? I was holding myself together like the bundles of china we'd seen on wagons and pushcarts. If the bundle came undone, I knew what I'd discover: everything inside would be smashed.

Once again we joined the crowds of people on the road, carried by a current that flowed in one direction: *away.* Some of the older people were being pushed or pulled in carts. Some had given up and sat on the roadside staring at their hands.

The blood on our clothes had hardened into smudges. The space beside me felt so cold. It began to rain, a dreary *tap-tap* on my metal bucket. I unfastened it and held it out to catch the water while we walked. All I could think about was Mutti lying outside, chilled and damp, her head uncovered, her hair getting wet. I longed for a cushion of time to be able to grieve her, but grief was a luxury. We had to keep moving.

In the next village, homes had been burned to the ground, their secrets gone, hidden in closets that were gone; the games once played in the attic that was now ground floor, now ash— gone. Gardens were strewn with the bones, guts, and heads of slaughtered pigs and goats. In one, we saw the bloated cadaver of a cow.

We took turns drinking from the bucket even though it made the water taste like metal.

I held Mutti's bag. With every step, I heard her voice.

- *Stay away from buildings that aren't damaged.* They were often the bombers' next targets. Ruined ones were safer.

- *Don't eat the dead animals on the road.* We didn't know how long they'd been there, and they could make us sick.

- *Stay out of the way of the tanks.* Tanks did not drive around obstacles. They drove over them.

The days and nights blurred into each other. We were so frightened by all the soldiers on the roads that we made almost no progress. Hilde got sick with a fever and I was terrified I would lose her as well. We didn't dare travel until she regained her strength.

By mid-April, word was that Marshal Zhukov's Red Army was attacking Berlin. Nighttime was filled with the drone of plane engines, bombs screaming in the distance.

Hitler was dead, people said. Suicide. Ambush. No, he was

alive. Captured. Escaped. *That man,* Mutti used to call him. *That man and his plan to be God.*

We slept in caved-in barns and burned houses. We found a cellar full of food and hid there for several weeks. We took off our bloody dresses and washed them in the river, then packed them away; it was too warm now to wear two dresses. By the time the food ran out and we got back on the road, we heard it was June and the war was over.

The war was over. I looked around, somehow expecting things to be different. Smoke rose in the distance, and a dead horse floated down the river. Someone had shaken and shaken the world until all the pieces were scattered.

Someone had shaken me too. I was a girl without parents, alone in this world but for Hilde.

"Did you know so many people wanted locks of Liszt's hair that he bought a dog and sent them dog hair instead?" I said to her as we trudged along. Liszt was not my favorite composer, but I was intrigued by this story. His hair must have been even nicer than Hilde's.

"Um, no, I didn't know that," she said without bothering to look at me.

"Did you know Mozart started composing music when he was five?" It felt like music was a long-lost friend and we were finally reuniting. Mozart, Brahms, Bach: we had so much to talk about.

Herr Goldstein and I used to have long conversations about the lives of the composers. I would come home from my lesson, supposedly with Frau Erdmann, and tell Mutti stories about Beethoven or her beloved Schumann while she baked bread or churned butter. As if Frau Erdmann knew a single thing about

Beethoven or Schumann. *In the beautiful month of May*, Mutti would sing. It was her favorite of Schumann's *Lieder*, and mine.

"Mozart was five?" Hilde said. "You'd better get busy. You're eleven years behind."

"I'm not going to be a composer. I'm going to be a performer." I clutched Mutti's bag against my chest. All day beside the road we'd seen burned-out tanks, boxes of old ammunition, and, notably, no pianos. "Did you know—"

"Enough already," Hilde said.

We passed a group of soldiers sitting beneath the trees. Some of them used their helmets as bowls to eat stew. I huddled closer to Hilde and we increased our pace. Even though the war was over, Soviet soldiers were Soviet soldiers; there was no predicting what they might do. I wished I could grab their helmets and dump the stew on their heads. My jaw tightened with hatred; my fingertips ached with it. There was hatred in my dirty hair; I breathed it in with the harsh smell of burning.

Another step. The next pine tree. A girl my age. Barely dressed, she lay dead beside the road, her privates exposed as if the thing that was supposed to matter most didn't matter at all. As far as I knew, her attackers might have been the men we'd just passed. *Savages.* The word made me feel prickly all over.

"You shouldn't look," Hilde said. "And anyway, there's nothing we can do for her."

I leaned over and covered her with her skirt.

"We're getting what we deserve," a woman said as she passed us. "The Soviets are paying us back."

The dead girl had a birthmark on her cheek, and one of her shoes was unbuckled. "What did she do to deserve this?" I said.

Hilde gave me the dirty-washrag look. "Keep your opinions to yourself."

"What's the point of having them, then?"

The woman nodded toward the dead girl. "She's German. The war was our fault."

"The war was Hitler's fault," I said. "It sounds like we're getting what he deserved."

"No," said the woman. "The Soviets are only doing to us what our men did to them. Burning down houses. Killing civilians."

I thought of our old neighbor who wore soft sweaters and read Goethe every afternoon to his wife. I thought of Papi playing Beethoven on his violin.

"Our soldiers wouldn't do things like that," I said. "They killed partisans." People who were a threat to them. "They destroyed military installations."

"Partisans. Is that what they taught you in school?" she asked.

And on the radio, and at our League meetings. "Who else would they have killed?"

The woman looked as though she felt sorry for me. "I'm not the right person to tell you."

As soon as she was out of earshot, I turned toward Hilde. "Tell me about what? Why did she say that?"

But Hilde was already chatting with a girl about her apprenticeship in horticulture.

Fine. In my head, I went through my favorite of Chopin's waltzes, the one in C-sharp minor.

I thought the second theme should be played slowly, but when I did that, Herr Goldstein stopped me. *It's a waltz, Katja,* he said. *Chopin didn't write his waltzes for dancers with wooden legs.*

Imagine this is a girl's first waltz ever, I replied, *and she finally gets to dance with the man she's been in love with since eighth grade, and all this time she didn't think he loved her back, but now he's asked her to dance. She wants to make it last.*

You shouldn't be going to his house for lessons, Hilde had whispered to me in our bedroom. *I'll tell Mutti if you don't stop.*

You mustn't tell. Not realizing she already had.

Things are getting bad for the Jews, she'd said. *You'll put us all in danger. And him too. He'll get into trouble for teaching you. You ever think of that?*

I had. But also I hadn't. I'd thought it, and then set the thought aside in its own box. If you couldn't see something, it wasn't there.

The air held the warmth of late spring. If we'd been home and things had been normal, Papi would have been teaching me to ride our old mare, Glücklich—Happy—despite Herr Goldstein's objections that I might fall and hurt my hands. *Glücklich won't throw me,* I'd insisted. *She's bombproof.*

CHAPTER SEVEN

CHINA, OR THE MOON

Here was what I thought: Ilse would be pretty, with soft blond ringlets and fancy dresses from Paris that she would let us borrow. She would be cheerful, and kind, and she'd have a bedroom for us, and food, because she would have planned ahead for distant relatives. And she'd have a piano, a beautiful baby grand that she kept dusted and tuned, and music books, and coffee sets that were probably different than Mutti's but just as dainty and pretty.

She would take us in and treat us like her own daughters—and then Hilde would have to forgive me. We'd sit together on her bed the way we used to and look at catalogs from the stores in the city, and I would point out the dresses I liked—even though I didn't care about dresses—and wait for her to tell me she liked the same ones.

Even so, as soon as we saw the sign for Fahlhoff, I began dragging my feet. Part of me wanted to keep walking forever, to be on the road and on the road and never arrive. I finally understood Schubert's unfinished symphony. He'd had six years to write the third movement but he never did it. If you didn't finish something, you never had to find out how it ended.

Soviet faces glared from posters fixed to buildings. The only face I recognized was Stalin's, with his bushy mustache, staring into the distance at something far more important than us. *Enjoy the war,* someone had scrawled in German on the side of a building. *The peace is going to be terrible.*

A woman on the street mentioned it was Thursday. I was surprised to hear Thursdays still existed. That was the day Mutti used to beat all the rugs. I'd enjoyed helping her, whacking them with a stick and watching the clouds of dust mushroom out.

"So?" I said to Hilde. "What do we do now?" There was no one around to tell us. It made me feel like I'd forgotten to put on my shoes.

Hilde straightened her shoulders.

"I don't need you to take care of me, you know," I said.

"Right." She waved Ilse's envelope at me. "Make it look like we know where we're going. Take that bucket off. It's ridiculous."

But I didn't. "Mutti would keep it." You never knew with a bucket; it had already come in handy for collecting water. I wrapped my arms around Mutti's bag and followed my sister, the bucket banging against my back.

Nearby was a crumbling building where scores of people, dirty and twig-limbed, were lined up. Their bundles and packs were piled beside them—some barely held together with unraveling twine.

I tugged on Hilde's sleeve. "Maybe there's soup."

"Yes, and maybe there's typhus. Mutti told us to stay away from crowds, remember?"

The residents of Fahlhoff crossed the street to pass that building—as if it had leprosy, or bad breath. Maybe I should have left the bucket behind.

"It's probably a transit camp," Hilde said. For people who had been displaced, like us. We'd had our place taken away from us. It made me feel all elbows and knees; no part of me belonged anywhere anymore. At least when Mutti had been with us, we'd belonged wherever she was. Now we were dandelion spores, at the mercy of the wind.

Up ahead, a tank blocked the road, along with a line of sandbags. The sentries standing at the blockade wore loose-fitting pants, belted shirts, and caps with the Red Star emblem on them. They stood at attention and kept their rifles at the ready. As we approached, one of them shouted, "*Stoyte*," and we stopped walking. The guards took one look at our identity cards and pointed with the ends of their rifles toward the skinny people with their bundles and packs.

No way were we going to end up in that place and get shipped off to who-knew-where. I yanked the envelope out of Hilde's hand and pointed to the return address. "Fahlhoff, see? We're not refugees. We have family here."

No response.

I tossed my wispy blond hair the way I'd seen Hilde do it a thousand times. The guards smiled at me, and one of them took me by the arm. My eyes widened in panic. *No, no, no.* I hadn't meant that.

Hilde grabbed my other arm. "She's my sister. She stays with me."

She wouldn't let go of me. With one hand she searched Mutti's bag for something to give the guard. What would be a fair trade for me? Mutti's green sweater? Her dented bowl? There was nothing, nothing, and nothing. Then she reached into my pocket, pulled out the doily I'd been carrying, and thrust it at the soldier, who was still holding my other arm.

He let go of me and took the doily with two fingers, the way I would have carried a dead mouse by the tail. Then he held it flat in his hand and blew his nose into it. *That's what I think of your trade.*

The second soldier laughed at the snot that oozed out of the doily holes into his partner's hand. Hilde grabbed Mutti's bag and hauled me past the soldiers. They hadn't said we could pass. But they didn't stop us, either.

We were through. We were in Fahlhoff.

CHAPTER EIGHT

WHAT YOU CAN DO WHEN YOU HAVE A MOTHER

As soon as we rounded the corner, we stopped to calm down.

My pocket felt a hundred pounds empty. "That was the most precious thing I had of Mutti's, and now it's gone." I thought of all her evenings of work, a fire in the grate, Papi's violin sitting in one corner; the way she would frown at each doily as it grew beneath her fingers, never quite satisfied with how it was turning out.

Hilde's jaw tightened. She wanted to shout at me, I knew she did, but she would never do anything to embarrass herself in public. She thrust Mutti's bag at my stomach. "God, when will you start being responsible? I can't always be there to rescue you."

"You do the flirty boy thing all the time."

"Not with Soviet soldiers, I don't. That's like playing with live ammunition."

"Thanks for the tip, *Scheisskopf.*"

"Everything would be different if Mutti was here." Hilde didn't even try to hide the blame in her voice. *It was your fault. You're the reason she's dead.*

I swallowed hard. If Mutti was here, I could have held her hand. And if it turned out Ilse was dead, or gone, Mutti would have had a backup plan, the way she used to keep a just-in-case cookie for us, or a piece of sausage. She would have suggested it, and I would have complained, because that was what you could do when you had a mother. When you didn't, you had to come up with your own ideas and not blame anyone if they went wrong.

A woman approached, and I decided I'd show Hilde I could be helpful. I stopped her to ask for directions.

Her face clouded over. "Dirty refugees," she said. "We don't want you here. Go back where you came from."

"Don't you think we'd go home if we could?" I said.

"Let's just walk," my sister whispered. "We'll figure it out."

The cobbled roads were slippery in places with oil from the tanks and trucks that had driven through. Americans, it must have been, because there were half-smoked cigarettes on the ground. Only Amis wasted cigarettes like that. Germans and Soviets smoked them until there was nothing left to hold. I gathered as many as I could and wrapped them in a piece of red paper I'd found on the ground.

"That's disgusting." Hilde fussed with her hair, combing it behind one ear over and over.

"No," I said, "it's treasure. We can use it to trade."

"I wonder if Ilse will have sticky tape for our photographs," Hilde said.

I knew it. My sister was doing it too—imagining how great everything would be once we found Ilse and Otto. "I think there'll be chocolate." My voice rose with excitement. "And a radio, and someone to teach me piano."

"You and your piano." Hilde pursed her lips the way Mutti used to do. "How about we move ahead to a life that doesn't revolve around that damn instrument?"

"What do you care? Your life doesn't revolve around it."

She tipped her head at me. "If I never hear the *Moonlight* Symphony again, I won't be—"

"Sonata."

"What?"

"It's the *Moonlight* Sonata," I said.

She let out a long sigh.

The narrow roads of Fahlhoff sometimes ended abruptly or turned into new roads, so we had no idea if we were walking in a straight line. When I spotted a church spire in the distance, I felt like we were trapped in some hideous nightmare. There would be a field nearby. I would suggest crossing it. Hilde would say it was a bad idea.

But there was no field. We seemed to be on the main road that led to the center of town. Fahlhoff must not have been close to anything important. It seemed largely untouched by the war.

We arrived at the church just as the bells rang the quarter hour. The church was part of a central square that included a park, the city hall, and a fountain with no water in it. A middle-aged man sat in the fountain, head bowed, hands resting in his lap. He had a graying beard and unkempt hair.

"Do you know where Isabella has gone?" He looked up at us with small, uncertain eyes.

"We're not from here," I said.

Hilde pinched me. "Yes, we are." She pulled on my arm to keep walking. "You can't say that to people or they'll send us away."

A Soviet flag flew above the city hall, but I could tell it was homemade. Darker sections of red showed the former shapes of swastikas.

We passed Fahlhoff's thousand-year oak, even though it wasn't a thousand years old; it probably wasn't even ten. Our town had had one too. A thousand years was how long the Third Reich was supposed to last. *Surprise.* The trees in the park were covered in messages, many of which had been written on the edges of newsprint that were nailed to the trunks: *Kurt, we're still alive and have gone to Oma's house,* and *the Jaeger family is in Leipzig.* I wished I'd thought to leave a message for the Goldsteins. How would they ever find me here?

I was studying the address on Ilse's envelope when a girl our age hurried toward us, her arms full of cabbages. She was blond and freckled, with a small pointed nose.

"Are you lost?" Her smile revealed a crooked front tooth.

Hilde pulled the envelope out of my hand. "Can you tell us how to get to Daschner's Damen und Herrenmode?"

"Sure. That's the clothing shop run by that hag. It's on Rosen-strasse."

My imaginary portrait of Ilse cracked down the middle. "Is she that bad?"

"Depends," the girl said.

"On what?"

She laughed. "I shouldn't speak out of turn. Go around the corner and then straight until you pass the bakery. You'll see Rosenstrasse on your left. I'm Liesel, by the way." She offered her hand awkwardly and we each shook it. "I'd give you a cabbage, but my mother would kill me. We own the grocery store. Oh God, Frau Daschner isn't a relative of yours, is she?"

"Sort of," said Hilde.

"Me and my big mouth," Liesel said with a laugh.

I liked her immediately.

"Be careful on these roads. There are still combat troops around." She rushed off toward the dim windows of the grocery store and banged on the door until someone with a gruff voice shouted, "Yes, yes, I'm coming."

Hilde stuffed the envelope into her bag and set off in a determined march, and I followed. The *Brauhaus* was closed. The butcher was closed. A sign in the bakery window said *No Bread*.

And then, there was Rosenstrasse. As the numbers on the storefronts went down, my pulse went up. Ilse would have dresses, nice ones with buttons and lace that you'd wear to meet friends for coffee and cake. Mutti had been to the shop once, long ago, and she'd talked about it for years afterward: the rows of dresses, the small stuffed bear wearing a miniature tailored suit, the sharp scent of eucalyptus leaves, which we knew as the fever-curing tree.

Mutti had sewn all our clothes. She thought bought dresses were extravagant and frivolous. *We are not a family of means,* she often said. She had never approved of Hilde's collection of catalogs.

Though once, when I'd had a recital, she had taken me on an outing, just the two of us, and bought me a dress with lacy edges. I tried to hide it from Hilde, but that was difficult: we shared a bedroom.

Why didn't I get a dress? she asked Mutti.

I'd hoped Mutti wouldn't mention the recital. My piano playing was already a thorn in Hilde's thumb: the extra money needed for books and lessons, the fuss Mutti made whenever I played her favorite Schumann. Herr Goldstein.

You're too sensible for such silliness, Mutti said to her, but I could tell by Hilde's fallen face that she wished God had given her a little less sense. Anyway, it didn't matter. On the day of the recital, when I wore my new dress, Hilde knew: piano had produced what begging and pleading could not.

As we walked along Rosenstrasse, we passed flower boxes, many empty, but a few with flowers in bloom.

"Gladioli," Hilde said in a voice of authority that made me want to pull their petals off.

Up ahead, I saw the wooden sign: *Daschner's Damen und Herrenmode*. But when we arrived at the shop, the door was locked, and wooden boards covered what must have once been a large display window. I peered between the cracks, but it was dark inside.

"They're not here," I said. Worse than not here. The place was shut down.

Hilde pointed to the windows on the second floor. "They might live upstairs."

Beside the door was a buzzer with a small nametag that said *Familie Daschner*. Hilde pressed it once, delicately, as though she were a neighbor coming over for *Kaffeeklatsch*. The sound echoed in my stomach. There was no answer.

"After all this?" I hammered on the door.

CHAPTER NINE

THE PRINCESS GETS
THE FIRST BATH

Above us there was movement at the curtained window. A minute later, a woman Mutti's age appeared at the door wearing a pretty flowered dress with puffy short sleeves. Even though it looked tired, it was as fashionable as the pictures Hilde and I used to admire in the catalogs. Her dark hair was done up in a tight braided crown and her house shoes had a heel. She had feet that pointed outward, like arrows—this way, that way—as if she couldn't make up her mind which direction to go. On her face was an expression as sour as fermented pickles. So much for cheerfulness. This was not the Ilse I'd imagined.

"*Mein Gott,* I thought you were soldiers the way you pounded on that door." She looked ready to smack us with a wooden spoon before we'd even said a word. "If you're here from Leipzig, I only have dresses to trade. No food. You'll have to try the farms on the outskirts of town."

She was shutting the door when Hilde said, "Auntie Ilse." Not just "aunt," but sweetened with a "tee."

Her eyes narrowed. "Auntie? Who are you?"

"We're Anna Siegert's daughters." Hilde's voice seized up on Mutti's name. "From Pomerania."

Ilse held the door at the ready, in case it became necessary to shut it in the middle of the conversation. "I'm not your aunt."

"Not exactly," I said.

"Not at all, to be precise," she said back.

"You played Piggy on the Ladder with our mother when you were younger." I couldn't believe it. Our entire lives depended on a silly game of string.

Hilde brought out the letter we'd been carrying. "See? You wrote to her."

Ilse held it up to the light, as if checking to see if it was counterfeit. Without a word, she tucked it into her pocket.

She eyed my dirty fingernails. "Where is she, then? This mother of yours who thinks I'm so great she comes all the way from Pomerania to visit. Now—when she needs something."

My sister's mouth opened. I knew she would try to soften the news of Mutti's death, maybe make Ilse feel sorry for us, but I could see in Ilse's tense jaw and steel-rod back that sorry wasn't in her repertoire. That girl, Liesel, had been right about her.

I stepped in front of Hilde. "Mutti is on her way. She should be here any day." It made me almost giddy to say it. Part of me wanted to believe it so badly. But the sensible part—which, I know, was very small because God gave most of the sense to Hilde—said, *On her way? Are you crazy?*

Hilde clamped a hand on my shoulder, but she didn't contradict me. Maybe I was crazy, but I was tired of having this war make all my decisions. It felt good to have some control.

Ilse folded her arms across her chest. "She's left you two girls to travel on your own? In these times? I find that hard to believe. Where is she, exactly? And why are you carrying her things?"

I loosened my grip on the bag. How did she know? "These are my things," I said. "She's in hospital." The lie felt like a hole, and every word I spoke made it bigger.

"With cholera, no doubt," Ilse said. "Or typhus."

"Nothing like that. She'll be better in no time." I fingered the identity card in my pocket. Maybe I should have left it with Mutti.

"Auntie Ilse," Hilde said. I knew that voice. It was the *please give me all your best pencils and I promise I'll be nice to you* voice. I'd learned the hard way to distrust it, but I was thankful for it now. "We've lost everything. The Soviets threw us out of our house."

"For heaven's sake, your father's parents are still alive, aren't they?"

"They live in Austria now," I said.

"Well, don't you have neighbors? This is all highly unusual." She clasped her hands in front of her.

I slipped my bag off my back and the bucket landed with a clatter, startling both her and Hilde. Mutti would have been annoyed.

"I suppose you can come in for now," she said. "We'll sort this out when your mother arrives."

We followed her inside the dark entryway and up a staircase that wound to the left. Might there be a piano up there? A small upright could maybe make it up these stairs, with three strong men and some ingenuity. As we entered the apartment, I looked around. That was the thing about pianos; there was no hiding them. All I saw was a violin case, which gave me a pang. Papi had planned to teach me how to play, but we'd waited too long. Did Ilse play? That didn't seem possible.

Hilde and I removed our street shoes and set them by the door. Every single thing we did felt like a luxury. When was the last time I'd taken my shoes off and felt a clean floor beneath my feet? When was the last time I'd shut a door—a real door, to a proper home? Probably it had been the side door to our farmhouse, when we'd left—forever. Even though these rooms were stuffy and smelled a bit like an armpit, I stood and breathed in the feeling of safety.

Ilse watched us as if we might contaminate something. "I don't have extra house shoes for you," she said. "You'll have to stay in stocking feet."

We waited in a corner of the sitting room, not daring to sit down. There was a bookshelf at one end of the room, and above it, the head of a wild boar. Its four sharp yellow tusks pointed dangerously outward, the snout as black as cast iron. The wallpaper was a faded pattern of trees and birds, and next to a lumpy armchair was a lamp with purple fringes on the shade. The very idea of a room where you could just sit, and not worry about having to jump up and leave, felt magical. I wanted to belong here. I wanted this to be my home, a place where I could curl up in the armchair and read a book. It looked so soft. But there were my elbows and knees all over again, sharp and in the way. I felt more like an intruder than a guest.

A door opened, and out stepped an older man with a wild fluff of graying hair and glasses that looked like they'd been stepped on. Everything about him drooped: his grand mustache, his pants held up by suspenders, his cardigan with stretched pockets that were visibly empty.

"These are Anna Siegert's daughters," Ilse said to him, as if she was describing an unusual species of wildlife.

The man stared at us. "Who?" This must have been Uncle Otto. He wrinkled his nose. I wondered how bad we smelled.

"*Distant* relatives," she said.

I wanted to poke her with one of her hairpins.

"They're waiting for their mother to arrive," Ilse added. "You remember Anna Siegert—from Pomerania. You met her once, years ago. She's in hospital, apparently."

Otto's whole mustache frowned. "You girls came all this way on your own?"

"Where are you headed?" Ilse asked. "Once your mother joins you."

Hilde examined her ripped knee socks, and I stuffed my hands into my pockets so Ilse would stop staring at them.

Finally Hilde said, "Mutti didn't tell us. She'll let you know when she gets here."

When she gets here. It was a reckless thing to do. How long before Ilse realized we'd lied? Then she'd ship us over to that crumbling building, where there was probably lice and typhus and definitely no piano. But that was a problem for Tomorrow-Katja to deal with.

Ilse tugged at her well-made collar. "We're barely getting by, you know. Those Soviet soldiers think they can take everything." She turned to Otto. "I don't know what Anna expects us to do with them." She would never have been so rude if Mutti had been with us.

"Well," Otto said. "It's only for a few days."

A whiff of cabbage, and my knees almost gave way.

"They're hungry," Otto said to Ilse. "Perhaps a slice of bread?"

Ilse led us into a small kitchen (a kitchen!). Every step on the tiles felt cushioned by the idea of home. She filled a kettle with water and set it to boil on the stove while we sat at the kitchen table, which was thick and wooden and had about two hundred years' worth of scratches and dents in it.

"The electricity has been unpredictable ever since Oberstrasse was bombed," she said. "All those fancy people across the river are in the same boat as the rest of us now." She clucked her tongue as she took out half a loaf of bread and cut two thin slices, spreading each with a tiny bit of lard.

Otto lumbered into the kitchen. With his big frame, he reminded me of a bear just after hibernation, his stomach slack and empty. "How long have you girls been on the road?"

Hilde said, "Twelve weeks," in her schoolteacher voice that was so much like Mutti's. *Twelve weeks, three days, and five and a half hours,* was probably what she'd wanted to say.

"They'll need time to recover," he said to Ilse.

"What they need," she said, "is a bath." She turned to us. "And I'll check your heads for lice."

"Let them eat." Otto opened a jar of peaches and put one slice on each of our plates. Hilde took dainty bites of hers, but I stuffed the whole thing in my mouth. It exploded with the sweetness of a summer evening. He gave us each another, even though Ilse made a face.

The kitchen played a song I hadn't heard in a long time: the kettle rumbled on the stove, cutlery clinked against plates, and could I count heat as a sort of music? An undertone of warmth, it made me feel heavy and sleepy.

Ilse made peppermint tea. Then she hauled out a large zinc tub and heated several pots of water on the stove. I didn't know a person could get hungry to be clean, but I craved warm water and soap almost as much as I did food.

In the meantime, she gave us *till your mother gets here* instructions:

- The kerosene lamps were only to be used when the electricity was out.

- We were not allowed into the shop.

- We would go to the forests and fields beyond the town to look for food.

- "The danger," Otto said—

- Regardless of the danger.

Mutti would have puffed up like an angry goose. She would have said, *I won't have you putting my daughters at risk.* But she wasn't here.

Ilse emptied the pots of water into the tub, and then she and Otto left the room to give us privacy. The water looked so clean, and Hilde's arms were caked with dirt.

"Let me go first for once," I said.

Hilde unbuttoned her dress. "Number one, no. And number two, no. You're dirtier. I'm older. And anyway, I was named after a strong and beautiful Norse princess."

Not this again. "No, you weren't," I said. "You were named after faraway Oma." Mutti's mother, who had lived in Berlin and died some years back.

"Yes, I was. And the princess gets the first bath."

Before I could argue, she climbed in.

I hadn't taken off these clothes in weeks. On the road, we needed to be fully dressed and ready to leave at the first sign of danger. I hadn't realized how filthy my hands were until I saw them next to my bare skin. No wonder Ilse had wrinkled her nose at us and strangers had called us dirty. We were.

An hour later we sat around the kitchen table. The dress Ilse lent me was loose in the chest, and the shoulders hung, but it had a pretty pattern of blue stripes, with short sleeves and buttons down the front. It was much fancier than anything Mutti would have made for us.

"Everything you need to know about a person can be told by the way they dress," Ilse said. "It's a good life lesson, girls. Keep your hems tidy and your buttons sewn tight and you'll always find a good job."

Hems and buttons? "Have you been outside lately?" I said.

Hilde kicked me under the table.

I had to remember: no matter how many ridiculous things Ilse said, she was our only hope.

Hilde took out the catalog photos she'd dragged halfway across the country and flattened them on the table.

"What do you have there?" Ilse asked.

"Dresses," Hilde said. "These ones are my favorites."

Ilse studied each page. "You have good taste," she said, as if this was unexpected.

Our clothes were soaking in water with potato peelings, our hair had been brushed and braided ("No lice, thank God," as Ilse put it), and she'd given us a second cup of peppermint tea. I forgot all about the cold welcome at the door. I hadn't felt this good in months. If only Mutti . . . I gulped back the sadness that welled up in my throat.

Otto poked his head into the kitchen. "You know, the boys' bedroom is empty. Maybe they can stay in—"

Ilse leapt to her feet. "Absolutely not. Helmut and Franz will be home any day."

I watched her face for cracks. *Any day* sounded like when Mutti was getting out of hospital.

The look on Otto's face was almost pleading. "They're family. Give me a chance to do something good, *Liebling.* Please."

But Ilse stood like a wall in front of us and said, "You are not to go in there."

After finishing the tea, we helped her clear a space in a small storeroom that contained old curtains and bolts of leftover fabric. There were no windows. She sent Otto to fetch blankets from somewhere downstairs. They smelled like they should have been hung outside to air, but I kept that opinion to myself. The prospect of sleeping indoors—not in a collapsed barn or burned-out house—overwhelmed everything.

"It's only temporary, you understand," Ilse said. "When your mother gets here, you'll have to move on."

She handed us each a broom and sent us out to sweep the sidewalk in front of the shop.

As soon as we were outside, Hilde said, "I can't believe you told her Mutti was alive. What are we going to do when she never shows up?"

"Make ourselves indispensable," I said.

Hilde put down the broom.

"That's not what indispensable means," I said.

"Shut up, *Scheisskopf.* I'm going to steal some of those gladioli we saw. You do the sweeping."

Usually I would have been annoyed that she had to say *gladioli* and not just *flowers* like a normal person. But I savored the victory like a sweet. Maybe Hilde had been born knowing better, but for once my sister thought I was right.

CHAPTER TEN

EVERYTHING IS BREAKABLE

After supper we went to our tiny room and sat on our musty blankets on the floor. Hilde took out her hairbrush.

"I still can't believe Mutti let you pack that," I said as she began brushing her long hair.

She huffed. "What about your music book? A hairbrush is small, and it doesn't weigh anything. She let you do whatever you want. If I'd wanted to bring a book, she would have smacked me just for asking."

"That's not true." But wasn't it? Sure, out of the two of us, I was the difficult one. Whenever there'd been responsibility involved, Mutti had called on Hilde, whereas I got the Every Bad Thing You've Ever Done speech—including my full name: "Katarina Wilhelmina (-for-my-grandmother-worst-middle-name-ever-) Siegert. This is just like the time you—"

But sometimes Mutti would talk about how, when I was older,

I would live in a house down the road and come over to help with the cows, and we would have *Kaffeeklatsch*—coffee and gossip. She would give me the seat of honor on her prettiest armchair, and wheel out the round table with cake, and serve coffee in her pretty coffee sets, the ones with the man and woman having a picnic under a willow tree.

I'd never been sure how her plan would fit with my vision of my future life—performing Beethoven and Chopin to standing ovations across Europe, plus cows. But we would have made it fit. *There's always room,* Mutti used to say, when she asked me to squeeze one more jar of pickled beets onto the cellar shelf.

Now there would be no coffee sets, no *Kaffeeklatsch,* no round table on wheels.

"Do you think Mutti's coffee sets are all broken?" I wondered if anything in our farmhouse had survived.

"What are you talking about?" Hilde said. "Why does it matter?"

"It doesn't. Let's not fight. Not now."

The vinegary new-fabric scent in the room was overpowering, but it was better than the smell of unwashed bodies on the road. I sat with my back to Hilde and stretched out my legs, the room so small my feet almost touched the wall. For the first time, I felt safe enough to unpack Mutti's bag. There was the green sweater she'd knit last winter, a tin bowl with dents in the bottom, a needle and thread, her silver thimble. One at a time I brought each precious thing to my face and smelled it.

Knit stockings. A spoon, a pot. I hoped Ilse wouldn't barge in. I could hear her bustling up and down the stairs doing God knew what. At the very bottom of the bag I felt a zipper. At first I thought it belonged to a piece of clothing—but no, it was a pocket.

I unzipped it and pulled out a gold locket in the shape of a heart. I clutched it to my chest, imagining it was Mutti's heart, beating. Hilde was beside me in a flash. "Where did you get that?"

"From the bag," I said, even though it felt like it had materialized from thin air. I opened the locket. Inside was a photograph of Hilde and me.

She tried to take it out of my hand. "It's not yours."

"It's not yours either." I held on.

"Give it. You have no right to keep it. You're the one who—"

"What? The one who what?" I didn't want her to say it. But also I did. I deserved it. I *was* the one who. Suddenly the locket was in her hand and she was shoving it into her pocket.

"That's not fair," I said.

Hilde's face said, *Oh yes, it's more than fair.*

The sound of gunfire outside shut us up. I huddled closer to Hilde and she wrapped her arm around me. On the road below us, soldiers whooped and hollered. It was the unhinged noise of too much schnapps. I wished there was a window so we could see what was happening.

"What if they come in here?" I said.

"They won't."

But they could. No one ever thought a thing was possible until it was happening. And if they did come in? One by one, they would line us up. My mind reeled as I thought of the soldier who'd shot Mutti—the photograph he'd crushed in his hand; the way his mouth had twitched as if he was remembering the taste of bacon.

There was a gentle tap at our door and Otto poked his big head in. "Are you girls all right?"

We nodded.

"Frau," yelled a soldier outside. I held myself absolutely still. Another chimed in. "Frau."

They sounded so close. My imagination hid them every-where—beneath us in the clothing shop, crouched in the narrow stairway, hanging from the rooftop. I couldn't help but think of Hilde's bedtime stories of men with knives. It was guns they had now, and these weren't stories anymore.

"They've been doing this every night," Otto said. "Keep quiet. Not a word. They'll pass soon enough." But he brought us our shoes, just in case. I put mine on.

Not a word. I wouldn't look at Hilde. One word was all it had taken to kill Mutti. I swallowed hard, and the darkness dropped into my stomach.

I slipped the silver thimble on and off my finger while tiny paws scritch-scritched in the walls. Glass shattered in the distance. So much was breakable now, things I hadn't even considered: Countries. Music books. People.

Neither of us dared to breathe until the conversations and laughter were long gone.

My hand ached with the loss of the locket.

When we finally went to bed, I wouldn't take off my shoes. I lay still, staring up at the ceiling and wishing I could enjoy the luxury of being in a bedroom—even if we were sleeping on the floor. I insisted on leaving the door open to let some light into the room.

"Hilde?"

"What?"

"Did you know Scarlatti wrote his cat fugue after his cat walked across the keyboard? He used the notes that the cat stepped on."

"Well, it must not be very good," Hilde said.

The lead motif did sound like something a cat could have come up with. I thought about the Goldsteins' cat. It had been black and white through and through. A tuxedo cat, it was called. *A true performer,* Herr Goldstein used to say, because male concert pianists often wore tuxedoes when they performed. Even the roof of its mouth had been black and white. I'd seen it once when the cat had yawned.

One day I'd arrived for my lesson and it was gone.

Why? I asked Herr Goldstein. It made no sense. He loved that cat.

The answer seemed prickly in his mouth. *We're not allowed to have a cat anymore.*

Not allowed? *What do you mean? Why not?*

Why not? Because the world was upside-down, he'd said, *and everyone seemed to be thinking with their toenails.*

I imagined their cat hiding beneath a stranger's bed, terrified, waiting for a sign it could go home.

"Do you think Jacob is ever coming back?" I asked Hilde.

She pushed herself up on one arm. "Jacob Goldstein? Why are you asking about him?"

The secret burst out of me. I was sure this was how criminals got caught. Sooner or later, you had to tell someone. "He had . . ." I struggled to find the words. "He had long eyelashes." And a smile that made his face beautiful. "After my lesson, I used to have trouble looking at him, so I would not-look, but what I really wanted to do was look with all my heart. Do you know what I mean?"

It felt good to tell Hilde. I realized I'd wanted to, but so many things had been in the way: her friends, with their way of excluding me by standing close to her; her own boyfriend, Paul. But since we'd left home, she didn't seem as old or sophisticated as she'd once been.

She fixed me with a long look. "No one's coming back. The war is over, and no one is coming back. Not even Ilse's sons." She set herself back onto the blankets and turned away from me.

Even though she was right beside me in the close little room, I felt cold and alone. "Ilse's sons are not my fault, you know." *And neither is Jacob.*

"I never said they were."

Maybe life was an uphill/downhill sort of thing. You spent the first part getting things—a family, school, friends—and then the rest of it losing them, until finally you were left with nothing.

It took me a long time to fall asleep.

CHAPTER ELEVEN

THE NOTHING THAT
WAS SOMETHING

I woke up to Yesterday-Katja's worries. The garden needed weeding. Had Hilde fed the chickens, or would I have to face our terrible rooster alone, armed only with a broom and some bad words? If the weather was good, Mutti would want to hang out the bedsheets. She would need help, which meant my hands would be tired for practicing.

And then the empty place in my heart reminded me that yesterday was gone, and everything with it.

When I rolled over, I realized Hilde was already up. The dark room had tricked me into oversleeping. I took off my shoes and slipped out.

"Ilse and Otto aren't awake yet," she whispered. "Make yourself busy."

We opened windows to air out the rooms, and swept and

scrubbed. By the time Ilse was up, I had found two potatoes in the back of a cupboard and was boiling them for breakfast.

She heaved a loud sigh. "Those were supposed to last us till Sunday."

Thank you, Katja, for preparing breakfast. You're such a lovely girl, I would like you and your sister to live here for the rest of your lives.

Ilse served Otto first, and we waited for him to start eating before we began. A salt mill sat in the center of the table. Such an ordinary object—it produced a lump in my throat. I hadn't seen a salt mill in months. I picked it up and held it with both hands, as though it might disappear if I wasn't careful. It was empty.

"In one of the barns where we stayed," I said, "we shaved pieces off the cows' salt lick and ate them. Mutti said we can't live without salt." Said. Says. Was she present, or past?

I wasn't sure if Ilse was frowning at the idea of eating animal food, or at my mention of Mutti.

Otto nodded. "That's good thinking." He patted down his hair. I imagined him on a windy day, the fluff of hair launching his hat straight off his head.

Ilse glared at the pieces of potato on her plate. "We'll have to trade some of the merchandise for more food."

I wanted to crawl under the table.

"I'll go," Otto said.

"Alone? No." When Ilse wrung her hands, they made a rasping sound, like wings. "And with your arms full of clothes? The soldiers will take them away from you. They think everything belongs to them now."

"I'll wear them," Otto said.

I imagined him wearing ten coats in June with his fluffy hair and crooked glasses, looking even more like a crazy bear than he already did. I passed him a piece of my potato, but he wouldn't take it.

"And the dresses? What will you do about them?" Ilse's braid was wrapped so tightly around her head it pulled out every anxious thought she had.

"I'll go with Uncle Otto." I sat up straighter. Maybe Ilse would let me keep the striped dress. I would wear the others over top and trade them one by one, like peeling the layers off an onion. I'd make sure the Soviets didn't get them. I would make the best trades, and be the hero, and then—

Hilde looked up from her plate and I tried to read her expression.

- *You'll just back out at the last moment.* Or,

- *Sure, you're making friends with the easy one.* Or,

- *None of this would be happening if Mutti was alive.*

"You'll take the side streets," Ilse said, speaking to Otto. "And you'll be quick about it. No dawdling or stopping to talk to the neighbors. And"—she turned to me—"no nonsense from you. I don't want you attracting any attention."

When I thought of those grim-faced soldiers and the *thunk* of their boots, I regretted my offer. But Otto was already putting on his shoes, and there was no way I'd give Hilde the satisfaction of stepping up to rescue me again.

I was about to follow him out the door when Ilse put a hand on my arm. "You wait here until he's ready."

Otto rumbled down the stairs while I stood there feeling like

I was in trouble with the teacher. But then Hilde brought out her catalog photos and asked Ilse a question about pleats, and I didn't feel like waiting anymore, so I left.

I expected Otto to be in the shop gathering the clothes we would be trading. I made my way down the dark stairway, growing more excited as I turned the corner and took the smaller flight of stairs to the bottom. Finally, I would see the shop I'd heard so much about. How I wished Mutti were here so I could tell her about it.

The door to the shop was closed. Maybe he was inside. But no, something else was open beneath the stairs.

"Uncle Otto?"

He hurried out from under the stairwell, his arms full of clothes, pushing the wall shut with one side of his body. It must have been on a hinge, like a door. Except there was no handle. No sign that a door even existed. I stood there staring, until he thrust three dresses at me.

"Put these on."

I chose the red dress first and stepped into it awkwardly. It was too long, and it made me feel like a little girl trying on her mother's clothes—something I had never done, because Mutti wouldn't have allowed it (though I felt sure Hilde had done it). The ache in my chest returned.

Two more over top and I felt bulky and too warm, like I was on the road all over again.

Otto wore three jackets, a second pair of pants, and a blue alpine hat. He carried two other hats in his hand.

I waited for him to mention the room in the stairwell—if it even was a room. But he didn't.

He doesn't want you to know about it.

Because if he did, he would have said something like, *Would you like to know a secret?* And then he would have opened the door that wasn't a door and shown me what was inside.

Instead, he'd hustled out and pretended it was nothing—which a person only did if that nothing was something big.

What was in there?

We stepped out into the bright day. It was quiet on the streets, but it was the silence of held breath. At its edges I sensed eyes behind curtains and bodies tucked into shadows. The air was warm, the trees were in blossom, and sparrows acted as though there had never been a war.

Otto walked like a man who was used to his stomach arriving before him, even though it didn't anymore. But he also walked quickly. I struggled to keep up.

"Where are we going?" I asked between breaths. Sweat trickled down the back of my neck.

"To the other side of the river. To find people who have something to trade." He looked straight ahead when he spoke, as if turning to face me might slow him down.

"Are there lots of hats in your shop?" Hilde fancied the ones with feathers in them.

"There are hats," he said.

Some of the shops we passed were boarded up, and a sign on their doors said *Empty*. It made me nervous. No one ever imagined the world could stop working all of a sudden, that shops would have nothing in them and money could be worthless. But anything could happen. Nothing was guaranteed.

When we arrived in the square, the man from the fountain was sitting in the middle of the road.

"You can't sit there, Herr Johannsen," Otto called to him. "You'll get run over."

But the fountain man, Herr Johannsen, didn't move.

"He doesn't have all the cups in his cupboard," Otto said quietly to me. Even though Otto was the one wearing three jackets in June.

He handed me the hats and went over to Herr Johannsen, lifting him to his feet and leading him to a bench by the park.

"This is much safer," Otto said.

"Have you seen Isabella?" Herr Johannsen asked.

"I think Isabella is in Berlin, isn't she?" Otto patted him on the shoulder, tipped his hat to him, and wished him a good day.

When Otto came back, I said, "Who's Isabella?"

"No one really knows. Herr Johannsen has been unwell for as long as anyone can remember."

"Is he dangerous?" I asked.

"No. He's more of a nuisance than anything. He follows people home, you know. Sometimes he gets quite worked up about Isabella—whoever she is."

I looked over my shoulder. I wanted to say something to Herr Johannsen. I knew what it felt like when the only thing you had in your life was the knowledge that the most special person in it was missing.

CHAPTER TWELVE

A WOMAN OF MEANS

The river was lined with old men and young boys, fishing. There was a musky smell in the air, and the gentle swish of moving water. Crossing the footbridge to the other side was like entering a different land. The streets were cleaner, the shops had brightly painted windowsills, and some of the half-timbered homes had decorative panels that were carved with wolves or the seashore. If Ilse's side of town was plain old knee socks, this was the see-through stocking side.

When we stopped in front of a large black door, I realized this wasn't a random visit. Otto lifted the heavy knocker and it came down like a fist.

A tall older man with a thin white mustache answered the door. "Can I help you?" He stood so stiffly in front of us it seemed like his screws were too tight.

"Herr Doktor Doktor, good day. Otto Daschner, from

Daschner's Damen und Herrenmode." Otto offered his hand. His voice had become slippery, his face red and sweaty from all the extra clothes he wore. "My niece and I have some very fine items to present to you in trade."

"Darling," the man called into the dark home behind him.

I stifled a groan, bracing myself for the appearance of his wife. There'd been a couple like this in our town: the age-spotted man who wore bow ties and pretended to be a doctor of everything, not just two things, and his wife who acted like she was a doctor simply because she'd married him.

The Frau Doktor Doktor in our town used to get upset if Mutti brought us to her door in dresses that were the wrong color for the season (even though Mutti had only one color—brown—and only one season: work).

The double doctor opened the door wider. I wasn't sure if this meant we were supposed to come in, but Otto pushed right through, so I followed.

Inside the entrance hallway was a grandfather clock even taller than Otto, with a long steady arm that swung back and forth. Its loud ticking made the rest of the house feel all the more silent. I was surprised the Soviets hadn't confiscated it. The lamps gave off a smell of kerosene, and on the wall was a glass case that housed what looked like spider specimens.

The home had probably been elegant before the war, but there was a scuffed, frayed look to it now, like a rich man down on his luck.

Two sets of house shoes slap-slapped down the hall.

"Who is it now?" A woman rounded the corner, a sour look

on her face. She was older than Ilse, but I could tell she was a woman of means. Her stockings still had some stretch to them, and she wore color on her face and perfume with a flowery scent. I could practically hear Mutti's voice next to me. *The world is upside down, but this one still needs her hat to match her shoes.* A younger version that had to be her daughter followed closely behind.

"Clothing," said the double doctor. "Again." He left the entryway to the women.

I felt embarrassed for Otto. Instead of presiding over his elegant shop, he was now a door-to-door peddler.

I waited for Frau Doktor Doktor to invite us to sit down. *Would you be so kind as to*—but she wasn't, so we didn't.

The girl and I locked eyes. She was probably Hilde's age, and had long hair that was even nicer than Hilde's, and wore pink lipstick. Her teeth were big, though, like a horse. *Handsome,* Mutti would have called her. Not beautiful.

I realized I was staring, and then remembered I was the one wearing four dresses, and my face grew even hotter than it already was.

"We're not interested," said the mother, before we'd even shown her anything.

"No," said the daughter. "I want to see the dresses."

I glanced at Otto, unsure of what to do. "Should I take them off?"

"For goodness' sake, we don't have all day." Frau Doktor Doktor huffed. "Just lift up the skirts to show us the colors." She turned to her daughter. "You don't really need another dress."

The war had barely skinned this family's knees—although I was certain the daughter would have disagreed. She would have listed the things the war had taken from her:

- her dancing shoes

- a red handbag that didn't match

- her second-favorite perfume

I lifted the dresses to show her, even though I knew there was no point. She barely looked at them.

Maybe the double doctor had taken pity on us and gone to the kitchen to find us something to eat. I held the wall to keep myself steady. The mother kept her eye on my hand, in case I left a mark.

"Could you make me one?" the daughter asked.

"A dress?" I said.

"Obviously."

"Oh. Not me," I said. "But my aunt could. Couldn't she, Uncle Otto?"

"I don't think—" Frau Doktor Doktor began.

"Mummy, please. Just one."

"We'll have to discuss it."

Otto said, "Perhaps your husband would like—"

"No," Frau Doktor Doktor said. "He would not."

"Is he a doctor of spiders?" I blurted.

She drew back suddenly, as though she'd stepped in horse manure. "He is an arachnologist, among other things, yes. Thank you for your time."

Spiders. It was a mystery to me, the lives some people chose for themselves.

Herr Doktor Doktor did not return with food. His wife held on to the open door, which was the sign that we were supposed to use it, so we did.

CHAPTER THIRTEEN

WHO ARE YOU, HERR HARTMANN?

"The next one will be better," Otto said to me after Frau Doktor Doktor had shut her big black door on us. "Many of our regular customers live in this neighborhood."

But it wasn't. The trouble was, people wanted food more than they wanted a new hat or a pretty dress.

We tried to stay on the shady side of the street. Even so, it felt stuffy with the extra clothes on. If Ilse had seen me sweating into her dresses, she would have stomped her this-way foot and yelled at me. Also, I didn't like the silence in the town. It felt like everyone was playing dead—or maybe they weren't playing.

Finally Otto managed to trade a hat for a small bag of flour, and I talked a woman into buying the red dress for six potatoes.

"You're a natural," Otto said.

"Will Aunt Ilse be happy?"

Otto let out a sigh: *Is she ever happy?*

I was so hungry I wanted to eat one of the potatoes raw, like an apple, but Mutti would have lectured me about manners.

We crossed the footbridge again and were on our way back to the shop when a fancy black Mercedes drove toward us. My chest tightened. I thought of Jacob, and Herr Goldstein, and the cat with black patches on the roof of its mouth. I thought of Frau Goldstein's delicious poppy seed cookies, and all the fancy black Mercedes-Benzes that the important SS officers and Gestapo agents used to drive around in.

But these weren't Germans. I noticed the caps with Red Star emblems. They were Soviets. They must have found the car somewhere, or stolen it. As they slowed alongside us, I edged closer to Otto.

"I'll do the talking," he said. "You say nothing."

It was sound advice, though I'd never been much good at following it.

The driver was an older officer with oiled black hair and an expression as grim as concrete. I was certain the younger man sitting beside him was his son, even though the only thing that said *kin* was his nose, which was as long and straight as the older man's. The young officer had dark eyebrows, a scar along one cheek, and the bluest eyes I'd ever seen. I could feel him staring at me. When I thought of the way Mutti had fallen beside me, all the grief I'd been carrying hardened into hatred. I wanted to glare, or spit at him, but I couldn't lift my eyes from the shiny black car.

The car stopped, and the men got out.

"*Dokumenty*," the older officer said.

Otto reached beneath his coats and dug into his cardigan

pocket. I had to lift two of the dresses to access my card. My face went hot with embarrassment.

The older man studied Otto's card, said something to his son in Russian, and passed the card to him. Then the older man looked at my card and said, in strongly accented German, "She is a refugee?"

Scheisse.

"No." Otto put his arm around me. "She's family."

The man tapped the card and shook his head.

"She left her ration card at home," Otto said.

The man clicked his tongue. "Refugee. Out."

The heat was making me dizzy. The memory of the Soviets kicking us out of our home was still too raw.

Otto passed him the hat he was holding and said, "Here. For you."

The man took off his army cap and tried the hat on.

Otto smiled at him. "It suits you. It looks good."

He tried to hand it back, but Otto said, "Keep it."

The man offered his hand and Otto shook it.

"Herr Hartmann." The son handed the identity card back to Otto.

I couldn't help a sideways glance. Herr Hartmann? But his name was Otto Daschner. Otto stuffed the identity card into a coat pocket and said, "Come, Katja."

The men got back into the Mercedes and drove away, leaving the sharp scent of diesel behind them.

I waited until I couldn't hear the car anymore. "Why did he call you Herr Hartmann?" I didn't want to make Otto feel uncomfortable, but what was I supposed to do when he had told an important lie right in front of me?

"Well, that's one less hat for us to sell," he said. "I suppose we should be grateful they didn't send you away."

So. He would do what he'd done with the room and pretend nothing had happened. *Make it small to keep it small.* That might have fooled some people, but it didn't work with me. As a younger sister, I was an expert at making somethings into nothings, so I recognized when it was being done to me. But I also knew better than to persist. He had stood up for me; he'd given away one of his hats.

"Those men are such savages," I said, and then wished I hadn't. It felt like the right word, but also the wrong one.

"Not at all," he said. "They were well groomed and respectful. Occupation troops, in my opinion. Didn't you notice the shoulder boards? That older fellow was a colonel general. Probably knows his Goethe better than we do."

I doubted that.

"Looks like our Soviet friends might be staying awhile," Otto said. "When your mother gets here and you girls move on, you'll want to leave this area and find the Amis."

Right. I'll tell her. When she gets here and we move on. So much for ration cards. We weren't indispensable after all.

Who are you, Herr Hartmann? I wanted to ask. *Why are you carrying false papers?*

When we got home, Ilse and Hilde were sitting at the table together looking at clothing catalogs. I wanted to knock Ilse out of the way. Hilde had never looked at fashions with anyone other than me. It had started when I was young and smart enough to know it was important. We'd always shared this as sisters; it was the only time she'd ever allowed me on her bed. With the catalog on our laps, we would dress ourselves in this silk scarf, that elegant evening dress, that fancy hat (with feathers for Hilde, even though I thought they looked silly, but I would never have said so, not during those moments).

"What do you think of the pleated skirt on page fourteen?" Ilse's tone made it sound like there could be a wrong answer.

Hilde gave a sensible response, as if she'd been thinking of pleats for weeks—which she probably had. I remembered Mutti mentioning how Ilse yearned for female companionship in her letters. That was one of the reasons Mutti had decided to go to Fahlhoff. "Three women coming to stay with her?" she'd said. "Ilse will be thrilled. All she's ever had in that house is men."

One of the photographs in the sitting room was of Otto and the two boys, with guns and a dead boar—probably the boar that now glared at everyone from the wall with its nut-hard eyes. I imagined a common language around the supper table—hunting, circuit boards, machines requiring diesel fuel—that had never included Ilse.

I pushed in and sat on Hilde's other side, pointing to a pair of dark blue shoes with a heel. "Remember how you always wanted some like those?"

Hilde shrugged. "Mutti says they're not practical for a girl my age."

"Nonsense." Ilse slid back her chair hard. "Fashion is not about practicality. It's a declaration." Then she noticed all the dresses I was wearing. "Take those off. You'll soil them."

I held up my bag of potatoes. "I sold the red dress."

She took the bag from me and set it on the counter. Otto still wore the extra pants and jackets. She straightened all three sets of lapels, blinking repeatedly as if holding back tears.

"It wasn't that bad, darling," he said. But his red face and the strands of sweaty hair pasted to his forehead told the truth. Mutti had described their shop as elegant. The wealthiest people in town had come to them.

"She wouldn't buy any of the dresses we brought," he said to Ilse. "But her daughter wants one—bespoke, naturally."

He must have been talking about the double doctor's family.

Ilse was quiet for a moment. "We might have enough of that checkered fabric to make her a dress, although I'll have to sew it all by hand now."

"Ach, she'll complain about the fabric, you know she will." Otto trundled out of the kitchen. "Nothing is ever good enough for those people."

Ilse followed him. "In these times? No one has anything new. She'll appreciate it."

I peeled off the dresses I was wearing and they puddled at my feet like the skins of old lives. "Sorry for leaving you alone with her," I said to Hilde, my voice low. Conspiratorial.

"I don't know what you mean," she said. "We had fun."

Oh. "We saw a Russian general and his son driving one of the SS's Mercedes in town. Otto thinks they're Occupation troops."

"And . . . ?" *I should care, because . . . ?*

"I met a girl your age on the other side of the river. She wore pink lipstick."

She perked up. "Pink? Really? Who is she?"

"The daughter of a double doctor. But I don't think—"

Hilde walked out of the kitchen without waiting for me to finish.

Later, on our pile of blankets, I asked if we could look at one of Ilse's catalogs together.

"I don't feel like it," she said, and took out her love letters from Paul.

CHAPTER FOURTEEN

A SOLVABLE EQUATION

The next morning Ilse handed us our clean, dry clothes. "There you are. All ready to go." *Your visit is over. It's been nice knowing you.*

I didn't want my old dresses back. She would never send us away in borrowed clothes. In my own clothes, anything could happen.

We went into our room to change.

"That cow," Hilde whispered to me. "After all the time I spent with her."

I took off Ilse's dress. I would miss the cool sensation of the fabric and how pretty it had made me feel. I'd wanted a chance to grow into it. Now it was back to the functional brown I'd always worn on the farm because it didn't show stains.

"We're not going anywhere," I said. "We're indispensable, remember?"

When we came out of the bedroom, Ilse and Otto were sitting on the sofa. He was massaging oil into her hands, working each finger at a time. It must have smelled nice, once—eucalyptus, like their shop. But the oil was rancid now and made my stomach turn over.

"We're going to look for food," I announced.

"Good. I'll take a kilo of bacon and a jug of milk." Otto winked at me.

"Sure thing," I said. *Because we're magicians.*

"Take the baskets in the kitchen," he said.

"You do understand," Ilse said to us, "there's no way you can stay here once the boys come home. Oh, they've got appetites, those two. You've never seen the like. I used to add flour to our eggs to stretch them."

Stretched meant see-through thin and not enough of, not quite the right ingredients. Mutti had been stretching things for years, and not just food: shoes that got handed down, paper we reused, sweaters that had grown too small and could be combined and re-knit into something bigger. How much could something stretch before it broke?

I hoped the boys didn't come home—but the thought pricked at me like bits of hay stuck in my knee socks. How could I wish that on anyone?

"I know how to trap rabbits," I said. Papi had taught me to make snares. I'd never done the actual killing, but Hilde was good at it.

"You're going to catch a rabbit?" Ilse pulled her hands, shiny with oil, away from Otto's, careful not to touch her dress. "I'll believe that when I see it."

I wasn't much good at mathematics, but I glimpsed an equation I could solve: Katja + one dead rabbit = three more days at Ilse's house.

Otto pushed himself up with an *oof.* "Head out of town, to the countryside. That's where the boys and I used to do our hunting. You might have some luck."

Out of town? That would mean a checkpoint on our return. Didn't he remember the confrontation we'd had yesterday with the Soviets? Maybe he was trying to get rid of us. I wanted to catch his eye, but he stood up and said, "I've got some wire you can use for snares."

Ilse rolled her eyes as he left the apartment, his footfalls sounding heavy on the stairs. Was he going to the secret room? I longed to run out the door and catch him at it, but I decided it was better that Ilse didn't know I knew about the room. A few minutes later he returned with a bird's nest of thin wire.

So. It wasn't just clothing that was stored down there.

"Wire is precious," Ilse muttered. "This better pay off."

I took the wire from Otto and sat on the floor to put on my shoes. Mutti would have scolded me for being unladylike, but I was preoccupied. What would we do about the checkpoint? What else was in that secret room?

Ilse turned to Otto. "I was thinking I'd invite Frau Doktor Doktor and her daughter over for coffee and cake."

Coffee and cake? Where would she get those?

"I'm telling you, it's not worth it," Otto said.

"She's our most faithful customer," Ilse said, "and she's the only one who can really pay. That's worth a little aggravation, don't you think?"

Hilde and I made our way down the dark stairwell. I glanced

at the wall that was actually a door. There was no sign that behind it was a room. No sign there was anything there at all.

"You know what?" I said to my sister.

"No, *Scheisskopf.* Not another one of your stupid composer stories. I do not have the patience." When she pushed the front door open, we were blinded by sunlight. "Now they'll expect a rabbit from us. Everything's going to be worse when we don't bring one home."

Fine. I wouldn't tell her about the secret room.

We stepped outside. How could the sun feel warm on our faces, *and* the only people we knew in Fahlhoff might put us out on the street?

"Farmers won't just let us set snares on their property, you know," Hilde said as we began walking. "What were you thinking?"

"They don't have to know," I said.

Hilde stood straighter, as though to emphasize that perfect posture and trespassing didn't go together.

"Girls." Otto appeared behind us. "Come with me. Don't tell your aunt. You can't wander around town without proper identification." He led us to the town square and into the *Kommandatura,* the local Soviet command they'd set up in the city hall. "These are my nieces," he said to a man behind a desk. "They'll be living with us now."

Not just for a few days? Had he guessed about Mutti, or was he making sure his rabbit hunters returned? "Do they have jobs?" the man asked.

Jobs. I bit my lip, but Otto said, "Yes. They're working with me and my wife selling clothing." He filled out some forms while Hilde and I stood in the corner with our heads down, hoping to blend in with the ugly green paint on the walls. The man registered us and gave us new papers and ration cards.

"There," Otto said once we were outside again. "Now you won't have to worry about the authorities. Good luck with your hunting." He winked at me and set off for home.

The idea of a rabbit only made me hungrier. And now that Otto had gone out of his way for us, I wanted to bring one home more than ever.

As we walked, the landscape grew greener. Late spring burst through hydrangea and lilac bushes—which I only knew were hydrangea and lilac because Hilde had fulfilled her older-sister duty of knowing better. We scuffed our shoes along the road the way we might have on any June morning. I swung my basket, waiting for someone (Mutti) to tell me to stop, gulping back the sadness that threatened to leak out of me all over again.

"Slow down, would you?" I said to Hilde. "My feet hurt." So did my heart.

A horse-drawn wagon passed us with a large dining room table strapped to it, driven by a soldier in a Red Army uniform. "Look at that," I said. "They're taking whatever they want."

Hilde stared into the distant hills. "We *should* get jobs. Actual ones."

"Where?"

"We know how to work on a farm. And farmers will need help, just like we did after Papi left for the war."

"How will they pay us?" I said. "Ever think of that?"

"They'll pay us in food. Sausages, eggs, milk. And we can bring it home to Ilse and then she won't throw us out."

I swung my basket until Hilde shouted at me to stop.

I didn't want her to be right—but she was.

CHAPTER FIFTEEN

THANK YOU, *SCHEISSKOPF*, FOR THINKING ON YOUR FEET

At the first door we knocked on, the people thought we were hamster women—women from the city who came to trade whatever they had for food. But then we showed them our hands (that was my idea): the hands of girls who (dug graves) knew how to work hard. They said *no*.

At the second farmhouse, we listed all the animals we'd taken care of (also my idea): cows, horses, chickens, geese, goats.

No.

At the third I said, "Do you have a piano?" and Hilde leaned on my toes.

"You girls are strangers here," said the woman at the fourth door. "Why should we bother with a couple of fish heads when we have enough trouble feeding our own?"

We weren't two girls with empty stomachs. We were Pomeranians—fish heads. Borders were borders.

The fifth farmhouse was a small place with white paint peeling from the walls. There were three apple trees in the front yard, and outside the door there was a decorative wall with a design of the Pomeranian griffin done in colored stone. I tugged on Hilde's sleeve and whispered, "They're fish heads too."

The woman who answered the door wore a carefully mended apron. There were dark half-moons beneath her eyes, and a sadness resting on her shoulders that made me think of my empty bucket. But something in the way she stood, ready to weather any storm, reminded me of Mutti.

She had strong hands, so big they looked like they belonged on a man's body. You could tell a lot about a person from their hands. Mine were small, but I had long nimble fingers, perfect for arpeggios. It had been a while since I'd thought about arpeggios.

The top of an envelope peeked from her pocket. I spied its black border and said, "I'm sorry for your news."

"It's old news now," she said.

But it stayed fresh for such a long time.

"You girls are not from Fahlhoff," she said.

Not this again. "We're from Pomerania, like you." It wasn't just the decorative wall; I heard it in her accent.

"We're staying in town," Hilde added quickly. "With relatives."

"Good," the woman said. "I've already taken in one boarder. I'm not interested in taking any more. What can I do for you?"

"We're looking for work," Hilde said.

"Work. Well."

"What my sister means is, we need to bring home food," I said, "or our aunt will throw us out."

The woman took a step backward. "Throw you out? Where's your mother? Surely she wouldn't put up with such—"

"Our mother is dead," I blurted. It was the first time I'd said it out loud.

One look, that was all Hilde needed to give me: I shouldn't have said anything. How many times had Mutti told me the wisest words were the ones you didn't say out loud?

"I'm sad to hear that." The woman introduced herself as Frau Weber. "Who is this aunt of yours? How could she think of turning out two motherless girls?"

It was like sight-reading a piece with a sudden key change. Even though you could see it coming, your fingers still got tangled up in the new sharps or flats. My head felt cluttered with all the contrary stories we'd told. Hilde's face went splotchy. Why had I mentioned Mutti?

"She's not really our aunt," I said.

"Maybe I know her," Frau Weber said. "What's her name?"

Hilde and I exchanged a glance.

"Ilse Daschner," I said, at the same time Hilde said, "Edith Schneider."

Frau Weber raised an eyebrow. "I don't know any Edith Schneider, but Frau Daschner, certainly. She owns the clothing shop in town with her husband. I used to admire their dresses in the window."

Great. Perfect.

"I haven't been by there lately," she added.

"It's closed," I said. "The windows are all boarded up."

"In that case, I should really stop in at her home and pay my respects," Frau Weber said. "Especially now that I've met you girls. Two extra people in her household—no wonder she needs more food. Doesn't she have sons?"

The sons, again. "Yes," I said.

Hilde stepped away from the door, pulling me with her. "We're sorry to have bothered you," she said to Frau Weber. "We won't take up any more of your time."

But Frau Weber placed a hand on each of our shoulders. "My husband and sons all died in the war. I have a boy staying here, but I could use more help."

An awkward silence followed. I mentioned rabbit snares.

"You can go ahead and set them if you like," Frau Weber said. "I doubt you'll catch anything, but it never hurts to try."

We went into her garden and I brought out the wire. Papi had always kept his coiled neatly. Otto's wire was a mess. My fingers struggled with the thin, flexible material, measuring out about fifty centimeters. Frau Weber used an ax to cut it. I twisted a small loop into one end and fed the other end through to make a noose. Then I made another, bigger loop, and attached the snare at an opening in the fence. We set another near the garden entrance. It felt strange doing it without Mutti. There was no one to say, *You set the snares, Katja,* so I could say, *I don't feel like it,* and Mutti could call me Katarina Wilhelmina and get cross with me.

Hilde asked about the boy, but he wasn't home.

"You can come tomorrow morning as soon as curfew's over to help milk the cows and clean the barn," Frau Weber said. "There's garden work—"

"Hilde apprenticed in horticulture," I said.

Hilde smacked me on the arm for interrupting, but she stood a little taller.

"Garden work," Frau Weber resumed, "and eggs to collect for the Soviets, and I hope to plow the field one of these days."

"Isn't it late for plowing?" I asked. Papi had never waited until June.

"Yes. But the Soviets make us share one horse and plow among all the farms on this road. I have to wait my turn." She flattened her hand against the envelope. "Why don't you girls top up the water troughs and then you can go out into the field and see if there are any potatoes left over from last year's harvest. Whatever you find, you can take home to Frau Daschner."

I winced at the mention of Ilse's name.

"And"—she went into the house and came out with a small chunk of salami—"please pass this on to her with my kindest regards."

Frau Weber left us to the troughs, which we filled quickly so that we could get to the potatoes. As we tramped through the long grass, crickets flew up around us. The field had a lush earthy scent that reminded me of the way Papi's coat used to smell. I grazed my open hand along the soft tips of the grass. "I shouldn't have mentioned Mutti."

Hilde looked as if she'd taken a bite of bitter dandelion greens. "How do you not understand when to speak up and when to keep your mouth shut?"

"I do understand."

"Do you?" She stomped the grass down as she walked. "What if she visits Ilse? What if she says something about Mutti?"

How could I have foreseen that Frau Weber would know Ilse? Lying was too much like playing chess, a game I'd never been good at.

We brought home some potatoes, as well as nettles and mushrooms from the nearby forest. Hilde hid the salami in her pocket. As usual, she was five moves ahead.

"No rabbit?" Ilse said.

"It's too soon," I said. "I just set the snares."

She held up a limp nettle. "This is not nearly enough food for four people. If you can't do any better than this—"

Hilde stood beside her, gathering up the mushrooms, and Ilse's nose crinkled.

She poked at the bulge in Hilde's pocket. "What do you have in there?"

Hilde had no choice. She took out the salami and set it on the table.

Ilse's face went slack. "Where on earth did you get that?"

I looked at my sister, my mouth clamped shut.

"We found jobs," Hilde said finally.

"Is that so?" Ilse set her hands on her hips. "That's interesting, for two girls who are passing through town. And where exactly did you find these jobs?"

"On a farm," I said.

"Whose farm?"

Neither of us answered.

"It's that Pomeranian woman, I bet." Ilse fell silent for a moment. Then her face twisted, as though someone had just toasted her with a glass of water. "Isn't she the one who lost all her sons?" Even Mutti, who was not superstitious, would never have toasted with water. It meant you wished death on everyone around you. "What's her name again?"

"What is her name?" I said.

Hilde didn't remember. "Her windows weren't as clean as yours," she said in her catalog voice.

Ilse gave a vigorous nod. Dirty windows were out of the question in her version of Germany.

"And she wore *Tracht*," Hilde added. "Like Eva Braun." Hitler's girlfriend.

"A woman like that?" Ilse said. "I'm not the least bit surprised."

I had to bite my tongue. Frau Weber hadn't worn a traditional Dirndl. The Nazis had wanted farm women to dress that way, but hardly any of them did.

"So." Ilse looked like she wanted to swat us with a broom. "When were you planning to tell me about this salami?"

I thought quickly. "It was going to be a surprise. We wanted Uncle Otto to be here."

With a sharp knife, she shaved off a thin slice and stuffed it in her mouth. "What will your new employer think when your mother arrives and you have to leave? When is your mother getting here, anyway?"

Hilde took the mushrooms to the sink to wash them, while I lined up my shoes.

I waited until my sister and I were alone in our cupboard of a room. "We should get jobs," I mimicked in her know-it-all voice. "Let's keep the salami. What does the Norse princess have to say now?"

Hilde used a small piece of wood to push down her cuticles. Her nails had become the most important thing in the room. "If you hadn't told Frau Weber about Mutti—"

I held Mutti's bag against my chest. "If I hadn't told her, we'd be having nettles for supper instead of salami, so thank you, Katja, for thinking on your feet."

"Thank you, *Scheisskopf*, for thinking on your feet." She threw the piece of wood at me and started brushing her hair.

CHAPTER SIXTEEN

HIND LEGS

Early the next morning Hilde and I stood at the entrance to Frau Weber's barn. Inside there were four cows, each with a calf—though the calves had already been separated from their mothers so they wouldn't drink all the milk. The barn was warm from the animals' body heat and smelled richly of their hides. A young man sat on a milking stool, humming softly as he milked one of the cows. After Papi was gone, that would have been me—except I would have done it properly.

"You haven't tied her hind legs," I said.

"Don't need to." The young man didn't even look at me.

"That's what you think. Then comes the day she decides to kick you and your full bucket of milk, which won't happen if you tie her legs." Papi had taught us everything about milking cows. Number one was cleanliness, which the young man also didn't seem to care about, because the cow's teats were dirty. Number two was leg tying.

"Frau Weber doesn't tie them," he said.

"See?" Hilde said to me. "Nobody wants your mustard on their bratwurst." She pushed past me and introduced herself. "And my loudmouth sister back there is Katja, but don't pay any attention to her."

When Hilde smiled at him, I knew she didn't have to worry: she would get all of his attention.

His name was Oskar, and he was only a few years older than us—an endangered species. Oskar had dark hair and brown eyes, and a complexion like a rough road. He looked so skinny I was afraid he'd snap in two. When something fluttered and crashed in the hayloft, he nearly fell off his stool. The cow startled and tried to pull away from him.

"Probably bats," I said. "Or an owl. The cows won't give as much milk if you spook them, you know."

My words made no impression on him.

Hilde chose the cow next to his and positioned her stool so she could talk to him. *Blah blah* about the books she'd read, and the dance hall we'd seen boarded up in town, and the bakery that never had any bread. I sat farther away and tried to think of something to say. *Did you know Mozart liked to imitate cats?*

Talking to Jacob had been different. The Goldsteins had been as familiar to me as a favorite shirt. After Jacob, well—there'd been no After Jacob. After he'd gone away, boys seemed pointless. They either died or disappeared.

Anyway, I was happier doing the milking in silence, listening to the warm, frothy liquid ping against the empty bucket and then whoosh once there was enough milk at the bottom. I couldn't bear to let my mind drift back to the time when Papi had done the milking. Mutti would be waiting in the kitchen for him with a second breakfast of cheese, thinly sliced ham, and pumpernickel bread.

Frau Weber bustled into the barn with cups and told us to have some milk before the Soviets came to take it. "Not too much," she said, "or they'll notice."

"How much milk do they take?" I asked.

"All of it." She looked like she wanted to bash something with a shovel. "It's the only reason they let me keep the cows. We do the work; they get the bounty."

The milk was still warm.

"Drink it slowly," she said, "or your stomachs will get angry."

The milk reminded me so much of home: our barn, and the must-be-done regularity of chores; Mutti warning me that if I made the cows wait too long to be milked they would get annoyed and poop on me. I went out to the pump and splashed my face with cold water to keep from crying.

When I came back, Frau Weber gave us our instructions. We needed to shovel the stalls, fork hay into the mangers, and fill the troughs with water. In the meantime, she moved hay bales to one side and slid open a door I hadn't realized was there. Behind it there were other stalls, containing chickens, another cow and calf, and two goats. Oskar rushed in to milk the cow.

"You're not to speak of these animals," Frau Weber said while she gathered eggs. "The Soviets don't know about them, so they can't take them away or impose quotas. And if you hear a vehicle in the driveway, this door is the first priority. It must be shut and hidden at all times. Is that clear?"

Hilde and I both nodded.

Frau Weber handed us shovels. We cleaned the secret stalls while she emptied the other buckets of milk into churns. When Oskar was done, he took the extra bucket of milk into the house, and then helped Frau Weber carry the churns to the road, where the soldiers would pick them up. We filled the water troughs and began mucking out the regular cow stalls.

I was wheeling a full barrow toward the manure pile, trying to keep it steady so it wouldn't tip, when Frau Weber cried, "Katja, come see. We've caught a rabbit."

The three of us dropped what we were doing and rushed over. Sure enough, there was a rabbit in my snare. It was still alive.

"We'll have to kill it," I said. Big tough hunter; as if I was the one who'd do that job.

"Won't it bite you?" Oskar asked.

"They never bite," I said. "It's their hind legs you have to worry about."

Oskar gave me a look like *not this again.*

I grabbed it from behind and Hilde wiggled it out of the snare. Then she said, "Yeah, yeah, give it to me, I'll do it."

She took the rabbit by the hind legs in one hand, and with the other she pressed her thumb into the back of its neck and wrapped her fingers around its chin. There was a snap, and it was done, the neck was broken. Hilde pulled on the head and legs a few times to be sure. My sister was fearsomely efficient at that job.

When I looked up, Oskar was gone.

Frau Weber put out her hands for the rabbit. "It's all still too much for him."

"What is?" I asked.

"Life. Death. Be gentle with him. He never wanted to be a soldier. He deserted his regiment months ago and was living in forests and garden sheds. I found him hiding in the barn and kept him in the house until the war was over."

I remembered the young German soldier with the sign around his neck. That could have been Oskar.

"I'll gut and skin the rabbit, and store it in the cellar until you go home," Frau Weber said.

"Don't you want to keep it?" I asked.

Behind her, Hilde rolled her eyes at me.

"I'll take the next one. You girls keep your aunt happy. Did she like her salami?"

"Yes," I said, careful not to show too much enthusiasm.

Frau Weber picked up a shovel and dug in the garden. I thought she was weeding, but then out came a jar of pears. She cocked her head. "You never can tell what this garden will grow."

Mutti would have thought up a clever plan like that too. And Frau Weber was like Mutti in another way: she never dawdled. There was always something useful in her hands. Even after supper, when we listened to the radio in the sitting room or I played piano, Mutti would be knitting socks, or mending an apron, or crocheting something pretty. *He who rests grows rusty,* she liked to say.

I wished I still had Mutti's doily to show Frau Weber. She would have appreciated the intricacy of the pattern, and how the things that weren't there were as important as the ones that were.

CHAPTER SEVENTEEN

EXAMPLE NUMBER THREE OF RABBIT STEW

That afternoon Frau Weber sent us home with four slices of bread in Hilde's basket and the rabbit in mine—both the meat and the fur. We'd eaten pears for lunch, with a small bite of sausage. My stomach gurgled as it woke up again. Before going home, we stopped in the forest to collect mushrooms. We also gathered nettles, and some ground ivy that smelled deliciously minty.

"Oskar seems a bit dull," I said.

Hilde laughed.

"What?" What had I missed this time? While I'd been feeding the secret chickens, she had spent her time talking to him.

"He knows people." The way Hilde said it made it seem like she knew people too, just by knowing Oskar.

"What's that supposed to mean?" I kicked at a rock. "Who does he know?"

"People who can get things."

"Like a piano?" As soon as it popped out of my mouth, I realized how dumb it sounded.

"For God's sake, can't you think of anything else?" Hilde said. "It's the black market. They can't run around with pianos under their coats. Anyway, I'm just saying, he's not dull. He's a friend worth having."

Maybe. I could already tell he didn't like me. I patted the top of my basket, still proud of the rabbit. "I got one. I did it."

"All you did was set the snare, huntsman. I'm the one who broke its neck." She unfastened her braid and tossed her long brown hair behind her until it caught the breeze like a flag. "You don't have to make a big deal of it. It's just a rabbit."

But a rabbit hadn't been *just* a rabbit for years now. I weighed the basket in both hands. It was heavy. This would be a lot of meat. "Ilse will make stew. If Frau Weber gives us some eggs, we can make a mixture to tan the hide. You'll have the beginnings of a pretty winter hat."

Hilde pressed her hands to her hair, probably already feeling the soft fur. "Maybe Ilse won't complain so much when we show up with that rabbit."

Now it was *we*.

"Example number one of rabbit stew," I proclaimed as we walked. It was like we were back on the road again with the borscht ladies, talking about food. "Add some mushrooms, which we're bringing, and parsnips—Ilse might have parsnips."

"Potatoes," Hilde said.

"No, wait. Sherry, oranges."

"Like anyone has those. Potatoes."

We passed through the checkpoint and turned onto a quieter cobbled street.

"Okay, Miss Sourpuss, this one's for you," I said. "Example number two of rabbit stew: potatoes."

"Finally," Hilde said. "Something sensible."

"And bacon," I threw in.

Before I could make it to example number three, the shiny black Mercedes rounded the corner and came toward us. This time the younger blue-eyed officer was driving. His cement-faced father was in the passenger seat and another man sat in the back. The car slowed to a stop before it reached us, and all three men got out.

"Keep walking," Hilde said under her breath, but we had to pass right by them.

I kept my head down and focused on their boots. They were big, and black, and looked a lot more comfortable than my worn brown shoes.

"*Nemetski,*" one of them said to us as we passed. I now knew that meant "mute ones." That was their name for Germans, because we didn't speak their language.

"Ignore them," Hilde said.

The two younger men kept pace with us, the long rifles slung over their shoulders bumping against their hips. One of them sported three wristwatches on his arm. I didn't dare turn around to see what Cement Face was doing, but I knew his eyes were on us; I could feel them peeling back my skin.

Cement Face called out something curt in Russian, and the two officers sped up to block our path.

"H—" *Say good day, not Heil Hitler.* "Good day." I hoped they would smile.

They didn't. The blue-eyed officer held out his hand, the universal sign for "Papers."

I felt slightly off balance as we handed Blue Eyes our identity cards. *We are getting what we deserve.* What did I deserve for causing Mutti's death? *You didn't cause it. It was the Soviets.* But my heart wasn't fooled.

The officer barely glanced at Hilde's card before giving it back to her, but he held on to mine. "Katarina." He pronounced my name slowly.

"We're just going home," I said, taking back my card.

"They don't understand you," Hilde whispered.

Cement Face's boots clicked across the cobblestones as he sauntered toward us. He pointed at Hilde's basket with his rifle. When she placed it on the ground, he kicked it over and the mushrooms tumbled onto the road. Some of them rolled away. The ones nearest him he squashed with his boot.

Something inside me exploded like a gunshot. "What's wrong with you people?" The hatred I felt was overpowering; I forgot to be afraid.

Hilde gripped my arm. "Are you crazy? Shut your mouth."

Blue Eyes stood so close to me I could smell the tobacco on his uniform. I felt sick. It was Mutti all over again, and me choosing the wrong time to speak out. I didn't want to look at him but I couldn't help it. His dark eyebrows made it seem like he was considering a terribly complex problem with two equally terrible solutions.

His father said something to him, and he took the basket out of my hands. Out came the rabbit by its legs, along with the freshly skinned fur. His announcement in Russian sounded triumphant and made the other men laugh. Blue Eyes handed me back the empty basket. "What's wrong with us," he said in perfect German, "is that we had to endure you krauts on our land for too long. It's your turn now." He put his large hand on my chin. It was warm, and as rough as the tongue of a cat. "We treat the Germans the way they treated us. Fair is fair." He gave my face a quick squeeze.

The men's boots made a clipped sound on the cobblestones as they walked back to the car with my rabbit and drove away. In a house beside the road, curtains twitched at the window and fell closed.

I pressed my empty basket against my chest, heart thudding. My first thought was, *Thank God.* They hadn't hurt us. We were okay. But hard on its heels was, *That officer just took my rabbit.* "Asshole," I muttered. "He's a real magician. He pulled a rabbit out of a basket."

Hilde smacked me on the head. "They are magicians. They make people disappear."

I held my ear. "That hurt."

"Consider yourself lucky. They could have arrested you. They could have raped both of us. You already got Mutti killed; I'm not letting you do the same to me."

My chin quivered. "Uncle Otto says they're only looking for fascists." I didn't know what a fascist was, but I was pretty sure I wasn't one.

"Uncle Otto is not a girl."

I couldn't look her in the eye.

Two older men stood on the corner like leftover pawns from a chessboard. Their hats and armbands marked them as members of the *Volkspolizei*, the People's Police. The fountain man, Herr Johannsen, strode toward them.

"I saw," he said to the police. "I saw the whole thing. That fellow took the girl's rabbit right out of the basket."

At least someone was on my side, even if he was missing a few cups.

The men didn't move. "Settle down, Johannsen. This is not your business."

"But it's true," I said. "Can't you do something about it? Make them give it back."

One of the men laughed. "Sure. All right."

The other patted my shoulder. "If there was something we could do, we'd do it. But we're only allowed to police the Germans. The Soviets can do whatever they like."

What was the point of that? I wanted to kick the policemen, both of them, see how they liked it.

"Have you seen my Isabella?" Herr Johannsen asked them.

"Oh, for God's sake," one of them muttered.

I marched back to where Hilde was gathering the mushrooms into her basket. She'd left the ruined ones on the road and scowled at me when I picked them up. With a grunt, she stood up, and we continued walking home.

"What if this is the way things will be for the rest of our lives?" My voice cracked. I hadn't realized I'd been storing this up. "What if the only thing that happens from now on is that we lose the things we care about?"

"Don't start," Hilde said. "Next comes the piano, I swear it. Do you know what's going to happen tomorrow?"

How did she always know more than I did? "No. What?"

"I don't know. That's the point. Neither do you. So don't worry about the rest of your life when you don't even know what you'll have for supper tonight."

I held my basket high. "I know what I'm not having."

Hilde let out a long-suffering sigh.

I made a list of hateful things:

- Soviets

- The way Oskar milked cows without any respect

- The way nothing meant what it was supposed to anymore. You were a coward if you refused to do something that was wrong; and if you spoke out when you were supposed to remain silent, if you spoke out . . .

I added to the list with more and more extravagance the closer we drew to Ilse's house. Chocolate was hateful, because there wasn't any. Long lazy rifles were particularly loathsome. Blue eyes? Despicable (even though mine were blue too).

I stomped up the stairs and crashed through the apartment door, adding it to the list, and Ilse rushed in from the sitting room yelling, "My God, are the wolves after you?" I added her to the list too. Thumping my basket onto the kitchen counter, I tried to stand proud. "I caught a rabbit."

"I was the one who killed it," Hilde said.

"Really?" Ilse said. "How big is it?" She picked up the basket, then immediately put it down again. "What happened?"

"Ivan took it." I fought the lump in my throat.

"I see."

Hilde unloaded her mushrooms, and Ilse frowned at the squished ones. "You couldn't have been more careful?"

The slices of bread evened things out. I could practically see the scales on her face, weighing us against the food we'd brought home. Stay? Go? Stay.

For now.

But I had something else on my mind. The time would come when that blue-eyed officer would have something to lose—and I planned to be there to take it from him.

CHAPTER EIGHTEEN

NOT A LOT OF PEOPLE, JUST THE RIGHT ONES

Every night Hilde and I left our bedroom door open so the light from the windows would wake us. We'd been working at Frau Weber's farm for a week—long enough to establish a routine. Usually Hilde woke first; then she'd shake me and we'd get up and dress quietly.

That morning when Hilde pulled on her knee socks, she said, "*Scheisse*. Look at all these holes."

The holes had been there for weeks. "You think the cows care?" Wait, that wasn't it. "This is about Oskar."

She picked at one of the holes. "Why would he matter?"

I pointed at her stocking. "You'll only make it worse if you do that."

"If I had a piece of coal . . ."

I knew that trick. Girls blackened their legs where the holes were, to make them less noticeable. I thought about the secret room beneath the stairwell. *I bet there's coal in there.* My imagination filled the room with impossible things: new shoes, sheet music. But if Ilse caught me down there . . .

Things like stockings had never mattered to me. While other girls drew seams on their legs, I'd been practicing scales and working out how to emphasize the theme in all four voices of a fugue. Piano made sense to me in a way that boys and stockings did not. There were right notes and wrong ones. A piece of music came with clear instructions—where to put your fingers, how fast or slow to play it, how loud or soft, where to add a pedal.

So I'd practiced, and I'd gotten better. Soon when I went to Herr Goldstein's house for lessons, instead of correcting my fingering he would listen with his eyes closed, tapping his hand on his leg. *It makes me happy, hearing you play,* he said. The rest of his life had shrunk to the size of an empty pocket, but in the cellar, he said, it expanded again. Once Jacob had come in to listen, barely breathing lest he break the spell. It had surprised me, the possibility that he admired me.

Why would I care about stockings when I had that?

While Hilde braided her hair, I tucked Mutti's green sweater back in my bag. I'd been sleeping with it every night. We tiptoed out of the room so as not to wake anyone. The door to the boys' bedroom was open, and as we passed the room, I heard breathing. Had one of the boys returned in the middle of the night? The idea that people were coming home made me feel weightless and full of light. Then again, if the boys came back, how much longer would Ilse tolerate us?

The small room was papered in dark green and reminded me

of the shaded corner of a forest. I wouldn't have been surprised to see a squirrel pop out from behind the wardrobe. There were hooks on the walls for hanging coats and things, and a pair of boots in the corner that I knew wouldn't fit me. It was a real bedroom, with two beds, and Ilse slept in one of them, dreaming her sons home.

An unexpected pang caught me in the ribs. Ilse was such a broom; I didn't want to like her. I didn't even want to feel sorry for her. But as we walked to the farm, I said a prayer for her sons to find their way back.

* * * *

As soon as we arrived at Frau Weber's place, Hilde sought out Oskar and they sat together to milk the cows. They sounded like old friends picking up in the middle of a conversation that had been going on for months. I was the outsider, the one who didn't understand the jokes and wasn't familiar with the names. So, when Frau Weber asked me to track down a lost goat, I was happy to escape the barn.

I walked the fence line until I found the spot where the wooden fencing had come down. Frau Weber's land bordered a forest, and the goat had escaped to the other side to munch on a tree branch. Sunlight came through the branches in patches, the light wavering and making the world look like it was underwater. There was no rumble of tanks out here, no explosions, gunfire, or shouting. There were only birds, the gurgle of water nearby, and the goat, eating. At last, a small corner of Germany the war had forgotten. I climbed over the broken fence, sat down on the cool moss, and allowed my heart to ache.

I didn't know what would happen for the rest of my life. Hilde had been right about that. But one thing I did know: it would be a life without a mother in it. One word, one small mistake, and I would pay for it forever. There didn't seem to be anything I could do to make things better—or to forgive myself.

I wondered if there had been a moment, after Mutti had been shot but before she had died, when she'd hated me for what had happened. Had it been her last thought? I longed to say goodbye to her one more time; I longed to say sorry. I wondered if I'd be saying sorry for the rest of my life.

The sound of water brought me to my feet. I followed it until I found a creek wandering through the trees. The air was cool here, and fresh. Squatting beside the water, I chose three stones and brought them back to the mossy spot. Herr Goldstein had told me once that it was a Jewish tradition to place stones on a person's grave. *It keeps the person's soul in this world*, he said. Plus, a stone couldn't die. It was a symbol that the memory of that person would be permanent.

I set the first stone down. It was for the *Zuckerei* Mutti used to make us whenever we were sick: egg yolk beaten with sugar until it was frothy and delicious. There'd been no faking with Mutti; she wouldn't make the *Zuckerei* when we were healthy. We had to cross a line of illness—a particular level of stuffy nose or chills— to earn the treat. Mutti would bring it to us on a tray, in a small glass bowl with a delicate silver spoon, and prop us up in bed to eat it.

The second stone was for the doilies she'd crocheted for no reason except that they were pretty. It made me think of Frau Weber's wall with the griffin made of stones. In a world where everything was either broken or it needed to be useful—or edible—I longed for the extravagance of pretty things that served no purpose.

The third stone was for Schumann's *Lieder*. Every year for the past three years I learned a new one for Mutti's birthday. I would practice it only when she was out of the house, so it would be a surprise. If Hilde was home and heard me singing, she would say I sounded like a cat in heat, but she'd never tell Mutti about the piece, and she wouldn't laugh on Mutti's birthday when I played it. Mutti would sit on the edge of the sofa, hands clasped in her lap, eyes closed, and when I'd finished, she would ask me to play it again.

I lined the stones up in a careful row, wondering if I could make something special with them. I wanted a place where I could sit and think about Mutti. Without a special place for grieving, the whole world became a person's sad memory. I was just about to head back to the creek for more stones when someone called, "Katja. What are you doing all the way out here?"

It was Oskar.

If only I'd seen him first, I might have hidden. I didn't want him to know about this place and spoil it. "I'm bringing the goat back for Frau Weber," I said. "The fence is down."

"I know. I saw it yesterday. I've come to repair it."

I'd seen how he worked on the farm. *Do you plan to do this wrong too?*

The goat was occupied with the branches, so I met Oskar at

the fence. "Hilde says you know a lot of people in Fahlhoff."

Oskar set down tools, wood, and wire, and then glanced up at the trees as if making sure there was nothing around to startle him. Being near him was like standing too close to an unexploded bomb.

"I don't know a lot of people," he said. "Just the right ones." He yanked out a stalk of grass and chewed on its end.

I had to ask. "Do you know anyone who has a piano?" If Hilde had been there, she would have given me a *God-you're-dumb* sigh.

"No," he said, "but I know where you can find one."

I studied his face for signs of a joke, but he didn't smile or even raise his eyebrows. "All right. Where?"

"Oberstrasse." He stuffed the long piece of grass into his mouth.

Why did that street name sound familiar? "You'll get a stomach ache if you eat grass." Hilde and I had wanted to do it on our journey over here. *You don't have cow stomachs,* Mutti had warned us.

Oskar fixed his dark eyes on me, pulled out another piece of grass, and stuffed the whole thing into his mouth.

I laughed. "Fine, pass me one." I'd never tested Mutti's theory. I crumpled the grass in one hand and put it in my mouth. It tasted the way it smelled: green, and a little gritty. Not the worst thing I'd eaten—not like rotting cabbage—and anyway, it gave me something to do with my mouth other than insult Oskar.

"Why do you want a piano?" he asked.

Why did anyone want one? Playing was the one thing that would ease the constant pressure I felt against my chest. If I played, somewhere Mutti would be crocheting, Herr Goldstein would be correcting my fingering, and Jacob would be standing around the corner with his ear pressed against the door.

"Where is Oberstrasse?" I asked.

He drew me a map on the ground with a stick. "You have to cross the footbridge to the other side of town."

The fancier side. "And where is the piano?"

"I promise you, you can't miss it. Do you play?" he asked.

"Yes, I play. What do you think?"

"I think you're angry all the time. I haven't done anything to you, you know."

A bird landed on the fence between us, looked at me, then at him, and flew off. Behind me were three stones instead of a mother. "I'm sorry," I said. "It's just, this isn't how my life was supposed to turn out."

"How do you know that?" he said.

"Because I know." There were supposed to be performances, and *Kaffeeklatsch* with Mutti.

"Right, I forgot." Oskar spat chewed-up grass onto the ground. "You know everything."

I shrugged. "I know you have to tie a cow's hind legs before you milk it."

He picked up the hammer. "I can't fix the fence until that goat is on the other side. You want me to catch it for you?"

I couldn't help but smirk. "Sure."

He climbed over the fallen fencing and walked toward the goat. The goat moved away. He called, "Come on, goat." The goat ignored him. He lunged; the goat leapt in the opposite direction. "I don't know why it won't—"

I rattled the grain I'd brought in a tin can and the goat lifted its head. Still rattling the can, I walked toward the fallen fencing and climbed over. As I expected, the goat followed, leaving Oskar alone on the other side.

"All right, you win," he said.

"If there really is a piano on Oberstrasse, then we're even," I said.

CHAPTER NINETEEN

LIKE MEDICINE

Hilde only agreed to come with me to Oberstrasse that afternoon because it was Oskar who'd told me about the piano.

Today we were bringing home two eggs, and one half-sausage each. Otto had rigged our baskets with a false bottom, which was where we hid our treasures. A layer of straw kept the eggs from breaking. Above the slats of wood we placed wild leeks and peppermint. That way, if anyone stopped us, the baskets wouldn't look empty.

As we walked, Hilde pulled a yellow hair ribbon out of her pocket.

"Where did you get that?" I asked.

"Oskar brought it for me. He can get things, I told you."

"He's sweet on you already?" I was dumbfounded. How had she done it?

She flicked her hair. "It's a ribbon, *Scheisskopf*, not an engagement ring."

But if Oskar was involved in the black market, then he had given away a hard-won item for free. "How do you think engagement rings get started?"

"Says the girl with all the experience." Hilde tied the ribbon around her braided hair.

I wanted to talk about Jacob, even though he'd never given me a hair ribbon, but I didn't want Hilde to ruin him. I didn't like her opinion about him never coming back. (Opinions weren't as good when they were someone else's, and even worse if you disagreed with them).

"All right, big talker," Hilde said, "here's your stupid Oberstrasse. But I'm not sure why we bothered."

We stood at one end of the street and looked down. Instead of buildings, there were mountains of rubble. Steel legs stuck out at crazy angles, as if the steel people they belonged to were drowning in stone. The few remaining scrawny trees were covered in dust. That was why the name had been familiar; Ilse had mentioned it had been bombed. Of course they had to drop the bomb where the piano was.

Damn Oskar. The next time I saw him I would make a loud noise when he wasn't expecting it. I picked up a brick and hurled it into what had once been someone's sitting room. The sofa was still there, white with plaster. "Great boyfriend you've chosen."

Hilde picked at her nails. "He's not my boyfriend. And anyway, you're not nice to him, so what do you expect? He played a trick on you."

We walked along the street, stepping over people's lives—a doll's head, the feathers from a quilt, a hairbrush. *Look away.* But even if I couldn't see the destruction, the crunch of glass made it sound like we were walking on bones. We passed sinks, and random walls with the pictures still hanging on them. A chimney stood by itself, trying to figure out what had happened to the house. Chimneys were sturdy things. They were the best survivors.

Mutti would have been completely distraught. *Ordnung muss sein,* was the way she had lived. *There must be order*—in the jars of beets and plum jam in the cellar, in the line of shoes by the door and the books on the shelves. There was order in music too. A disordered orchestra was nothing but noise, and this place was a thousand disordered orchestras all playing at once.

And then—my breath caught in my throat. There was the piano, as unlikely as the daffodils that bloomed beside dead bodies. It was a miracle it had survived. The house around it was mostly collapsed. I ran toward it, not looking where I was going, tripped as I climbed up the rubble, and skinned my knees. I didn't care if the eggs had broken. For once, there was something more important in the world than food.

It was a black Steinway upright, though the color was already fading from exposure to the weather. *The weather.* Who left a piano outside? The changes in temperature, the moisture—you weren't even supposed to put a piano against an outside wall in your house. The soundboard would probably be warped. The strings would be rusty, the keys sticky, the hammers rotten.

It was out of tune, and one note, a high E-flat, was missing. This wasn't the precise sound of my piano at home. There was a tinny echo to it, the notes unsure of who they were. But . . . it was music.

I played three chords, and then the scale of G. My hands looked different on the keys: dirtier, older. My stiff fingers objected to the movement, but with a few more scales they warmed up.

How strange to be playing outside. I imagined the sound echoing off trees, drifting on the breeze all the way to Mutti. She used to love listening to me practice, even though I often played the same sections over and over to get them right.

At first I played standing up. Hilde walked away—this was her nightmare come to life—but she returned with a wooden chair. I sat and played Chopin's *Minute Waltz*, stumbling in the beginning because I liked to play it fast. The piece loosened something inside me and made me feel free for the first time in months. By the end of it I was laughing.

"What's funny?" Hilde stood beside the piano, eyeing me the way people looked at Herr Johannsen whenever he asked about Isabella.

"Chopin wrote this after watching a small dog chase its tail," I said.

"Is this another one of Herr Goldstein's stories?" She crossed her arms and turned away. "Anyway, I thought this was a waltz. What does it have to do with dogs?"

"Nothing." Everything.

I played the first two movements of the *Moonlight* Sonata. My out-of-shape fingers struggled with the big stretches Beethoven required of pianists (*He must have had huge hands*, I'd said once to Herr Goldstein. *No*, he'd said. *The keys were smaller back then.*) But I was amazed at how my fingers remembered the way. The keys were routes to their favorite places.

As I played, Hilde stopped commenting, stopped frowning,

and closed her eyes. The tightly wound spring of my sister finally let go. I'd only ever thought of her as jealous of my playing. Not once had I suspected she might enjoy it.

By the end of the second movement, a small crowd had gathered on the road. Sound carried, and music was like medicine. It worked for any ailment, especially a broken heart. The silence on the street was poorer now that the piece was done.

"Please play more," a man called. It was Herr Johannsen.

Seeing all those people gave me even more energy. I was doing the thing I'd been born for, and making strangers happy—it was on their faces. I wished Mutti could see me, and Herr Goldstein.

"Ilse is expecting us," Hilde said in her peas-in-straight-rows voice. "We're supposed to help with supper."

"You go. I'm not ready." I clenched and unclenched my hands, relishing the strength that had returned to my fingers, and soaking in the joy the music had created.

"Stop acting like this," Hilde said.

"Like what?"

"Like you're the extra sausage. I've had more than enough of living with a prima donna." She took her basket and walked off with wood-plank posture. But she was only pretending to go home. While I played *Für Elise*, she picked through the remnants of a bombed building, waiting for me.

I remembered Debussy's *Clair de Lune* and most of the variations on Mozart's *Twinkle, Twinkle, Little Star*, which started deceptively easy but became more complicated as the variations developed. The destruction around me disappeared. I forgot about being hungry, or expendable, or inconvenient. Mutti sat on the sofa crocheting while she listened, Herr Goldstein beside her nodding and saying *Ja*. But only once, because I was making mistakes.

When I reached the end, the audience applauded. I looked over and the breath stopped in my chest. There in the front was Blue Eyes, the Soviet officer who'd taken my rabbit, standing completely still and holding his cap in both hands. He looked ready to fall to his knees. Well. My breath rushed out in a huff. I hoped the ground at his feet was covered in broken glass.

I stood up.

"Don't stop," he said. "Katarina."

Like I cared that he remembered my name.

I looked straight at him. "That's it for today."

Several people cried out in protest.

"Do you know any Schubert?" asked Herr Johannsen. "Schubert was Isabella's favorite."

Even though it hurt me to leave the piano, I now knew where it was. I could come here every day and practice. Maybe Frau Weber would have a tarp I could bring to protect it from the rain, though that would only be a temporary arrangement. The piano needed a proper home.

Ilse's house? What if she kicked us out?

I would ask Frau Weber if she could keep the piano at her house.

Then I noticed a truck on the road, and soldiers standing beside it. They approached Blue Eyes. One of them pointed at the piano, then looked back at the truck. They were going to take it, the way they'd taken that dining room table—the way they were taking everything.

I forced myself to walk away. If I didn't, the anger rising inside me would get me in trouble. My feet slid through the debris as I stormed over to where Hilde was waiting. I didn't want to look back—I didn't want to see them take the piano—but I had to.

But they weren't taking it. Blue Eyes scowled at the men and shook his head, and the soldiers returned to the truck and drove away. The piano stayed.

Maybe I should have thanked him. Instead I tugged on Hilde's arm and said, "Let's go."

We walked along Oberstrasse toward the center of town. Someone was following us; I could feel eyes on my back. I turned, certain it was the Soviet officer—but it was Herr Johannsen.

"Who is that man?" Hilde said. "He's a weirdo. I don't like him."

"Otto says he's harmless," I said.

She picked up her pace. "He makes me uncomfortable."

Anyone who didn't tip their hat with a polite *Guten Tag* made my sister uncomfortable. "Relax," I said. "He's fine."

"You and your piano," Hilde said. "You're going to put us in danger, just like before."

"What are you talking about? It's nothing like before."

My first teacher, Frau Erdmann, had a daughter named Edith who was just my age. Edith had greasy hair and smelled like sweat, and Frau Erdmann used to make me play awful duets with her that were ridiculously simple.

Lessons with Frau Erdmann were all right—until the afternoon I came to her and said, *I want to learn Chopin's waltz in C-sharp minor.* She fussed with her eyeglass chain. *That's far too complicated for you, dear.*

No, I said. *It's too complicated for you.*

She whisked the duet book off the music stand. *Go to Solomon*

Goldstein, then. He's the one who should teach you.

Who?

No one. She glanced at the walls. *Nothing.*

I went home and told Mutti, *I need a new teacher: Solomon Goldstein.*

Solomon Goldstein, she said, as if the name weighed a hundred kilos. *Impossible.*

Papi said the same.

Why? I asked. *Have you heard of him? Is he not taking new students?*

Not Aryan students, Papi said. *I doubt he's even allowed to have a musical instrument.*

What? *Why not?* I said. *He's a piano teacher.*

Papi changed the subject to cows. There was always a lot to say about the cows—their calves, the quality and quantity of milk, the sales in town.

That night I heard him and Mutti talking.

Frau Erdmann says she has great talent, Mutti said. *She thinks we should send her to the city for lessons.*

Ridiculous, Papi said. Stettin was too far away, and we couldn't afford it.

What about Solomon Goldstein? But it seemed Frau Erdmann hadn't mentioned him.

The idea echoed in my head like the theme in a fugue. All four voices took it up—subject and answer, *Solomon Goldstein*—until I found out where he lived and showed up at his little house.

Impossible, he said, when I introduced myself. *I can't teach you. I don't even have a piano.*

Both of those things turned out not to be true. The piano was hidden in the cellar, where the sound didn't carry. All I had to do was play for him once. Herr Goldstein agreed to teach me if I swore to continue my pretend lessons with Frau Erdmann and not breathe a word of the secret lessons to anyone.

Why can't I tell? I asked.

He did not talk about cows. *I'll get in trouble.*

What kind of trouble?

The serious kind—the kind that involves the SS and the Gestapo. The men in long leather coats who drove big black Mercedes-Benzes. People kept their heads down whenever they passed.

For a long time I told no one. My playing improved dramatically. Frau Erdmann didn't teach me anymore during our lessons, and she didn't make me play duets with Edith. She just listened. Once a month I'd take her Mutti's payment, and though I wanted to keep a portion of the money for Herr Goldstein, I didn't dare. I didn't want to give Frau Erdmann a reason to tell on me.

Anyway, I didn't think she would. Whenever I performed at recitals, she took the credit for my success, and I didn't contradict her.

I could only pay Herr Goldstein in the food I stole from our pantry.

It's better than money, he reassured me.

The secret grew wings inside me until it had to take flight. I told only one person about Herr Goldstein: Hilde.

It was a mistake. She was horrified.

You can't go there, she said. *You mustn't. Don't you pay attention at League meetings? Haven't you seen* Der Stürmer?

The weekly newspaper. Who could miss it? *The Jews are our misfortune* was printed in bold type across the bottom of every issue. On the radio, at school, at meetings of the Young Girls' League—everyone knew things were bad. But I didn't understand.

Our misfortune, I asked Mutti. *Why?* The Goldsteins were the only Jews I knew, and Herr Goldstein was the most fortunate thing that had ever happened to me.

That is not your concern, she said.

Everything about my piano lessons became black-is-white— the wrong notes, pretending to be the right ones. Herr Goldstein had to hide his piano in the cold cellar—the worst room in the house for it. He couldn't teach, couldn't perform. Misfortune had found him.

"Are you even listening?" Hilde tugged on my arm, and the noises of Fahlhoff rushed back at me: Russian singing, shouting, the backfire of a truck. "Mutti always said we should be invisible, and quiet. But you have to be the center of attention, as usual. I saw that officer standing there, listening. The one who took our rabbit."

At home, Hilde had repeated over and over, *You shouldn't be going there, someone will see you, someone will find out*—until finally she told my secret to Mutti.

Papi would have put a stop to the lessons immediately. But by then, he was gone to war.

It's dangerous. Mutti echoed Herr Goldstein's earlier warning. *For him—and for us.*

But by then he didn't want to stop. *You're making such good progress*, he said. *Besides, teaching you is a perfect act of defiance.*

Mutti began sending me with food, candles, blankets. And still I showed up weekly at Frau Erdmann's house for my useless lessons, keeping up the ruse—until a neighbor's house was searched by the Gestapo and a black Mercedes took one of them away. Herr Goldstein himself told me I had to stop coming.

"All I did back there was play," I said to Hilde now. "It made people happy. Is that so bad?"

I never told Mutti, or Hilde, but even after my piano lessons with Herr Goldstein were finished, I'd sneak over to visit him and sit with their cat (before they'd been forced to give it away) and sample Frau Goldstein's poppy seed cookies (before their milk ration card was taken away and they were banned from purchasing any food that was in short supply). That was when Herr Goldstein doctored up the third movement of the *Moonlight* Sonata for me and, later, gave me his copy of Schumann's *Lieder*.

Sometimes I'd catch a glimpse of Jacob, still studying, growing into a thinner stick-version of himself with dark circles under his eyes. I'd bring milk from our cows, hidden in a jam jar in my bag, and butter I'd stolen from our kitchen.

"You don't think of the consequences of your actions," Hilde said as we neared the square. "You never have."

At one point, the Gestapo paid us a visit, searching our home, the barn, and all of the sheds, as if we were hiding something.

But we weren't.

CHAPTER TWENTY

THE KOHLENKLAU

The girl from the grocery store was crossing the square—Liesel, the one who'd told us how to get to Rosenstrasse—and I waved to her.

"Enough already," Hilde said. "I'm going home."

"I'll come in a bit."

"At least give me your basket," she said, "so Ilse won't complain." Ilse didn't care if I showed up, but my food had better arrive.

I crossed the street and caught up to Liesel. She'd been kind to us; I hoped we might be friends.

Once again her arms were full, but this time she carried a bulky potato sack. The way she looked at it, then looked away, I knew: whatever was in there, it wasn't potatoes.

"How's Frau Daschner?" she said with a teasing lilt.

I laughed. "You were right. She's a hag." A pinch of conscience reminded me that despite Ilse's unpleasantness, she had still taken us in. But I wanted Liesel to like me. She seemed so sure of herself. "And you know what it depends on?"

"What?" Her eyes twinkled.

"Nothing. She's a hag all the time."

When Liesel laughed, it was a small victory. "I didn't want to alarm you," she said. "Do you have to stay there? Where are your parents?"

My gaze fell to my dusty, scuffed shoes. "My father died in the war."

"Mine too," she said. "And your mother?"

I'd already made the mistake of blabbing to Frau Weber. "My mother is on her way," I said. "We had to leave her in the hospital." There was a hitch in my voice.

When Liesel put down her sack to hug me, I nearly started to cry.

"I'm sure she'll be here soon," she said.

I took a deep breath, willing the sadness away. I was still buzzing with the energy of Chopin and Mozart. "You'll never guess what I found on Oberstrasse."

She smiled. "Something good, I can see by your face."

"A piano."

She glanced at my hands. "You play." It was a statement, not a question, and I detected a hint of admiration in it.

"Yes." *It's the beating heart of my life*, I wanted to say, but it was one of those things that sounded better in my head.

"I always wanted to learn," Liesel said. "But . . ." She tipped her head toward the grocery store.

"I could teach you. I've been playing for years. I want to be a concert pianist. Maybe that seems stupid." Because, *look around, for God's sake.*

"Not at all. I want to be a schoolteacher—if I can ever get out of that stinking store." Liesel hoisted the sack with a grunt, and made a big show of adjusting it on her hip.

I knew she wanted me to ask. "What's in the bag?"

"Promise you won't tell?" She pulled me around the corner. "My older brother always said I was no good at keeping secrets."

A younger sister. I liked her even more.

She shifted the bundle as if it was a fat baby, and I saw its improbable contents: coal.

"How did you—"

"I've made friends with one of the soldiers." The way she stuck out her chest, I knew *friends* wasn't quite what she meant. "He's helping me steal coal from the trains."

"Isn't that dangerous?" I noticed now that her fingertips were stained black. It made her hands look strong.

"Sure. The trains are guarded."

And the guards had guns.

"But the soldiers spend most of their time playing chess," she said. "All they really want is to go back to their families. My friend took a bunch off one of the coal cars and hid it for me behind a building. You should come and get some while you can."

The blood moved faster in my body. Stealing from the Soviets? I loved the idea of doing anything that would hurt them. And Liesel was doing it. But—

"I'm delivering this batch to a woman down the street who has three small children," Liesel said. "Then I'm going back for more.

Your dress is brown—that's good. It won't show the coal stains."

"I don't know. If we're caught—"

"Don't be a soft egg. Say you'll come." She squeezed my hand, a glint of mischief in her eye. "Wait for me here. I won't be long."

She ran off before I had the chance to answer. I sat on a bench in the square, facing the thousand-year oak.

You should go home.

Hilde would shit her knickers if she knew about this. And if something bad happened, who would be the reckless one? Me, as usual.

But—this was coal. Soviet coal. We needed it for cooking; we'd certainly need it for heating in the winter. Bringing home a whole bag would guarantee several more days at Ilse's place, maybe even a week.

And—Liesel was a friend who wasn't my sister: my judgmental, moody, unforgiving sister who'd been forced to endure me for most of her life. Hilde would never do anything like this.

Exactly. You should go home.

But when Liesel returned, I was still sitting on the bench.

She plunked herself down next to me and let out a long breath. "The tree that thinks it's so important." She nodded at the oak. "It reminds me of my mother."

My heart pinched at how casually she scorned her mother. I would have done the same, if I'd still had one.

From her dress pocket she took out a soft leather sack and untied the drawstrings.

Tobacco. My mouth fell open. "Do you know what that's worth?"

She didn't even look up as she flattened a small piece of newspaper on her leg. "My friend brings me as much as I want. It's makhorka, Soviet tobacco." She placed a pinch on the newspaper, then rolled the paper with her small fingers and twisted the ends. Her hands were just the right size for this delicate job. I used to marvel at the way Papi had managed it with his thick, calloused fingers.

She caught me watching and I looked away, embarrassed.

"Would you like one?"

When I was younger, I thought of smoking as something only soldiers and film stars did. But since the war had ended, I wouldn't have dreamed of burning tobacco when it could be traded for something to eat. "I don't think—"

"Come on, live a little." She prepared one for me and lit them both at the same time so as not to waste an extra match. I took a long suck on mine and burst into coughs.

Liesel laughed. "Don't inhale right away. Take smaller puffs, like this."

We smoked in silence for a few minutes. I watched the way Liesel did it and tried to hold my cigarette with the same casual grace. I did feel like a film star, but the tobacco had a bitter taste and made my throat dry.

"Is your soldier friend also your boyfriend?" I asked.

"Yes, but don't tell my mother. She'd kill me."

Don't tell my mother. What a luxury. There was no one around to care if I smoked or had an inappropriate boyfriend. Hilde disapproved of everything I did on principle, but who said I had to listen to her?

"His name is Dmitri. He was studying literature at university before he was drafted." Liesel kept her blond hair tied back in a ponytail, but a few of the shorter pieces had crept out and fell into her face. She had a sprinkle of freckles across each cheek. I hadn't realized I wanted freckles.

"Is he nice to you?" I thought of the girls I'd seen on the road, bloodied and left for dead.

"Of course," Liesel said. "And he protects me. The other soldiers know. They stay away. Or else." She mimicked shooting a gun.

After we finished our cigarettes, we walked to the grocery store together. It was dark inside, and the woman behind the counter was round-faced and grumpy with her customers. In my town, the grocer used to hand out sweets to children whenever he had them. This woman did not seem to believe in sweets, or handouts, or children. Then again, she had a reason to be grumpy. There was almost no food on the shelves.

"Liesel, where have you been?" she barked.

"Mother, meet Katja," Liesel said.

I raised my hand to say *Heil Hitler*, then remembered and, flustered, pretended I'd wanted to do something with my hair. Liesel grabbed hold of my arm and pulled me through the store faster than her mother's voice could carry. Mutti would have been mortified at my bad manners.

In the back room, she thrust two empty potato sacks at my chest. I bit my lip as I realized she intended us to fill them—with stolen coal. This didn't seem like such a good idea anymore.

"Let's go," Liesel said. "The Kohlenklau waits for no one."

I laughed, despite my nerves. The Kohlenklau—the coal thief— was a cartoon character that government officials had posted all over public buildings and near light switches during the war. Dressed in black, with a bag of stolen coal on one shoulder, he was meant as a warning for people not to waste electricity.

We hurried out the back door before Liesel's mother could catch us, and I followed Liesel to a checkpoint. She nodded at the men while my heart thumped and my neck got sweaty.

I started to smile, but she said, "No, don't. They'll think you're simple. Or insane. Soviets need a good reason for smiling."

As soon as we were out of earshot, I asked, "How will we get past them once we have the coal?"

"You worry too much."

Sure I did. Her Soviet boyfriend would defend her if she got caught stealing, but what about me? They could send me away, or shoot me on the spot. There were no laws anymore, except one: don't get caught.

We approached the train station, a brick building with soot-darkened walls. Civilians stood on the platform in clusters: old men in worn caps, and women with thick ankles carrying battered suitcases. Children in short pants hung on to skirts, a doll or blanket tucked under one arm. Many of them looked as if someone had spun them around in the dark and then set them loose.

Other people paraded around the station dressed in mismatched outfits—prisoner-of-war jackets, worn-out trousers, and capes. As they passed us, whispered offers of *soap, flour, cigarettes, butter* floated in the air. People carried bundles under their coats. I watched cameras change hands. A cuckoo clock. Some fancy porcelain.

Several girls stood in the shadows, their arms empty.

"I guess they've got nothing to trade," I said.

"You're kidding, right?" Liesel said. "Don't you know they're prostitutes?"

My face grew hot. "Obviously I'm kidding." I was thankful the light bulbs on the platform were still darkened from the blackouts.

A freight train sat on parallel tracks behind the passenger station, guarded by Soviet soldiers. "We're in business," she said.

We stood off to the side watching two soldiers load a rail car with oil paintings, and German typewriters they probably couldn't use, and a wooden sideboard I could imagine stacked with delicate coffee sets and tiny sugar spoons. The piano on Oberstrasse could have been among those treasures.

"I guess we shouldn't feel bad about stealing from them," I whispered. "They're helping themselves to all of our stuff."

"Actually?" Liesel said. "I never realized how rich we were until I saw the loot that was leaving our country. Dmitri says the Soviet Union is nothing like this."

I let out a sharp breath. "That doesn't make it right, what they're doing."

Liesel shook the hair out of her eyes. "Nothing is right. But we invaded them, remember? This is *reparatsii*. Reparations. When you think of it that way—"

I didn't want to think of it that way.

Near the entrance to a large wooden building, two men in uniform sat on upturned crates playing chess. They each had a glass of tea.

"What are they holding between their teeth?" I asked Liesel.

"Where have you lived all your life? Those are sugar cubes. They like their tea sweet."

How did they resist popping it into their mouths and sucking on it until it dissolved? Their rifles lay at their feet like trained dogs.

She pointed to the side of the building. "The coal's around back."

"But how will we—"

"One of those men is Dmitri."

I tried to get a better look at him, but the men were hunched over the chessboard and their caps shaded their faces. They seemed to be in the middle of an intense discussion. One of them was counting as he spoke, bending first his baby finger, then the ring finger, then the middle one.

"He'll help me distract the other soldier," Liesel said. "You go around and load up the sacks. Wrap your hands in these"—she handed me two long strips of coal-stained fabric—"or else you'll give yourself away later."

Did Dmitri even speak German? And anyway, *No. I don't want to. I can't.* This was crazy. I could feel Mutti burning holes in my neck from wherever she was glaring. *Katarina Wilhelmina*—before I'd even done anything. It was a pre-emptive Every Bad Thing speech because she knew how this would turn out.

But Liesel was already walking toward the men. *She only has to talk to them. She's making you do the dangerous part.* I couldn't. But did I really want to face her afterward and tell her I didn't have the guts?

Coward. This was what happened to . . .

All I had to do was move my legs. It was called walking. So I walked. Just a little walk in the freight yard. I hummed one of Schumann's songs to keep myself calm. *In the beautiful month of May*—even though it was June. *I'm sorry, Mutti.* But no, I wasn't. I would finally be hurting the people who'd taken my mother from me. They deserved it. All they did was take and kill and destroy.

This could be the beginning of a campaign of sabotage—all of it, revenge. I picked up my pace, energy surging as I reached the building and scurried around to the back where there was a small mound of coal.

My hands shook as I wrapped them in the filthy scraps of fabric. It was hard to open the potato sacks with paws instead of hands. I held the first sack open with my teeth until there was some weight in it. Liesel's laughter rang in the background. Then came a man's voice—Dmitri's? I struggled to scoop the coal into the sack. Even with my hands covered, the pieces were rough and I couldn't help but worry about my fingers.

I heard another deeper voice, more laughter. My ears were keen for the click of a rifle, but it didn't come. What was Liesel saying to those men? Did she even speak Russian? It sounded like she was being so nice to them. And anyway, how did girls like her and Hilde always know what to say to men, when I couldn't string three words together to ask for a cup of water?

My heart raced. What would I say if someone caught me back here? *I'm lost.* And also, meanwhile, loading a bag with coal. *Where's the passenger station? Isn't this it?*

A shadow fell upon me. I startled and dropped the bag.

It was Liesel.

"What the hell are you doing?" she said in a hoarse whisper. "You're taking too long."

She grabbed the second sack and filled it quickly while I finished packing the first one. We tore the rags off our hands and stuffed them in our pockets.

"Go, go, quickly," she said. We walked as casually as we could toward the passenger station. Sweat trickled from my hairline, but I didn't dare wipe it away. Despite the rags, my fingertips were black. All I needed was streaks of black down my face, and then I really would look like the Kohlenklau.

As soon as we were far enough away I regained my courage. "We did it. We got away with it."

"We did." When Liesel smiled, my whole body felt warm with pride.

"You're lucky I was there," she added. "You'll need some practice, but I'll make a coal thief out of you yet."

We took a different route back, one that bypassed the checkpoint. When we reached the square, Liesel hugged me and said, "Hurry home. Don't get caught."

She walked toward the grocery store. I was crossing the park when, behind me, I heard a loud voice call, "*Stoy.*" I stopped in my tracks and looked around, but the voice hadn't been directed at me. It was Liesel who'd been ordered to halt.

I hid behind one of the trees. A Soviet officer stood in front of her with two other men. When he poked at Liesel's bag of coal with the tip of his rifle, she placed it on the ground. She said something to him in Russian that sounded confident, but it didn't help. He opened the bag and took out a lump of coal.

"Who helped you?" he asked in German. "You couldn't have done this alone."

Here it comes. She would give me away. Or worse, they would shoot her. They'd shoot both of us.

No, surely not.

But they could. Anything could happen.

"No one. I swear." She seemed to purposely avoid looking in my direction. "I had permission. Ask Dmitri Pavlukhin," she said with authority in her voice.

The officer spoke to his men. One of them picked up the sack of coal, while another led Liesel away.

As soon as they were gone, I ran to the clothing shop, thundered up the stairs, and burst into the apartment.

"My God, you'd think a wild boar was loose in the streets," Ilse said. "What would your mother say about such behavior?"

Then she saw the bag in my arms. "What do you have there?"

When I showed her, her face softened so much even her braids seemed to loosen. I waited for her to ask where I'd gotten it. *I stole it,* I wanted to say. *From a freight train.* But then she might scold me for doing something so dangerous. It *was* dangerous, but I'd done it.

My heart still pounded at the thought of Liesel having gotten caught. Dmitri would help her; that was why she was with him. But I could barely sit through supper thinking about it.

That night in our room I handed Hilde the piece of coal I'd saved for her, wrapped in a dirty strip of fabric. "For the holes in your knee socks," I said.

She took it without thanking me, but early the next morning I saw her use it.

When we left for work, there was a note at the Daschners' door.

The Kohlenklau strikes again.

L.

I tucked it into my pocket. We were friends. Maybe there was already something in me that was just like her.

CHAPTER TWENTY-ONE

SCHNAPPS, SACCHARIN, AND BEETHOVEN

The barn was a peaceful place to be early in the morning. The dawn light was gentle, the cows' low, heavy breathing soothing. Oskar sat in the corner milking one of the more docile cows. Hilde went to fetch a stool. Before I could talk myself out of it, I hugged him, even though he still refused to tie the cow's hind legs.

Oskar stopped milking and went so rigid it was like hugging a plank of wood. When I let go, it took him a moment to snap back into his usual shape. "I'm guessing you found the piano," he said.

I stroked the cow at the soft spot behind her ears. "Yes. I don't know how you knew about it, but thank you."

The cow snorted, and Oskar resumed the rhythmic music of milking. "I find things," he said.

I lose them. "Could you get me some sheet music?"

He laughed. "Most people ask for schnapps, or saccharin. You want Beethoven."

Hilde let out a pained sigh.

"As a matter of fact, I do. The third movement of the *Moon-light* Sonata." The most complicated movement by far, but also my favorite.

I hadn't bothered telling Frau Erdmann I wanted to learn it. What was the point? *Oh no, dear,* she would have said, *the third movement is far too difficult for a girl your age.* But when I told Herr Goldstein, his eyes had brightened behind his gold-rimmed glasses. *It's the perfect piece of music for you,* he said. *You'll play it brilliantly.*

I wouldn't have the benefit of his careful arrangements anymore. I'd have to go through the music myself bar by bar and knock off the top or bottom notes of the chords that were too unwieldy for my hands. And then—to learn it without his guidance? To not be able to play it for him once I'd mastered it?

Oskar's eyes narrowed. "What will you give me?"

So much for free hair ribbons. I caught Hilde's smirk as she settled herself on the milking stool. In my pocket was all the tobacco I'd collected off the streets, wrapped in red paper. I pulled it out and showed it to him.

"That's it? You don't have anything else?"

Let's see. I had one pair of worn-out shoes, but they were on my feet. I had Mutti's green sweater, and her dented bowl, and her thimble—but those were not available for trade. And—nothing. I had lots of that.

"Forget it." I drew my hand back, but he reached for the tobacco and stuffed it into his pocket.

"I'll see what I can do."

Outside, the grass was covered in dew. I grimaced at the thought of all that moisture swelling the wooden parts of the piano and throwing it even more out of tune.

"The piano must belong to someone," I said. Though ownership was becoming such a tenuous thing. If something was in your hands, you owned it. *Zapp-zarapp* was the Soviets' way of thinking about it. *Help yourself.*

Oskar stroked the cow's large brown flank. "I heard it belonged to an older man and his wife. I don't think they survived the bombing."

If I kept the piano, it wouldn't be stealing. I wondered which of them had played. Maybe both. "Do you think Frau Weber would agree to keep it at her house?"

He hesitated. "You'd have to find a way to transport it here. That's the real problem. The Ivans are the ones with vehicles, and if they get that piano on a truck you might never see it again."

I remembered the truck that had been waiting on Oberstrasse to cart the piano away. Oskar was right. I'd have to be happy with it where it was, for as long as it lasted—which seemed true of most things now.

CHAPTER TWENTY-TWO

HOW FAR WOULD YOU GO?

"We're not going to Oberstrasse every day, you know," Hilde said that afternoon when I turned toward the footbridge to cross to the other side of town.

"I am." Even though my feet felt heavy after a long day of chores, the promise of playing urged them forward.

"I'm not coming with you."

I fidgeted with my sleeves. "Then don't come."

I handed her my basket and turned to cross the narrow wooden bridge. The long line of people fishing beside the river didn't seem to have changed. I looked down into the turbid water and wondered if anything lived in it.

My sister's absence was fine while I was still annoyed, but it became less fine when I realized I would have to walk alone. My heartbeat went from quarter notes to racing sixteenths as I made my way along streets where the only pedestrians were men in Red Army uniform. Around me was the sound of a language I didn't understand, and the crack of bootsteps I did.

Maybe the piano wouldn't be there.

Had it ever been there? Had the whole thing been a dream?

I ran the rest of the way to Oberstrasse and climbed the mountain of rubble: it was there. My newly acquired sitting room smelled of plaster dust, burnt wood—and dampness. How long would it take for the damage to be permanent? And how long before Blue Eyes decided it belonged to him?

But as soon as I played, my worries floated away.

Chopin broke my heart, and mended it by breaking it again and again, with every sweet and sad note. A broken heart, I was learning, made it easier for the music to find its way in. I sensed an audience forming on the street and sat taller, adding a flourish to the end of my pieces and drawing out the minor chords in the first movement of the *Moonlight* Sonata. I wanted everyone to feel Beethoven's agony at going deaf while writing the most incredible music—music he would never hear, except in his head.

Even though Herr Goldstein told me Beethoven had dedicated the sonata to a student he was in love with, I still believed it was all about despair. The first movement was full of sadness. Liszt had called the second movement a flower between two chasms. But the third movement—that was where the fire was. That was where Beethoven let rage speak in a most beautiful, compelling way.

When I finished playing the calmer second movement, I looked over at the audience. There were more people today than yesterday. And their faces—the clenched teeth and furrowed brows were gone. People were smiling; some closed their eyes. I spotted Liesel in the crowd and played my favorite Chopin waltz just for her. Then I slid back down the rubble and onto the road.

I headed straight for her, but was stopped by several people who asked if I would come back tomorrow. I assured them I would. Others shook my hand and thanked me for playing. Nothing could match how I felt, seeing how happy people were. It made me think of the way Herr Goldstein used to look whenever I played in his cellar—as if every bad thing in his life had melted away. At the time it hadn't seemed like much to give him—a temporary release from his misery—but I saw in these people's faces that it was.

When I looked up to find Liesel again, she was halfway down the road. I ran to catch her.

I waited for her to tell me she loved the performance, but all she said was, "Oh. There you are."

"I'm so glad you're okay," I said. "After last night."

"With no help from you." She smiled her crooked smile. "Hiding behind a tree like a frightened squirrel."

"Well," I stuttered. "I don't have a Soviet boyfriend to protect me." My voice came out an octave higher than usual.

"I guess you can't have everything."

A cloud passed over the sun, and the world darkened for a moment.

Then she tossed her hair. "Come on. I don't feel like going back to work yet."

I let out my breath.

We went to the same bench by the thousand-year oak and she produced two more cigarettes. It had been so long since I'd had a friend, so long since having friends had been possible—someone you could meet on a bench in the square. Someone to talk to and laugh with.

I sat beside her and she gave an exaggerated frown. "The freight train left this afternoon." That was why she was out of sorts.

"*Scheisse*." I'd liked the way the coal theft had made me feel: fierce. More powerful than Ivan. The same way smoking a cigarette, rather than pocketing the tobacco, made me feel a little less desperate. I probably should have saved the tobacco for Oskar, but at that moment, with Liesel, I wanted to be extravagant.

She lit our cigarettes and passed me mine. We chatted about the small things in our lives—chores and customers, Dmitri's fascination with cigarette lighters. She told me she and Dmitri took long walks along the river holding hands. He was teaching her Russian. She knew all the parts of the body. All of them.

"I've never had a boyfriend," I said.

The way she smiled, it looked like she was sucking on a chocolate. "I could have an officer if I wanted. But Dmitri is—special. I'm lucky."

Herr Johannsen loped past and she waved at him. "Have you found Isabella?" she called in a friendly voice. People in the square looked over at her.

"Don't encourage him," I said under my breath.

Herr Johannsen stopped near the dry fountain. "Have you seen her?" His whole face twisted with concern.

Liesel rolled a cigarette and took it over to him. "She'll come, don't worry. She'll be here any day." The way she lit his cigarette for him, it made me think she was on stage. Then she returned to me.

"Should you really say that to him?" I said softly. "What if this

Isabella person never comes back? What if she's dead?"

"All he wants is a bit of hope," Liesel said. "Isn't that what anyone wants?"

We smoked in silence for a minute.

"Someone hid him, you know," Liesel said.

"Hid who?"

"Herr Johannsen. Because he's soft in the head. The Nazis would have taken him away, but someone saved him."

I remembered how cold it had been playing piano in Herr Goldstein's cellar during the winter. What might it have been like to live there for six years? Did Herr Johannsen ever come out for fresh air? I wondered if he'd had anyone to talk to.

"How far would you go?" Liesel said.

"What do you mean?" I took a careful suck of the cigarette so I wouldn't cough. It made me feel a little sick to my stomach, but I didn't want to put it out. Was she talking about sex? The last thing I wanted was to say something stupid again, like the comment about the prostitutes in the train station.

"I mean, would you risk doing something heroic like that? Even if you knew your family would pay the price?"

I swallowed hard. Had it been heroic to take piano lessons from Herr Goldstein? Yes: for him. At first, I didn't understand the risk he was taking in teaching me. Even when I did, I deemed it worthwhile—because I wasn't the one risking my life. Not like him. Later, maybe, when I snuck him food, but was that heroic? Or just human?

Heroic would have been hiding someone for six years. Heroic would have been saving Mutti. It was another equation I understood only too well: heroic = dead.

"You're the one who's a hero," I said. "Helping people all the time." I was just a frightened squirrel.

"What about you?" Liesel tilted her head. "Here on your own, while your mother is still in hospital. You and your sister were very brave to travel all that way without her."

Something cracked inside me. "She's not in hospital," I said. "She's dead, and it's because of me, and I lied to Ilse and told her Mutti was on her way." It felt awful to admit it. Every word was heavy. Maybe Liesel wouldn't want to be friends with me anymore now that she knew this.

And yet, there was something about telling the truth that lifted the boulder I'd been carrying on my shoulders.

She took my hand in hers. "I'm sure your mother's death wasn't your fault."

"It was. I spoke out when I shouldn't have. The Soviets thought it was her, and they shot her."

"That doesn't sound like your fault," Liesel said. "You weren't the one with the gun."

I shook my head. "Ask my sister. She'll never forgive me."

She gave my hand a squeeze. "We all have things in life we regret—even your sister. Give her time. She'll come around."

But Liesel was wrong. Time was only pushing us further apart.

"Our neighbors hid three Jews," she said. "During the war. And they were caught, and the whole family got sent to the death camps."

"Death camps?" A lead ball settled in my stomach. "There wasn't actually such a thing." There'd been rumors, but Mutti had never believed them. *It's an exaggeration*, she'd told us. *Propaganda*—made up by the Allies to turn Germans against their leaders.

"I saw Jews being taken away," Liesel said. "Streets cordoned off, buildings emptied, the Gestapo going door-to-door to find the ones who were hiding."

I took a drag on my cigarette and allowed the smoke to burn my throat. Taken away. *We're moving, Katja.* "But they weren't taken to death camps."

"The train from Fahlhoff left full and came back empty," Liesel said. "The luggage stayed at the collection area. We all knew something terrible was going on. We kept our mouths shut, else we'd be on the next one." Liesel stared into her lap.

Moving? Where are you going?

Poland. Of all places.

Why?

They had to, Herr Goldstein said. There was no choice.

Jacob looked up from his books, dark half-moons beneath his eyes. I held his gaze. It was the last time I saw him. That was the day Herr Goldstein gave me the book of Schumann's *Lieder.*

Please tell your mother, Frau Goldstein said. *Tell her we must speak to her.*

And I did, with Hilde perched in the corner of the kitchen frowning and shaking her head. Talking in a low voice with Mutti after I left the room. *I knew it would come to this,* I heard her say. *I told you to put a stop to it.* The next day Frau Goldstein came to our house. I was on my way home from school and saw her leave, walking with her head down. I called out to her, but she didn't look up.

What did she want? I asked Mutti and Hilde.

Something we didn't have, Hilde said.

Mutti sent me out to feed the chickens, and though I pressed the question, neither of them ever answered it.

"Katja?" Liesel's voice brought me back to the bench.

I wanted to tell her about the Goldsteins, as if talking about them would ensure they were still alive. But I couldn't even say their name.

"What you're saying about camps—it's not possible." I rubbed my arms, suddenly feeling cold. All those people—dead. Wouldn't everyone have known what was going on? How did you keep that a secret? "What did they do with the bodies?"

"Some were buried in mass graves. Most were cremated," Liesel said. "There were big ovens."

Ovens?

We'd had ovens at our farm, so big we used to play in them when we were little and they were cold. Mutti had baked thirty loaves of bread at a time. Though that felt made up. Did we really have a farm? Did we have bread, as much as we wanted? I tried to imagine the Goldsteins stacked like loaves of bread. It was an unbearable image. "It's not true," I said.

"No, Katja, it is. People are saying now that they were against it all from the very beginning, but they voted for the Nazis. We got what we asked for."

"My parents didn't vote for them," I said.

"Well, enough people did. They were elected."

"People didn't know what they were voting for," I said.

"They should have," Liesel replied. "Who didn't have a copy of *Mein Kampf* at home?"

"True," I said. The book was given out free to newlyweds and soldiers fighting at the front, and it was good insurance to have a copy sitting on your bookshelf. "But nobody read it."

"Whose fault is that? Anyway, it makes me sick that I did nothing. I was too afraid." She blew out a long stream of smoke. "But how can you not know about the camps?"

How? Because it was not possible to know Herr Goldstein and also believe in those camps.

Hilde was the one who'd warned about how bad things were getting for the Jews. She was the one who kept saying I had to stop going to my lessons. But how could I? I glared at the thousand-year oak. The cigarette smoldered until it burned the tips of my fingers and I threw it to the ground.

"Anyway," Liesel said, "that's why I steal coal, or anything that falls off the back of a wagon."

Falls off. I was pretty sure she meant anything she'd pushed off herself.

"That's why I'm with Dmitri," she added. "Well, one reason anyway. I care about him. I'm not a *Schlampe*." A slut.

I winced at the harsh word. "I didn't think—"

Liesel put a gentle hand on my shoulder. "I know you don't. But some people do, and I don't care. I'll do what I can to help anyone who needs help—which is what I should have been doing during the war."

A vehicle rounded the corner and I startled at the sight of the black Mercedes. The Goldsteins—might I have saved them the way someone had saved Herr Johannsen? And maybe the bigger question: Would I have taken the risk? I wanted to say I would have; I would have done anything to save them. But it was an easy thing to believe, now that I couldn't actually do it.

The air around us was heavy with the smell of diesel. *Drive on. Please.* But the car slowed to a stop ahead of us, the driver's door opened, and the arrogant rabbit thief stepped out.

"Now there's a handsome one," Liesel said under her breath. "The commandant's son."

Cement Face was the commandant? I should have guessed by the way he strutted around.

"Any girl who nabs him would be lucky," she added.

I ignored her. "What do you want?" I called out.

"Mind how you speak to him," Liesel said. "You don't want him as your enemy."

"Miss Katarina," he said as he came toward us.

"You know him?" Liesel whispered.

"I wondered if you would play piano today," he said.

"Oh," Liesel said. "Figures."

But I barely heard her. I watched the officer's face as he drew closer, until I could see the ragged edges of the scar that ran down his left cheek. "I already played. You missed it. Too bad for you." I struggled to control my temper. He wore the uniform of the men who'd murdered Mutti, and he wanted me to play him a tune?

Liesel turned to me, her eyes strange, as if she was squinting into the sun. "You never told me about him, you sly thing. Sounds like the two of you are old friends." She poked at my calf with her toe, and then offered Blue Eyes her hand. "I'm Liesel. And I apologize for my friend here being so rude."

He barely shook it. "Might I coax you back to the piano?" he said to me.

I pressed my shoulders against the bench. "I don't think so." I had something he wanted, and he couldn't take it away. *He could take the piano.* But he wouldn't. I wasn't sure why I knew that, but I did. I thought of Hilde and the yellow hair ribbon Oskar had given her, which I was certain she hadn't asked for.

"I'm sorry about the rabbit. I shouldn't have—"

"No, you shouldn't have," I said. "Was it good, by the way? Did you prepare it with the bacon you stole from somebody's farm? Did you marinate it in wine and vinegar?"

"Of course not," he said. "We don't have those kinds of items."

"My goodness, Katja, what's gotten into you?" Liesel said.

My heart raced back and forth between anger and fear. He could shoot me. It would take nothing—a swift decision and one finger on the trigger.

Liesel looked up at him. "Would you like to sit down?" She moved closer to me to make room on the bench, but he remained standing with his head down. Finally he walked away and got back into the car.

"Apparently you have an admirer," Liesel said after the Mercedes pulled away. She was smiling, but it sounded to me like it bothered her.

"I don't care," I said. "I don't like him."

She crossed her arms and made a fake-stern face I was sure she'd copied from her mother. "What have you been doing behind my back, young lady? I insist you tell me right now."

"Nothing. I'm telling you. The Soviets killed my mother. How could I ever have anything to do with them?" Then I remembered Dmitri. "I mean—you understand, don't you?"

"Sure," she said. "I suppose you can afford to be choosy."

"What's that supposed to mean?" A woman's voice from down the road interrupted us with a sharp cry of, "Liesel!"

"I should be going," Liesel said. "Here"—she handed me some wax—"Dmitri gave it to me. The soldiers use it to clean their artillery barrels. If you melt it down and put a string in the middle, you can make it into a candle. If you don't mind Soviet wax, that is."

That beat burning strips of linen in a dish of lard, which Hilde and I had been doing in our room at night so as not to waste precious kerosene. But our makeshift candles were dim and smoky, and they reeked of pig. I pocketed the wax and said goodbye, though the conversation lingered like a wrong note.

People in ovens? Mass graves? Liesel had to be wrong. Who threw a piano teacher into an oven? Or a teenage boy? Germans? Had we done this terrible thing?

On the back of the note Liesel had left by our door, I'd written my own. *Has anyone seen the Goldsteins?* it said. *Solomon, Rivka, Jacob*, and the name of our town. I'd left my name, and the address of the Daschners' shop. I pushed the paper onto a nail in the tree that no longer held a message. It looked so flimsy, the faint hope that a stranger passing through might actually know where they were or what had happened to them. There were probably seventy million people in Germany, and thirty million of them were looking for someone.

CHAPTER TWENTY-THREE

PEOPLE LIKE HAVING CHOICES

"It's taking your mother an awfully long time to get here," Ilse said during supper.

We were eating herring. Ilse had gotten it from the fishmonger's wife in exchange for one of her dresses. I was tempted to tell her she'd gotten the short end of that deal. The fishmonger's wife had given her brown herring, which meant it had been sitting against the barrel wood. No respectable Northerner ate brown herring. We fish heads knew better.

Hilde and I exchanged a quick glance before cutting our herring into small pieces. We'd been living with Ilse and Otto for nearly two weeks now. How much longer would our hospital story be plausible?

Otto put a hand on Ilse's arm. "The girls must be very concerned." He turned to us. "Which hospital is she in?"

I poked Hilde under the table.

"It's in Leipzig," she said. "I don't remember the name."

"I know Leipzig quite well," Otto said. "I used to travel there all the time for the shop. It shouldn't be hard to track her down. Maybe we could try to get some news."

"That would be a huge relief," Hilde said.

I struggled to swallow the piece of herring in my mouth.

"That employer of yours," Ilse said. "Surely you remember *her* name now."

Hilde poked me back.

"Frau Weber," I said carefully. Any sudden movement and the name would explode.

"Does she have any more salami?" Ilse's tone suggested the answer had better be *yes*.

"We can ask," I said.

* * * *

After supper, Hilde and Ilse settled themselves at the kitchen table to study clothing catalogs—an event to which I had not been invited.

"Every girl should have at least two dresses," Ilse was saying. "One for working, and one for looking pretty."

I tried to give Hilde the eyebrow, but she wouldn't look at me. She and I each had two dresses—but they were both brown and functional. I'd grown out of my recital dress a long time ago.

While Ilse went on about Hitler's girlfriend, Eva Braun, wearing Gretchen dresses that made her look like a milkmaid, Otto called me into the sitting room.

"Wait here," he said, and scurried out of the apartment.

I sat on the lumpy armchair. Where was he going? To the secret room? I was dying to follow him, but I forced myself to stay put.

He knows that you know. But also he didn't. You could hold both ideas in your head at once and believe them equally—I'd done it numerous times. But since he'd made it into nothing, I would keep it as nothing. That way I could sneak down and explore the room without anyone suspecting it.

A few minutes later he returned with a square bottle of schnapps and a tiny glass. He put a finger to his lips and then poured amber liquid into the glass, as full as it would go. Holding it level, he brought it to his lips and sipped it without spilling a drop. The tips of his mustache were wet. He handed me the glass and whispered, "Just a small one."

Papi would never have—

And if he had, Mutti would have given him the eye of fury. She couldn't yell at him, so it would have been *Katarina Wilhelmina . . .* all over again.

I took a sip. It tasted bitter, almost smoky, but it warmed my throat as it went down. I handed the glass back and Otto set it on a small table beside him. Then he took the violin out of its case.

"Oh!" I couldn't conceal my delight. "You're the one who plays." The violin had been silent for so long I was convinced it belonged to one of the boys.

"Shut the windows and draw the curtains." He pointed with the bow. "If the soldiers hear the music, they'll take the violin away."

Like they'd almost taken the piano.

But I couldn't stop my mind from leaping further back in time, to another piano hidden in a soundproofed cellar.

"That shouldn't be allowed," I said.

"Ah," Otto said. "It's because music is powerful. They jail poets for speaking the truth. They take away music because it creates joy."

Yes. He understood.

I did as he asked, even though it made the room stuffy. I could smell the sharp odor of Otto's armpits, and probably mine as well. Ilse only allowed us one hot bath per week—the rest of the time we used cold water to combat the dirt from Frau Weber's farm. Mutti always said water was water, but I still believed it worked better when it was warm.

Otto tuned the violin the way Papi used to: first the A-string with a tuning fork, and then the others, two at a time. He stood with his feet in a V, then moved his left foot forward. *For balance,* Papi had explained.

I sat beside the fringed lamp and held my breath. What would he play?

Instrument under his chin, he began with a piece by Mozart. Three seconds of playing and I knew he was as good as Papi. My eyes fell shut. The piece was supposed to be accompanied by cello, but I played an imaginary piano accompaniment on my leg instead.

Otto played three more pieces before setting the violin down and taking another sip of schnapps. When he sat on the sofa across from me, his pant legs hiked up, revealing skinny ankles covered in dark hair. He leaned forward, resting his forearms on his legs the way Papi used to before telling me a story.

"When our shop was open," he said, "I was the one in charge of the window display."

"Really?" I'd been certain Ilse had taken charge of the windows. I played with the fringes on the lamp, letting them spill through my fingers. "Did you have mannequins?" The first time I'd ever seen those life-sized models was when Mutti had taken me to the shop in town to buy my recital dress. They had painted faces and real hair. If Hilde had told me about them, I wouldn't have believed her.

Otto had a faraway look on his face. "We had two," he said. "A man and a woman. I'd choose one of the pretty dresses your aunt Ilse had made, for the woman mannequin, and a suit I'd purchased from our tailors in Leipzig for the man."

"Don't you sew?" I asked.

"*Nee, nee.* These hands." He opened his eyes and held up his long fingers. "They're good for violin, but they're all thumbs when it comes to sewing. Ilse is the dressmaker. I was the one who'd make the trips to purchase fabric and men's clothing. But I had a flair for the window display." He winked at me. "My favorite part was choosing a hat for the man, something with personality."

I pictured Otto standing out on the road in front of the shop, stroking his bushy mustache as he decided who this man was, whether he smoked cigars, read newspapers, or rode horses. "Did you give them names after you dressed them?"

"Always," Otto said. "*Guten Tag*, Frau So-and-So, I would say, and *Danke*, Herr Mucky-Muck."

I would have named them too. "Did the man and woman's clothes match?"

"Naturally. The display had to be pleasing to the eye, but I also wanted the mannequins to look so real a person could imagine them climbing out of the window and walking down the street."

"That would have been something to see," I said.

"Yes." Otto leaned forward. "Especially because the mannequins never wore shoes. Couldn't you picture it? There they'd be,
strutting down the main streets of Fahlhoff dressed in the finest
clothes in the city—and as barefoot as beggars."

We both laughed.

"Why haven't you reopened the shop?" I asked. "Wouldn't it be
easier than going door-to-door with all the clothes?"

Otto made a face. "A shop full of beautiful clothing? How long
before someone broke in and stole everything?"

Ilse bustled into the room holding the catalog. "Such a party
you're having in here." She frowned at the violin and the half-full
glass of schnapps on the table. "Here is the style of dress I will
offer to Frau Doktor Doktor and her daughter when they come to
visit. Simple, but elegant." She pointed for Otto to see.

"Well." He turned the catalog to face me. "What do you think,
Katja?"

I wasn't used to having an adult ask my opinion.

"Give me that." Ilse reached for the catalog, but Otto held on
to it.

I wanted time to prepare my answer, but if I didn't speak up
she would take back the catalog and leave the room. "I think it
depends on what they want, and also what style would suit them.
Either way, I'd offer them a choice. People like having choices."

Ilse looked at me as if I'd sprouted horns. She pulled the drapes
wide and threw open the windows, and Otto put the violin back
in its case.

That night I laid on our blankets on the floor, picturing
Rosenstrasse as it might have looked before the war—sidewalks

crowded with shoppers carrying cloth bags full of groceries, men in hats, women wearing shoes that matched their handbags, people carrying parcels tied carefully with twine. Did I also see the people who carried nothing? The ones who walked with their heads down? They were easily overlooked. Soon they'd be impossible to miss with the yellow stars sewn onto the front of their coats.

CHAPTER TWENTY-FOUR

OUR LITTLE STREET
IN FAHLHOFF

When I got home from playing piano the next day, I could hear Hilde in the kitchen talking to Ilse. Instead of heading upstairs, I stood in the landing and eyed the Daschners' private door that led into the shop. I'd been so curious, for so long. Just for fun, I turned the handle, expecting it to be locked. But the door clicked open.

The only light came from the gaps between the window boards, but it was enough. The broken glass on the floor crunched beneath my shoes. I picked up a blue velvet dress that was covered in boot prints and ripped down the seam. Mutti had said the shop smelled of eucalyptus, but that scent was overpowered by the horse manure strewn across the floor. An oval mirror stood in one corner, shattered. Framed photographs lay on the ground, broken.

"I didn't think they'd come to our street."

I wheeled around. Otto stood in the doorway.

"Our little street in Fahlhoff," he said. "Otherwise we would have been better prepared." Even his wild tuft of hair looked like it didn't believe this could happen. *Like our little town in Pomerania.* No one ever thought a war could end up in their sitting room.

He entered the shop and crossed to the customer door, unlocking it and pushing it open. A small bell jingled, and the room filled with light and fresh air. Neither of those things felt like they belonged in this dark, broken place.

I picked up one of the photographs. "Doesn't Aunt Ilse want these back?"

Otto righted the hat stand. When he nodded, his whole head seemed like a burden. "After we heard them take the sewing machines away, we didn't have the heart to come in here."

"What was it like? Mutti told me it was beautiful."

"There were chairs," he said. "And a small table over there"—he pointed to a corner of the room—"where I sat to do the accounts and take my coffee. We never rushed our customers. Sometimes they spent half a day in the shop looking through magazines, chatting to Ilse about fashion. She hated the traditional German outfits. The styles from Paris were her passion."

His head sank to his chest and he stared at the broken window glass on the floor. "Six years. We survived six years of war and never had a problem. And then the war ends, and everything falls to pieces."

"But it's going to be okay, right?" I wanted words to be a guarantee, the way they used to be when I was little and Mutti would reassure me that a new day made everything bright again. "The Soviets won't stay forever."

He picked up a piece of glass, then put it down. "It won't be like before."

Nothing is like before. That was how the suffering started, when you thought too much about *before.*

I longed to make Otto feel better. "You'll have a window again soon. That way people will be able to see your mannequins."

"The mannequins are gone." The empty pockets of his cardigan drooped outward.

"But maybe you'll find them." Who would steal mannequins? What could you even do with them? "And we can fix the dress. Mutti has needle and thread in her bag." Damn it. "I mean . . ." What did I mean? The story I'd told about carrying the extra bag became confused in my mind. "She gave them to me to take care of." It seemed so real, I wanted it to be true.

Otto took off his crooked glasses and rubbed the bridge of his nose. I wasn't even sure he'd heard me.

Make yourself indispensable. "Come on, Uncle Otto. At least we can clean it up. It will go faster if we both do it."

It felt funny telling a grown man what to do. It felt even funnier when he went upstairs to fetch some rags, a broom, and my bucket.

Part of me wished Otto hadn't told me about the window display. It made the dream of things returning to normal so much more unlikely. I wanted to help him set one up. He would probably let me name the mannequins. I could open the door to the shop and hear the little bell dingle, and a customer would be inside standing before the large oval mirror, Ilse crouched at her feet with a row of pins in her mouth—the way Mutti used to when she was taking up a hem.

I gathered the broken frames and photographs while Otto swept the floor. Then he placed the bucket in the middle of the room and we dipped our rags in and moved to opposite ends.

As soon as we started washing the wood floor, I could have sworn it doubled in size. I snuck glances at Otto, scrubbing on his knees. Papi would never have—

"Aunt Ilse wishes we'd never come here, doesn't she?" I said.

Otto patted down his fluff of hair. "I wouldn't say that. The situation just needs some smoothing out. She'll be happy about the shop."

When we were done, we shut and locked the customer door, making the bell tinkle with such a gentle noise I felt sad for it. We went back upstairs and I waited for Ilse to comment on the mop or my armful of broken photograph frames. Instead, she kept her head down over the stove, the steam from the boiling sugar beets curling the wisps of hair that had escaped from her braids.

I was about to take off my shoes when Otto said, "I almost forgot. Someone stole the shoemaker's scissors. He asked to borrow a pair of ours." He handed me a set of tailors' shears with their odd-looking handle. "They're not meant for cutting leather, but I suppose they're better than nothing. Would you mind dropping them off for him?"

I kept my worn old shoes on. It occurred to me the shoemaker was someone I should make friends with. The pharmacy had no medicine. The dance hall was closed. But the shoemaker had shoes.

CHAPTER TWENTY-FIVE

THE SHOEMAKER'S WIFE

I was going to carry the scissors in my hand, but Otto suggested putting them in my basket so no one got any ideas. They slid around the bottom as I walked down Rosenstrasse. I looked forward to visiting the shoemaker. I loved the smells of leather and shoe polish. Maybe he would let me try on a new pair of shoes, even if we both knew I couldn't afford to buy them.

I entered the square and walked past the grocery store, hoping to run into Liesel, but I didn't see her. The grocery display window was empty. One year in our town there'd been a chocolate heart hanging in the grocer's window on a long red ribbon. I had walked past it every day after school and admired it. I'd even asked the grocer if I could work there and be paid in chocolate heart, but he'd had nothing for me to do.

So I'd stolen the money from Mutti. She had found it in my pocket—a discovery that had launched the Every Bad Thing speech she was so fond of: *Katarina Wilhelmina, this is just like the time you—*

The display window was another thing to add to my long list of impossible things. Imagine a chocolate heart on a red ribbon, hanging in a grocer's window. Could there be anything more absurd?

Farther down the road, Soviet soldiers knocked on one door after the next.

"Fascist? Fascist?" they asked. Otto had explained they were looking for Nazis. It was part of the cleanup they were doing after the war.

I thought of all the things that needed cleaning:

- Daschner's Damen und Herrenmode, still, but also:

- Me.

- The refugees and displaced persons walking along the road, a cloud of hopelessness raining down on them constantly like ash.

- The past. The past could use a good scrub. It burned our eyes and made the days darker and more sinister. But there was no way to clean that.

Closer to the shoe shop I heard shouting—a mixture of Russian and German. Soviet soldiers were beating someone up—another suspected Nazi, probably. I pressed myself into a doorway and peered down the road: three soldiers, one older man.

Liesel would have found a way to stop this. She would have walked over and diverted the soldiers with something clever, a made-up story about Dmitri needing them in the square. She wouldn't even have hesitated. Already I'd waited too long. This was where cowards were born, surely—in that moment of hesitation. What would happen if I intervened? The soldiers would turn their attention on me, and I'd be the next girl dead by the roadside with her privates exposed.

A couple of overweight *Volkspolizei* lumbered toward the fight, but the soldiers didn't even look up.

I was about to head on to the shoemaker's when the pungent stench of diesel filled the air. The black Mercedes rounded a corner and stopped down the road. Out stepped Blue Eyes. He strutted toward the scene in his important way, shouting in Russian.

I edged around the corner, slipped between two buildings, and emerged almost right behind the officer's car.

I knew I should just walk away. But I couldn't. That black Nazi car—how could I not think about the Goldsteins? And . . . death camps? When the Gestapo had shown up at our door, everything about them had been cold. Even their black leather coats had winter sewn into the lining. And now the Soviets were driving that car. The Soviets, who were just as cold, who pointed their guns at women—at Mutti—and ended their lives.

I pressed my hand flat against the black body of the car. It was warm. My fingernails weren't sharp enough to do any damage to the paint. But when I opened my basket, there were the scissors Otto had given me.

We treat the Germans the way they treated us. Blue Eyes' words echoed in my ear. Well, fair *was* fair. I took out the scissors, looked both ways, and made a deep scratch across the passenger door. Wait till I told Liesel about this. For once, I wasn't a coward. I would have revenge—and then Hilde would have to forgive me for Mutti. I longed to see Blue Eyes saunter back to his car, the smug look on his face turning to outrage when he saw the scratch.

But scratched paint wouldn't stop the car from running. I studied the tires. The tread looked thick and difficult to puncture, but the side of the tire was smooth, maybe thinner. It took one quick thrust, and then came a hiss of air that thrilled me at first—and then terrified me. What had I done?

Somewhere behind me a door slammed shut, and in a panic I hurried away. My heart raced at top speed. *Don't run.* Only guilty people ran. I was fifty meters down the road when I realized the fighting had stopped. I glanced back and saw Blue Eyes helping the German man to his feet.

Fifty more meters and I realized the scissors weren't sliding around in my basket anymore. Had I dropped them? I looked back at the ground near the car, but now the door-knocking soldiers stood in the way.

Blue Eyes was scolding the soldiers who'd been fighting. I would wait. Surely the door-knockers would go away. But they didn't. And sooner or later Blue Eyes would turn around—sooner, now. I turned onto another road, feeling as though I'd left a murder weapon behind. What if something on the scissors identified them as belonging to Otto, or to the shop? I racked my memory but, aside from the oddly shaped handle, I came up blank.

Everything was looking at me, even the windows on the street. I wanted to run, but I forced myself to slow down and focus on a spot on the road a few meters ahead. I passed three Soviet soldiers taking turns trying to ride a bicycle. Each of them rode in awkward wobbling circles, their knees coming up to their shoulders, laughing every time the bike toppled over. My clothes felt like they'd been buttoned the wrong way. But no, it wasn't my clothes; it was my skin. What if someone stopped me, right here on the street?

I shouldn't have vandalized the car. Blue Eyes had done the right thing, and I'd done the wrong one. I wanted to go back and fix it, but there was no going back.

I ran all the way to the clothing shop and crept up the stairs. I dreaded facing Ilse in this state. Maybe she wouldn't be home. But when I opened the door, I could hear her in the kitchen commiserating with Hilde about sugar beets.

I slipped off my shoes, hoping to sneak through the sitting room to our bedroom, but Otto was there.

"You're back already?" he said.

Back? From the shoemaker. The scissors. *Scheisse.*

"What did my black-thumbed friend have to say?" Otto asked me. *Blame not the cobbler for his black thumbs,* Mutti used to say whenever she was dusted all over with flour from baking.

"Not much," I said.

What if he asked about the scissors?

I dropped them.

I lost them.

But Otto would speak to the shoemaker, and then he'd find out I hadn't given him the scissors at all.

"Did you see his wife? You must not have. She's such a talker." Otto's pleasant conversation made me feel even worse.

"She wasn't there," I mumbled.

I would go back to where the car was parked. Right now. I'd go back, find the scissors, and take them to the shoemaker. No one would be the wiser.

CHAPTER TWENTY-SIX

MOTHER OR NO MOTHER

As soon as Otto went back downstairs to the shop, I entered the kitchen—with the intention of passing straight through to put on my shoes. The longer I waited to retrieve those scissors, the less chance there was that they would still be there. Though who was I kidding? Scissors were precious; no one who passed them would leave them lying there. Even if they didn't need them, the scissors could be traded for something else.

"Well, look who it is." Ilse stopped chopping the mushrooms Hilde had brought home. "It's about time you decided to help out instead of gallivanting around the neighborhood."

The broken frames and photographs from the shop were spread across the table. The kitchen was hot and humid, and I already felt clammy from the afternoon. Sweat beaded up on my nose. Hilde was rinsing beet greens in the sink and wouldn't look at me.

"I was helping Uncle Otto," I said. "I'm going back down right now."

She wheeled around. "You have no business being in the shop. No right."

Anger spiked in my body like a fever. "We were cleaning up. I was being kind."

"Kind. Hmm. Do you know what I found today?"

It was her favorite type of question: one I couldn't possibly know the answer to, but which I *should* know if I was a decent person.

The hiss of air from the flattening tire sounded in my head. I had to get those scissors. Hilde gave me one quick warning glance over her shoulder. What was going on?

When Ilse whipped a folded card out of her apron pocket I nearly cried out. It was Mutti's identity card. I yanked it out of her hand. I couldn't stand to think of her touching it. That card was the closest thing I had to Mutti herself.

"Would you like to tell me how you have this if your mother is in hospital?" Ilse asked.

I put the card into my pocket and flattened my hand against it. *Think*. There were three main reasons why a person might have their mother's identity card:

- because she was dead,

- because she was dead, and

- because she was dead.

Otto would know what to say. He'd have a phrase he would

repeat to calm Ilse down, the way Papi used to shush our horses with a Na, na, *you're all right*. But Otto was downstairs. I had the feeling Ilse had waited for him to leave.

"I'm keeping it for Mutti," I said. "For when she arrives."

"Is that so?" Ilse stood with her hands on her hips, her large face looking more square and mannish than ever. "In what world does that make sense? There are checkpoints everywhere. What will she do without her *Kennkarte*?"

My mind raced. "People steal them in hospitals. For false identities." I felt like I was running on an icy pond, feet slipping beneath me. "We decided it would be safer if I took the *Kennkarte* with me." And then something else occurred to me. "Why were you looking in my bag?"

"Mind your tone, young lady," Ilse said. "This is my home, and you girls are guests here. That card was not in your bag; it was in your mother's bag, I'd swear on it, or else I'm a three-horned cow."

"Mutti gave us some of her things to bring ahead," I said. "There wasn't room for her to keep them in the hospital."

"Is that so?" Ilse said. "I'll get to the bottom of this situation sooner or later."

Hilde moved from the sink to the stove. "Would you like me to strain off the beet juice, Auntie Ilse?"

"Don't *Auntie* me. You girls were supposed to bring home more salami. Let that juice settle, and keep the pulp. We'll be eating it for supper this evening. And understand—the moment my boys come home, the two of you will leave. A refugee camp will accommodate you, mother or no mother." *No mother*, her face said. She turned on her heel, thumped out of the apartment and down the stairs.

Mutti used to feed beet pulp to the horses. It tasted like cardboard. "She is a three-horned cow," I muttered.

Hilde didn't even laugh. All the sugar had been boiled out of her too.

"Don't worry," I said. "We're not going to any camp." Although I didn't feel confident about that at all. Just last week, a neighbor's son had arrived home—missing a hand, but home.

I edged toward the door. If I hurried, I could slip past Ilse and run back to where Blue Eyes had parked his car.

The car with a slashed tire. It was probably surrounded now by investigating soldiers. How could I have been so stupid? Even if no one found the scissors, I wouldn't be able to get anywhere near them. But I had to try.

Hilde's head popped up from the stove. "Where are you going?"

"Nowhere."

"Nowhere, with shoes on. Don't you think you've done enough for one day?"

Footsteps sounded up the stairs.

Ilse returned with a bulge in her apron pocket that was probably a potato. "Help your sister," she snapped at me. There was no hope of leaving now.

As I put on my apron, I wondered how Otto planned to smooth Ilse out. There were things in this world that did not take well to smoothing. I'd known a girl once in school who'd had the wooliest, curliest hair I'd ever seen. Otto would not have been able to smooth that over, no matter how hard he tried.

CHAPTER TWENTY-SEVEN

A TURNIP-SIZED SECRET

That evening I lay on the blankets in our stuffy little bedroom. "What are we going to do?" The room felt smaller and stuffier than ever. "It's only a matter of time before she kicks us out." Despite the circumstances, it felt good to make us into a team again: me and Hilde against the world. The candle I'd made from Liesel's wax flickered and hissed in the dark room.

Hilde sat cross-legged beside me brushing her hair. "I don't know why you ever kept Mutti's *Kennkarte*. Ilse's bound to figure everything out now."

So much for being a team.

But something else swirled through my mind. *What am I going to do?* There had been no opportunity to sneak out before curfew and rescue those scissors, and I couldn't go out on the streets after dark. The scissors would have to wait until tomorrow, and by then there was almost no chance they'd still be there.

And if a stranger picked them up?

It wouldn't be the worst thing. They would be well and truly hidden. I'd have to think about what I would say to Otto. Maybe I'd admit to losing them.

And if the Soviets found them?

Hilde held up a piece of broken mirror she'd found in the wreckage of Oberstrasse, examined her hair for I don't know what, then set the mirror down and brushed some more. One rhythmic stroke after the next: it was a sound that insisted everything was all right.

"Oskar might get me some see-through stockings," she said.

Of all the impractical things to want. But I understood. See-through stockings were like doilies—extravagant, pretty, and useless. A vote in favor of a mended world.

"How does he get these things?" I asked. "What does he have to trade with?"

Hilde knew. She had a secret in her mouth the size of a turnip. But she wouldn't tell me. She loved keeping secrets, especially from me, because she knew how badly I wanted to know everything.

In my opinion, secrets had categories:

- If they were about someone else, they were fun to tell.

- If they were about you, they were only fun to tell if they were good. I wasn't sure yet if Hilde would think the car was a good secret or a bad one. Liesel would think it was good. I was dying to tell her.

- Secrets about secret rooms should never be told.

"And by the way," she said, "you need to stop doing things that put us at risk."

My God, did she know? Was it written between the creases on my forehead? Lodged like blood beneath my fingernails?

"This is not just about you," she said. "What you do affects me too."

"What are you talking about?" I said.

"The *Kennkarte*, obviously. Unless you've done something else I don't know about."

I willed my face to stay still. "What will you have to trade Oskar for the stockings?" It would give me an idea of what I'd have to come up with for some Beethoven.

She flicked her hair back. "Nothing."

What? "So he *is* sweet on you."

She didn't answer.

"Well? Don't you like him? I mean, he's pretty nice, even if he knows literally nothing about how to take care of animals."

She put down her brush and studied her nails. "He's only okay. His skin is so . . . And he's jumpy as hell."

"So you just flirt with him to get things from him," I said. At least Liesel actually liked Dmitri.

"Mind your own business, *Scheisskopf*." Hilde took out her stack of love letters. "Anyway, I can do what I want. I was named after a strong and beautiful Norse princess."

I sighed. "That is not the reason Mutti chose your name."

"Yes, it is. And if you remember the story, Brunhilde vowed to marry a man with only exceptional qualities. He had to be stronger than she was."

"Who said anything about marriage?"

"You did, before. Anyway, shut up already about Oskar. He's nice to work with, but that's all. When Paul comes back—"

"Do you actually think Paul is coming back?" I covered my mouth with one hand. I couldn't believe I'd said that out loud.

"When Paul comes back," she said, "we're going to have sex and use condoms." Her wide eyes meant she had said something shocking and I was supposed to react.

"Good for you." I knew what condoms were in theory, though I'd never actually seen one. I didn't want to give my sister a reason to laugh at me, so I rolled over and went back to brooding about the black Mercedes.

Would Blue Eyes have noticed the flat tire right away? Possibly not. It was on the passenger side. He would have started the car and tried to drive away. The tire would have made that *whap-whap-whap* sound I'd heard on the road a few times, like a wet towel smacking the ground. He would have stopped and gotten out. And that's when he would have seen not only the tire but also the scratch. *And the scissors?*

No, he wouldn't have even noticed the scissors because he would have been too preoccupied by the car. He would have had a moment of confusion at the unexpected scratch, those three seconds when the world has put its pants on backward. Then he would have understood: Sabotage. Vandalism. No possibility of driving the car unless someone changed the tire. Maybe him, if he knew how. Kneeling on the cobbles, getting his uniform dirty. Being scolded later by one of his superiors: *Look at you, Ivan, you're a mess,* and, *How could you have let that happen to the fancy Nazi car?* Maybe his father would take away one of his shiny medals for a few days as punishment.

And then what?

I wanted Hilde to know I'd begun a campaign in revenge for Mutti's death: first the coal, now this. I wanted her to be proud of me, and hug me, and bring out one of the catalogs. We could sit side by side with our legs stretched out the way we used to, and imagine dressing in fancy clothes that we would never in a thousand years be able to afford.

But if those scissors were traced back to me, it wouldn't matter what Hilde or anyone else thought. I had to go back and get them.

Something glinted in the candlelight. It was Mutti's locket, cradled in Hilde's hands.

"Can I hold it?" I asked.

"No."

CHAPTER TWENTY-EIGHT

WHAT GIRL IN HER RIGHT MIND WOULD—

Early the next morning I tried to think of a reason to walk in the wrong direction to Frau Weber's farm so I could look for those scissors.

"The shoemaker has a new pair of shoes in the window," I said. "They're blue. You'll love them."

"Don't be ridiculous," Hilde said. "He wouldn't leave them in the window overnight. Come on, already."

She walked to the farm as though the road was on fire. So much for Oskar only being *okay*.

All day the scissors cut into my thoughts. What if someone...? What if the Soviets...? And what would I tell Otto? The overture to Rossini's *Barber of Seville* picked up my worries and ran in circles with them, getting louder and faster in my head, as his music tended to do. Signor Crescendo, people used to call him.

The main theme was stuck in my head.

But I was also bursting to tell Liesel about the vandalized car. I imagined her eyes widening, freckles multiplying in excitement. I wanted her to think of me as a hero. Even more—I wanted her to look at me with the same admiration as when Blue Eyes had spoken only to me.

Ilse had told us to come home straight after work, so there was no time to play piano. When she asked us to go pick up rations at the grocery store, I jumped at the opportunity. I was hoping to go alone, but Hilde followed me down the stairs.

"Let's go see those shoes I was telling you about," I said as soon as we were out on the street.

"They're going to be a disappointment," Hilde said. "You've built them up too much."

A huge disappointment, yes, *because they don't exist.* "You'll see," I said.

I headed back to the road where Blue Eyes' car had been parked, then slowed down.

"What are you doing?" Hilde asked. "What are you looking for? I thought you wanted to go see the shoes."

"Nothing."

Might someone have kicked the scissors onto the road? No. No one who stepped on them would leave them there. I had to admit it. The scissors were gone. *It's fine.* Whoever had picked them up had no idea they'd been used to vandalize the car. It was the best way to get rid of them.

We reached the shoe store and Hilde peered into the window.

"So? Where are these wonderful shoes?"

I gave a cursory look. "He must have sold them."

She unbraided her hair and it blew away from me—as if even her hair could hold a grudge.

When we arrived at the grocery store, there was a line-up humming with conversation. If people were waiting, it meant something good was available. We stood at the end of the line.

"What do they have?" I asked the woman in front of me.

"I heard it was butter," she said.

"There's no way it's butter," said someone closer to the door. "They always say it's butter, and then it ends up being cabbage."

"Or nothing," said someone else.

We'd been in so many line-ups I could now recognize their personalities. There were dull line-ups where people shuffled forward and barely spoke to one another, and there were energetic ones like this one, where conversations erupted between strangers and everyone was allowed to have an opinion. Those were my favorite kind.

At first I thought the energy was all about the butter. But then a woman nearer to the front of the line asked, "Who do you think did it?"

"Whoever it was, he must have testicles of steel," said another woman. "Good for him. I salute him."

"Did what?" I had a feeling.

"Ruined that fancy black Mercedes," the first woman said. "The one the commandant drives around in with his son, the *Hosen-scheisser.*" The coward—literally, someone who shit his pants.

A coward? Was he?

Word had spread even quicker than I'd imagined. I tried as hard as I could not to puff out my chest. They thought it was a man. Because only a man would be brave enough to vandalize a

Soviet vehicle. Ha! *It was me,* I wanted to shout. *I did it.*

Hilde stood taller beside me. Good posture was her body's automatic reaction to trouble. It was all those years in the League of German Girls; they figured a straight back could fix anything. "What happened to the car?" she asked.

"Someone slashed the tire and gave it a nice long scratch down the side," said the first woman.

I glanced at Hilde, hoping to catch a smile or a raised eyebrow. But she kept her gaze staunchly forward, as though slashed tires were a toy she hadn't played with since she was four.

"Ach, you shouldn't salute the person who did that," said an old man who'd sauntered up behind me. "It was foolishness." He spoke *Plattdeutsch*—Low German—like many of the people in our town had done. Mutti had always cautioned us against picking it up, as if it were a disease. *If you ever get a good job and you sound like that,* she used to say, *everyone will recognize your low background.*

I turned to face him. "Foolishness? Why would you say that?"

"Because these are Soviets," the man said, "not some French *Sitzpinklers*." A Frenchman sitting down to pee. A woman nearby snickered. "The commandant is in a rage about his damned car, which means he won't stop until he finds out who did it. And if he doesn't find out, he'll punish us all."

The heat in the air felt thicker, and the bad smells crept out of their corners. What if one of the soldiers had found those scissors? I felt dizzy. How was it possible word had passed this quickly? *It's okay.* They thought a man had done it. Because what girl in her right mind would—?

Thank God my sister wasn't looking at me. Sooner or later

something on my face always gave me away, and she and Mutti could spot it no matter how nonchalant I tried to be.

"You're overreacting," I said to the old man. "Whoever did it will get a slap with a dirty washrag and nothing more. If they're caught."

"Destruction of a Soviet officer's property?" The man laughed. He was missing several teeth. "They'll send that person to Siberia, you see if they don't." The way he said Siberia, a name with weights attached to its ankles, made it sound like hell.

"The car is German," I said.

His laughter was wry. "Everything belongs to them now, or haven't you noticed?"

I imagined Mutti finding out. She'd make that face, the one when it looked like her apron strings were too tight. She'd use my full name. I'd have to listen to the Every Bad Thing speech for at least half an hour, and probably miss my supper.

There was no butter at the store, and Liesel's mother was especially grumpy because of all the excitement the rumor had caused. "Move along, move along," she kept saying.

As we waited for our rations in the dimly lit store, Liesel bustled out of the back room, kerchief askew. She caught my eye and nodded toward a corner stacked with German army coats no one wanted anymore. Hilde was busy talking to some lady about where to find carrot seeds. I sidled over.

"Did you hear about the car?" Liesel whispered.

"Yes. Everyone is talking about it." I'd wanted to be excited, but a tiny corner of my voice was tinged with dread.

"I have to admit, when I first heard about it, I wished I'd done it." She picked at a bloodstain on one of the coats with her fingernail. "The one person I knew it couldn't be was you."

The frightened squirrel. I crossed my arms at my chest. "It was me," I said—quietly, but with force.

At first she laughed. But I didn't laugh with her.

"*Mein Gott.* You aren't kidding."

"You mustn't tell," I said.

"Of course I won't tell. It's brilliant. Although—"

"What?" For the first time I noticed a dusty smell in the grocery store.

"It's a shame we didn't talk it over first. You should have only flattened the tire," Liesel said. "A flat tire could be caused by anything. There's glass all over the streets. But a scratch? It's a punishable offense. And it's the commandant's car."

In other words, that old man was right. "I didn't think of that."

"Anyway, it's done," Liesel said.

Imagine if she knew about the scissors. Leaving them at the scene of the crime was the work of a panicker. I longed to ask for her advice, though. The words were almost out of my mouth when Hilde came up behind her.

"I still think it's magnificent," Liesel added.

Hilde's eyes narrowed.

Stop talking. But there was no way for me to transmit that message to Liesel without my sister seeing.

"The baker's making Russian black bread, I just found out," Liesel said. "But he only has it early in the morning. People line up at night, behind the dance hall."

"What about curfew?" I said.

"Screw curfew. You should sneak out. We'll go together."

Hilde glared at me from behind Liesel.

"I can't."

"Come on, don't be such a little sausage," Liesel said. "We can wrap our shoes with rags so they don't make noise on the cobblestones. Keep half the bread for ourselves and give the other half to families."

I could hardly meet her eye. Liesel was willing to risk the heroic to help other people, regardless of the danger to herself, whereas I had merely been reckless.

Hilde moved to stand beside me. "She's not going with you, so forget it." She hooked me by one arm and pulled me away. "That girl is trouble," she said between her teeth. "Don't you dare get involved with her. I'll bet any money she's the one who ruined that car."

We left the grocery store with a shrunken cabbage, one small packet of beans, and one packet of meat to be identified never.

* * * *

It was after supper when the banging started on the door downstairs. Hilde and Ilse were studying dress patterns. Otto had poured a glass of schnapps and was about to play the violin. I was his audience of one. He grimaced, snapped the case shut again, and took it to his bedroom.

"Open up," someone shouted outside.

Ilse appeared in the sitting room doorway, eyes wide. When Otto returned from the bedroom she rushed over to him. "What do we do?"

"I'll go down," he said. "See what they want."

"What do they ever want?" she said. "You shouldn't."

"It will be worse if I don't. They know we're here. The lights are on."

She held on to him. "Be careful." Her eyes lit on the bottle of schnapps. "Take it with you, just in case. So you have something to give them."

I could tell Otto didn't want to, but he took the bottle under one arm like a misbehaving child and went downstairs. "I'm coming, I'm coming," he called.

The three of us huddled near the door, listening.

"We look for information," said a man with a strong Russian accent. "The commandant's car."

Every muscle in my body went stiff. *The scissors.* They'd found them. They had traced them back here.

"Forgive me," Otto said politely. "I don't know anything about the car."

I could barely breathe.

The soldier said, "If you have information, you come to the *Kommandatura*. There is a reward."

A reward. I wondered what they were offering.

"If I hear anything, I'll get in touch with you immediately," Otto said.

The entryway fell silent.

"*Chasy*," the man said. Wristwatch. "Do you have?"

"I do not," Otto said. "Please. Put the gun down. You can take this instead."

A murmur of Russian words was exchanged, and then *thank you* and *you're welcome*—as if Otto had given them the bottle of schnapps willingly. The door clicked shut and he came back up the stairs.

I looked at Ilse with the tiniest bit of admiration. Her quick thinking might have saved his life. Already we could hear banging at the next door, and the shout to *open up.*

I lay awake that night thinking of the groups of soldiers that would be knocking on all the doors in Fahlhoff. They wouldn't be happy until they found someone to blame for this.

What had I done?

CHAPTER TWENTY-NINE

MEN WITH KNIVES, PART TWO

When we arrived at Frau Weber's farm the next morning for work, Oskar was not in the barn. Neither were the cows. One of them was in the vegetable garden eating the lettuce, two were standing outside the barn door waiting to be milked, and one was missing, along with all the calves.

"What's your boyfriend up to now?" I said with a frown.

"He's not my boyfriend," Hilde said.

Irresponsible was what he was. I should have known. Not tying the cow's hind legs was only the beginning. He couldn't even shut the barn doors properly. Great. Frau Weber would come out, see the cows, and blame us for Oskar's incompetence. We rounded them up and did the milking without him, both of us annoyed by the extra work.

But after we'd taken care of the animals in the hidden part of the barn, he still hadn't shown up.

"Something's wrong," my sister said. "Do you think he's been caught?"

I didn't know much about the black market except that it was illegal. It seemed more likely Oskar had made off with the calves, traded them, and run away.

But Frau Weber hadn't come to the barn yet either. By now, she'd usually brought us something to eat. Plus, there were quotas to fill. The Soviets expected everything to be ready when they came by. Frau Weber never missed those pickups, even though she muttered and swore about the soldiers as she poured their watered-down milk into churns. What could be keeping her?

We went to the house and knocked on the side door. Silence. I shaded my eyes and peered in through the glass, expecting to see Frau Weber up to her elbows in flour and unable to answer. That was not what I saw. There were broken dishes on the floor, and chairs upended. The rack of small silver spoons had been taken off the wall and broken in half, spoons scattered everywhere. I tried the door. It was unlocked.

Hilde put a hand on my arm. "Whoever did this might still be in the house."

Thank you, sister with the men-with-knives bedtime stories.

We entered, stepping gingerly around the shards on the floor. The house smelled stale, like tobacco, and was utterly silent. Had Frau Weber and Oskar fled? Had they been taken away? I listened for voices or footsteps but heard nothing. In fact, I heard so much nothing that a worse thought than the men with knives came into my head: *they're dead.* Frau Weber and Oskar, both. Dread crept up my legs, making it hard for me to move. Around every corner I was sure I would find blood, a body.

Then I heard a groan. I pointed to the bedroom and motioned for Hilde to come with me. The door was shut. She nudged me to open it.

"You do it," I whispered.

My sister didn't move. "You're the one who does things."

Translation: *you're the one who does stupid things.* I turned the doorknob and pushed the door open with a long creak. The room was dark. A noise came from the corner and I wheeled around.

Oskar's hands and legs were tied with rope, his mouth stuffed with a rag. I raced over to him. There was a stench of urine around him, which I pretended I couldn't smell. He glanced at Hilde, then away, as I removed the rag and unfastened the ties.

"I tried to stop them," he said, his voice hoarse.

I opened a window for some fresh air. Frau Weber lay curled and lifeless on the bed.

"She's been out cold for hours," Oskar said.

Hilde bent toward her. "Frau Weber?" She stroked her hair.

Not again. Please not again. "Check her pulse."

Hilde pressed a thumb against her wrist. "She's alive."

I sat on the bed near Frau Weber's legs. I wanted to grab hold of them and not let go. She was supposed to be the sturdy one, but she looked so small. Her lip was puffy and there was a large bruise on her cheek, though I suspected those were the least of her injuries.

"What happened?" I asked.

"Soldiers," Oskar said. "Three of them. I tried to stop them, but I couldn't . . . I couldn't . . ."

"You're lucky they didn't kill you," Hilde said.

"They came to the door asking about that vandalized car," Oskar said, "but they were so drunk, and we didn't know anything. They hurt her, and then they smashed everything and left. I don't know what they did in the barn."

My mind recoiled from what Oskar had just said. *This was my fault.*

"The calves are gone," I said. "And one of the cows."

There was blood on the sheets. What had he and Frau Weber lived through last night?

This would have happened with or without me.

Not true. Without me, there would have been no vandalized car. No door-to-door searches.

I had dropped a boulder into a pond, thinking the ripples would be predictable.

"Go take care of the quotas," Hilde said to Oskar. "Let me help her. This is a woman's job."

He looked grateful to be excused from the room.

"I can help too," I said.

"You don't understand what she's been through," Hilde said.

"Stop treating me like a baby. Of course I understand."

Frau Weber moved her head. "Tea," she said in a shaky voice.

Hilde gave me a pointed look. "Put water on. And bring warm cloths so I can help her wash."

I rushed into the kitchen to heat water. I'd make the best tea of all time, to make up for— No, that would not make it up. Part of me wanted to confess my role in this, but there was no way I'd get the words out. I would have to find another way to fix this, if such a thing existed.

I set the tea on Frau Weber's nightstand, then stood in the bedroom not knowing where to put myself. Hilde held Frau Weber and sang to her. I felt small, and smaller. A breeze fluttered the curtains as I passed Hilde a warm cloth. I hated the way a room could be so oblivious to what was wrong in it. But I realized: what was wrong in it was me.

I decided to clean up the mess in the kitchen. If Frau Weber was anything like Mutti, a disaster in the kitchen would break her. The smell of cigarettes lingered in the air. The men had spat on the sitting room floor and put out their cigarette butts on the rug. I gathered whatever could be mended, swept up the things that couldn't, and went out to the vegetable garden to survey the damage. The cow must not have been in there for long. Only one corner of the garden had been destroyed.

At least the soldiers hadn't figured out Frau Weber's system of hidden food. She used twigs to mark the places where she'd buried things. You couldn't see them from afar. Even up close, you wouldn't know what they were, unless you knew what they were. I chose one twig and dug. It was always a surprise to see what came up. This time, it was a small bag of barley that had been stored in a sealed jar to keep the bugs out. Treasure, buried like carrot seeds: as if by burying a spoon, one might grow a silverware bush.

I was thinking about what I might make with the barley when a rattle came from one of the snares. There, caught and struggling, was another rabbit.

"Hilde!"

I waited for her to come running. Instead, it was Oskar who appeared. When he saw the rabbit in the trap, he backed away.

"No, you don't," I said. "I'll need your help. This is something we can do for Frau Weber. We can prepare her a meal."

I took the rabbit by the hind legs and instructed Oskar to ease its head out of the snare. He thrust his hands into his pockets. I was about to say something rude, but then I remembered he'd been in the room while the men were raping Frau Weber.

"It's all right," I said. "It won't hurt you."

"You're going to kill it," he said.

"Yes, Oskar. That's how we get rabbit stew."

It was different when you'd grown up on a farm. I knew where my food came from. Papi had been slaughtering pigs and geese since I was a little girl. When all you did was show up at the dinner table to a plate of roast beef, it was easy to forget the middle part, where the cow went from being alive to being meat.

Then again, Hilde had always been the one with the stronger stomach. Sure, I knew how to kill a rabbit; Papi had taught me. But I'd never actually done it. Now I had no choice.

Oskar pulled the snare off, I held the wiggling rabbit by its warm hind legs—and me with my brave thoughts, I almost let it go. I'd seen so many dead things lately.

He shielded his eyes with one hand. "Is it over yet?"

All I had to do was snap its neck. There was no need to think about it. So I did. Not as quickly and efficiently as my sister, which made me sad because the rabbit suffered more than it should have, but I did it. Was this how soldiers had made their way through the war? Not thinking about it. Just doing it. How often could you do that before it changed you?

In the kitchen I found a sharp knife and sent Oskar away while I skinned and gutted the rabbit. I heated the stove, improvising a stew as best I could without wasting any of Frau Weber's precious food. Soon the kitchen smelled fragrant with the simmering meat. Why couldn't this have been a regular meal, on a regular day?

The bedroom door opened and Frau Weber teetered toward the sweet-smelling kitchen. "What is this? What did you do?"

When I showed her the stew, she patted my cheek. "You're a good girl."

If only that were true.

I insisted Frau Weber go back to bed. How would she sleep there tonight, knowing the men might come back?

After I finished cleaning the house, I went to the barn to find Oskar. "Frau Weber needs a dog," I said. "For protection."

He didn't respond.

When the rabbit stew was ready I took charge of it, scooping it into bowls and serving it with the thinnest slices of bread. Frau Weber sat in a soft chair with a blanket around her shoulders. I brought a bowl over to her, but she looked right through it.

"You should eat," I said. "It will make you feel better." Her lip looked so sore and swollen I didn't dare bring the spoon to her mouth.

She didn't move. "You eat. That will make me feel better."

I sat at the table with Hilde and Oskar. The stew wasn't as rich and fine as Mutti's would have been, but there was so much meat—enough that when I chewed and swallowed it, I didn't have to pretend to make it bigger. We tried not to eat with relish, but our spoons crashed against the sides of the bowls, breaking the awful silence in the room.

CHAPTER THIRTY

THE NAME WITH WEIGHTS ATTACHED TO ITS ANKLES

I worried about what we might find the next morning at Frau Weber's farm—had the soldiers come back? But when we arrived, the large wooden barn doors were open, and Oskar sat on a stool milking one of the cows the wrong way, as usual.

"You're pulling too hard on her teats," I said. The hind legs weren't worth mentioning anymore. "She'll kick you if you don't stop that."

He didn't even break his rhythm. "You should see the pistols I got."

Pistols?

"For protection," he added.

"I said a dog, Oskar."

"Dogs get shot. One pistol for Frau Weber, and one for me. I swear that will never happen again."

I remembered the soldier with the twitchy mouth, the sound so explosive it made my head hurt; Mutti falling instantly and not getting up. A gun might solve Frau Weber's problems, at first— and then it would make them much worse.

Hilde brought her stool over and placed it right next to his.

"Does Frau Weber even know how to fire a gun?" I asked.

Germans weren't allowed to possess guns and could be shot if anyone caught them with one. But knowing how to use a gun was one thing. Being willing to use it was something else. If you were willing, it took less effort to pull a trigger than it did to snap a rabbit's neck.

The barn filled with the sounds of milk hitting the bucket, Oskar's low voice, and my sister's giggly laughter. Oskar hadn't bothered to answer my question about Frau Weber. When my sister was near, everything else disappeared. I went to the far side of the barn and milked the other cow, opening and closing my hands around its teats, trying to imagine what it would feel like to hold another person's life in my hands.

When I went into the house to check on Frau Weber, I expected her to be wrapped in a shawl, clutching a mug of hot chicory coffee. Instead, six bullets were lined up on the kitchen table in a tight row, and she sat in front of them cleaning the barrel of her gun with some cotton wool stuck to the end of a screwdriver. She hadn't heard me come in. Or if she had, it was less important to her than the job she was doing. The crockery might have been smashed, but the gun seemed to have put her back together.

"Brutes," she said.

I couldn't look at her. The bruises on her face were a dark purple, and her lip looked painful. She hadn't said *savages*, but that was the word I heard, the one that had caused the sky to fall on me.

Would this have happened if I hadn't vandalized the car?

"I dare them to come through that door a second time," she said.

I held one of the bullets in my open palm. It was heavier than it looked. "Is this really a good idea?"

She set down the weapon. "Pass me that rag. You think I'll end up in Siberia because I have a gun?"

The man in the butter line-up had mentioned that place. "What's in Siberia?"

"The worst of their forced labor camps." Frau Weber wiped down the outside of the gun, giving attention to every crevice and corner. "That's what people say, anyway: winter twelve months of the year, and summer the rest of the time. There are too many prisoners and not enough food. They work you and work you until eventually you wear out and die. I'm not going there, Katja, so stop worrying about me."

They wouldn't send me to Siberia just for wrecking a car, would they? And was it wrecked, really? A flat tire could be changed. A scratch could be repaired.

I trudged back to the barn and opened the secret door to feed Frau Weber's hidden chickens. Behind me Hilde and Oskar were having a quiet conversation about sugar beet mash. It made me wonder if he was making alcohol from the mash and selling it on the black market. People were making it from potatoes. Why not beets?

Morning dragged its feet into afternoon. I thought maybe we could go home early, but then a neighbor brought over a scrawny horse and Frau Weber asked us to help prepare the field for plowing.

"Don't you want to rest?" I asked.

"A resting body creates a thinking mind, and I don't need to think just now. What I need to do is work—especially while we have the horse. That field will be full of rocks. I'll need all three of you to follow behind me and fill up the wagon."

But Frau Weber was in too much pain to walk. We settled her on a chair in the shade and picked the rocks on our own.

By the end of the afternoon, my back and arms were aching, and my hands were filthy and sore.

"Wash your face," Hilde said before we left. "I'm not walking with you if you look like that."

Like it mattered. I pumped cold water into a bucket and splashed my face to make her happy.

We walked back toward the center of town. As we neared the road where the car had been parked, I imagined myself as a bird, flying overhead, screeching a warning at the foolish girl with scissors in her hand. *Don't do it.*

I glanced in the direction of Oberstrasse.

"If you're going to play that stupid piano again today, I'm going home," Hilde said.

I'd been longing to play piano, but my hands hurt. What I wanted to do right now was talk to Liesel. "Yes, I'm going."

"Fine." She grabbed my basket and turned toward the clothing shop.

CHAPTER THIRTY-ONE

THREE PUNISHED SOLDIERS FOR A *FÜR ELISE*

"How much money do you think they're offering as a reward?" I sat next to Liesel on our bench and she passed me a lit cigarette.

"It won't be money," she said. "Money's useless." She waved her cigarette at me. "This is what they'll give."

Sure. Cigarettes were the new currency.

"What if someone saw me do it?" I said in a low voice. I wondered for the hundredth time who had found those scissors.

Liesel blew out an aggressive stream of smoke. "Stop worrying. If someone saw, you'd already be arrested. The only people who know are the ones you've told. You haven't told anyone besides me, have you?"

I shook my head. "No one." Unless Hilde had figured it out, but she would have said something if she had.

"Well, then." Liesel leaned forward and her whole face changed.

"Guess what?"

Those were two of my favorite words, because they always perched on the edge of something exciting. "What?"

"Dmitri says he wants to marry me."

Oh. "What will your mother say?"

Liesel laughed. "We might have to elope. Imagine. You'll be calling me Frau Pavlukhin."

Mutti would never see me get married. I swallowed hard to make the thought go down.

"And that officer?" Liesel said. "The one who likes you?"

Blue Eyes. "He doesn't," I said.

Liesel rolled her eyes. "His name is Arkady. Captain Arkady Voronov, son of the commandant, if you please. Miss Fancy-Pants."

I frowned. "Stop. He has nothing to do with me."

"Anyway, I have inside information for you. Dmitri told me *everything*."

"I don't even care." Something twitched beneath my left eye.

"Dmitri says Arkady is engaged to be married to a girl in Moscow. She's from a rich family. It's a big deal."

I took a careful puff of my cigarette. "Good for him."

"Whatever he's doing flirting with you, it's nothing but a diversion." She cocked her head at me. "I hope you're not heartbroken."

"I told you. I have no interest in him." A breeze rustled the messages on the trees, hundreds of papers whispering *Ich suche—I'm looking for* . . . I thought of the one I'd written about the Goldsteins. No one had contacted me—not that I'd expected it. But I had hoped. I'd heard of a tracing service through the Red Cross and wanted to write to them, but there was still no post.

"Did the soldiers knock on your door a few nights ago?" I asked.

"No. We heard them going to other places, but they leave us alone."

Because of Dmitri. "My employer—"

"The woman on the farm?"

I nodded. "Frau Weber. She . . ." I knew it would make me feel better if I told. Liesel wouldn't judge me. She had a generous heart. And anyway, how could I have predicted the vandalism would have such a terrible consequence? "A few nights ago, she—"

I was interrupted by the sound of men singing in Russian. Not just singing—harmonizing. Liesel and I sat completely still.

"It's stunning," she whispered.

Though I had no idea what the words meant, the song hollowed out a place in my chest and made me want to cry. We stood and followed the sound to see who was making this exquisite music, crossing the square and peering around a corner.

We shouldn't have looked.

It was him, Blue Eyes. Captain Arkady Voronov. The one who'd saved my piano. *Engaged to be married.*

The one whose car I had ruined.

He was with Wristwatch Man and two others I didn't recognize. They had their arms around each other and stood swaying in the middle of the street. Passersby stopped to listen. Curtains were opened, windows unlatched. Herr Johannsen sat cross-legged by the side of the road with his eyes closed. I had no doubt everyone was thinking the same thought as me: How could men who beat people up on the street, and break into farmhouses to rape women, be allowed to have such magnificent voices?

Blue Eyes looked right at me. Of all the people to run into . . . When he stopped singing and walked toward us, Liesel tugged on my arm to lead me away.

"You mustn't talk to him," she whispered. "You've got guilt written all over your face."

My legs felt like they were bending the wrong way as I took one jerky step and then another.

"Katarina," he called. "Stop."

"I don't have an alibi," I said softly.

"You were at work," Liesel said. "Your sister will vouch for you. And you know I'll never tell. We're partners in crime."

Blue Eyes—Captain Arkady Voronov—drew closer. Right now I had to stop thinking about the sound the tire had made when all the air hissed out of it. *Did you know every time Beethoven made a cup of coffee, he counted out exactly sixty beans?*

"I'll handle this," she whispered. "Good afternoon, Captain," she said.

He didn't even look at her. "I thought you'd be playing piano today," he said to me. Where had he learned to speak such good German?

"Katja is busy this afternoon," Liesel said.

Did you know Schubert was so short—he was so short, that— I showed him my hands, willing them not to shake. I had washed them at Frau Weber's house, but my fingernails were still filthy and my hands were covered in scrapes. "I've been picking rocks out of a field. My hands are too tired for piano."

He stood at attention in front of me. He didn't seem to be missing any medals. "Picking rocks? Do you live on a farm?"

"No," Liesel said quickly.

"I work on a farm," I said.

"Which one?" Captain Voronov asked.

I thought of Frau Weber's swollen lip, and a flush of rage passed through me. "The one your barbarian soldiers broke into a few nights ago."

Liesel gasped. "You never mentioned this."

Captain Voronov's significant eyebrows nearly met in the middle. "What are you talking about?"

I hesitated. It had been difficult enough to broach the topic with Liesel. I had no idea how to talk about what had happened to Frau Weber with a man. Especially not with this man. But maybe this could be my way of making things up to her. She would never report the incident, but I could.

Captain Voronov's eyes wouldn't leave my face. I looked away, then back at him, fixing on his neck to avoid his gaze. "Three soldiers. They tied up the boy that stays with Frau Weber. They . . . they hurt her, and broke things."

He still hadn't looked away. "I was not aware of this."

"Maybe you should keep better track of your men."

Liesel murmured a cautionary "Katja."

"Frau Weber is terrified they'll come back," I said.

"They won't." He straightened his already straight tunic and adjusted the rifle that hung from his shoulder. "I'll make sure of it. Tell me where—which farmhouse?"

I had never paid attention to the address, so I described Frau Weber's house. "There's a decorative wall next to it done in colored stones."

"The guilty parties will be punished," he said. "I believe in justice."

Sure. Those men deserved it. But what would justice look like when it came to the vandalism of the car? What would punishment look like?

He put a hand on my forearm. "Please play for me today."

Liesel stiffened. "We promised to help my mother."

"Only a few simple pieces," Captain Voronov said, "if your hands are tired."

It felt like we were making a deal: three punished soldiers for a *Für Elise* and some of Chopin's waltzes.

"Liesel," came a surly voice from around the corner. "Where are you? For crying out loud." Everyone in the square must have known Liesel's mother by her voice.

"Come on. We have to go." Liesel put out her arm for me to take, but I shook my head.

"I'm going to play."

Her face reddened. "Well. Don't come crying to me later." She gave me a look that went beyond Hilde's customary disappointment. She was concerned, naturally, but I needed to do this for Frau Weber.

CHAPTER THIRTY-TWO

DEATH RUNNING BACKWARD

Captain Voronov waited for me to say something, but all I could think of was the long scratch along the passenger door of his car. I walked in the direction of Oberstrasse and he kept pace beside me, his boots on the cobbles going *whap-whap-whap* like a flat tire.

"I know your name," he said, "but you don't know mine."

Yes, I do.

He offered me his hand and introduced himself.

Anyway, why was he bothering? He had a girl in Moscow waiting for him. Surely it was only a matter of weeks before he took his (scratched up) Mercedes and drove home with the rest of the Soviets. He made it sound like they were planning to stay. For once I understood how Ilse must have felt when we'd shown up at her door with our rucksacks and bucket and a not-so-casual hello.

"If you know any Tchaikovsky—" he began.

"I don't." But I did. Herr Goldstein had taught me the *Dance of the Sugar Plum Fairies*, which I loved.

We walked in awkward silence, and I thought of things I could (couldn't) say:

- Who changed the flat tire on your car?

- What is the reward?

- Who is the girl in Moscow? What does she look like? Will you really marry her?

You don't care about the girl. But thank goodness Hilde had insisted I wash my face.

"Nice weather we're having."

Mutti would have been proud of me. Hilde would have hit me on the head with her basket. Bad enough I didn't know how to talk to boys. That had always been her specialty. But this soldier wasn't a boy; he was a man. And not just a man—a Soviet man. And not just a Soviet man—the man whose car I'd ruined. I shouldn't have been talking to him at all. Hilde would have thought up a polite excuse and gone straight home.

We arrived on Oberstrasse. The piano stood there like a stubborn horse refusing to abandon a scorched field. I hadn't bothered protecting it with blankets; I knew they'd be gone by morning. It was lucky there hadn't been much rain, but still— "The piano won't last long outside," I said.

"You're right," Captain Voronov said. "It must be moved."

He followed me into the house that no longer had walls or a roof and stood beside the piano watching me.

"I can't play with you hovering like that." I pointed to the bathtub farther away—bathtubs were also good survivors—and said, "Sit there." Away from me, where I couldn't see him.

I warmed up with some scales, trying to coax strength back into my hands. It didn't take long. I began with a slower Chopin waltz, and then moved into my favorite, in C-sharp minor.

When I finished, the captain's cap was off and his eyes were closed. Chopin in a war zone was almost as unlikely as a chocolate heart on a red ribbon. And yet, I'd just proven it was possible. Was it better to keep believing anything was possible? Or was it safer to protect an aching heart by closing certain doors? A heart couldn't break so easily if you knew some things were unattainable—but it wouldn't be much of a heart.

I played the *Minute Waltz*, imagining the small dog chasing its tail. I played the first movement of Beethoven's *Moonlight Sonata*—a man for whom music should have been impossible. Yet he'd grown fiercer about it the deafer he'd become. He'd written his best music at the most hopeless time in his life.

And then I played my favorite of Schumann's *Lieder*, "In the Beautiful Month of May." The opening bars were in the minor key, but they didn't stay there for long. Throughout the song Schumann switched from minor to major, as though unable to decide if he was happy or sad. It made sense. He'd been in love with a woman whose father didn't want them to marry, so he'd spent an entire year writing poetry and love songs.

Behind me, I heard singing. And then it wasn't behind me anymore. Captain Arkady Voronov stood with one hand on the piano, his face opening like a cherry tree in full bloom. I'd never played Schumann with someone who could sing. His rich, deep voice turned the music into a physical place. A field—the one where Mutti had been killed. But this one wasn't muddy and stomped and barren. It was a field of expanding green—lush, fragrant—and there was Mutti standing in the middle of it. The music brought everything back to life. Even death could run backward—which, it turned out, was no more ridiculous than chocolate hearts and moonlight sonatas.

My heart burst open. If Arkady's blue eyes had been stones, I would have kept them in my pocket for luck. By the end of the piece I was in tears.

In the silence that followed, the spell broke. We were back in a bombed house, and I was the girl in trouble, and he was the enemy. I wiped my eyes with my sleeve, embarrassed that I'd cried in front of him.

"Another," Arkady said. "Please."

I couldn't speak. I couldn't even look at him. All at once I felt uncontrollably angry. Lucky stones? No, the equation was simple: Soviet officer who was engaged to a rich girl in Moscow + German girl whose mother was killed by Soviet soldiers ≠ eyes like lucky stones. Ever. There was comfort in that. If something was impossible, you never had to consider it or worry about it. It was a door that fell shut on its own, and stayed shut.

I stood so abruptly I knocked the chair backward. A crowd of listeners had formed, and I pushed myself through them, racing down Oberstrasse with glass and gravel crunching beneath my shoes.

"Katarina," he called behind me.

All I wanted was to be safe in my room, with Mutti's green sweater pressed against my face.

CHAPTER THIRTY-THREE

THE MOST
FAITHFUL CUSTOMER

I burst through the apartment door and sent it smacking against the wall.

"Here she is, with the hounds of hell barking at her feet," Ilse shouted.

Hilde poked her head out of the kitchen. "Ilse's got company."

My stomach flipped over. "Who's here?" Had Frau Weber finally shown up?

But Hilde tossed her hair back and said, "Some lady, with her daughter."

Oh God, not *them*.

Hilde was making coffee, or rather roasted chicory pretending to be coffee. Three flowered coffee sets I had never seen before were laid out on an embroidered cloth. In the middle of the table was a plate of small round cookies that Ilse must have made with ground acorns, because there was no flour. I leaned forward and inhaled the sweet spice of gingerbread. Mutti had loved to bake.

Hilde coughed, and when I looked over, she revealed the cookie she'd hidden in her apron pocket for us to share later. Then she took another look at me. "What's wrong?"

"Nothing." I chewed the inside of my cheek and wondered if my eyes were red from crying. Playing Schumann had upset me, but I'd also loved it—more specifically, I'd loved it *with him*. I wanted to tell Hilde about Arkady, but *Remember the officer who took our rabbit?* didn't fit well with *My heart is a melted mess*.

The sound of excited conversation burst from the sitting room. Ilse was talking about bolero jackets, whatever they were, and how nylon had revolutionized women's fashion.

"Katarina," she called.

I braced myself to be assigned an outlandish chore.

"Come in here and greet Frau Doktor Doktor," she said.

I trudged into the sitting room. The clothing catalogs were open on the table, and Ilse was all dressed up in one of her faded creations. Frau Doktor Doktor sat next to her on the sofa, still wearing her street shoes, her vanilla perfume permeating the room. Her horse-toothed daughter perched on the edge of the armchair as if she was afraid it might soil her dress.

"This is the younger sister." Ilse extended an arm in my direction.

"We've met," I said.

"Have we?" Frau Doktor Doktor studied me like I was some specimen of beetle that had crawled into her kitchen.

"Imagine," Ilse continued, "two girls on my doorstep and no mother in sight."

Not this again. "She's on her way," I said a little too forcefully. I could tell Frau Doktor Doktor wanted to ask a hundred questions, so I offered her my hand and tried to sound like a girl who still had a mother. "Good day, Frau Doktor Doktor, I'm pleased to see you again."

"Serve the coffee in here please, Hilde," Ilse called.

I winced, and went to help my sister so she wouldn't feel so much like a servant.

"Isn't she pretty?" Hilde whispered.

What? "Which one?"

"The girl. Her name is Carlotta." Hilde got that faraway look that meant she was imagining herself doing something ridiculous, like having lunch with Carlotta in a posh restaurant somewhere where there was actually food.

"She's well put together," I said, "but that's all about money. You can't buy pretty."

I carried out the coffee and plate of cookies and set them on the table, which I could already see would be too small to hold the coffee sets. The women would have to balance them on their laps, which wouldn't happen at Frau Doktor Doktor's house. I gave Carlotta a second look, thinking maybe I'd been wrong. No. Those teeth. Hilde must have been bewitched by her stylish dress and pink lipstick—and the perfumed life they belonged in.

"Did you hear about the reward they're offering for information about the vandalism?" Frau Doktor Doktor said.

I took my time arranging the cookies.

"They're making a big deal about nothing, in my opinion." Ilse swatted my hand. "Stop touching them."

Frau Doktor Doktor's mouth fell open. "Nothing? It's the commandant's car."

"True," Ilse said quickly. "Well, yes, vandalism and all. It's monstrous."

"What's the reward?" I asked. "Cigarettes, right?"

Ilse glared at me. This was a conversation to which I had not been invited.

"No," Frau Doktor Doktor said. "It's chocolate."

I nearly knocked over the plate of cookies. Chocolate?

"Don't you wish you knew who did it?" horse-toothed Carlotta said. "I'd make something up if I could think of someone to blame it on."

"Hush." Frau Doktor Doktor leaned forward. "Rumor has it whoever did it will be hanged in the square."

I kept my eye on the stains in the rug. Why did rumor have to have everything?

Hilde brought in the coffee sets and I poured the coffee.

"Cream and sugar?" Frau Doktor Doktor said.

I studied her long sharp nose and determined chin, the way her smile had an I-know-better edge to it. Whatever planet she lived on had a better-stocked grocery store than this one. "There is no cream," I said. "Or sugar."

"Have we run out?" Ilse said.

I caught my tongue firmly between my teeth. Sure, we'd run out. In 1944.

Carlotta took a sip of coffee, made a face, and set her cup down. I could tell she wanted to say something, but one look from her mother and her mouth stayed shut. The cookie she'd taken stayed on her plate, untouched. Good. I'd eat it later.

Hilde hovered near her, trying to seem nonchalant. "What do you do?"

Carlotta's expansive forehead rippled. "What do you mean?"

"I just finished my apprenticeship in horticulture," Hilde said. "I'm hoping to find a job in flower arrangement—once things settle down."

Ilse gave her a strange look. "When your mother arrives, you girls will move on. You won't settle here, in Fahlhoff."

Hilde's face reddened, and I felt sorry for her.

"My husband thinks Carlotta might be musical," Frau Doktor Doktor said. "We're looking to purchase a piano, but the Soviets have taken so many of them away."

"I know where one is," Hilde said in her Sunday-manners voice.

I tried to catch her eye, but her attention was fixed on Carlotta. "Katja found one. Right in the middle of the street."

If there had been anything sharp within reach, I would have stabbed her with it.

Frau Doktor Doktor put down her cup. "How unusual. A piano is not the sort of thing one generally finds."

"It's not in the middle of the street." I shifted my weight and looked down at my shoes—my street shoes, which I was still wearing. Frau Doktor Doktor wouldn't get scolded for hers, but I would, and there was no way to slip them off now without causing an uproar.

"You should come with us," Hilde said to Carlotta. "Katja can teach you."

"I'm not a good teacher," I mumbled.

"I can't have my daughter wandering the streets. It isn't safe. Where is this piano?" Frau Doktor Doktor looked at me for the answer.

I wanted to lie, but what was the point? My sister was so

desperate to impress Carlotta she would have corrected me. "Oberstrasse," I said.

"Well, that's very unlikely." Ilse's voice came out higher and louder in the presence of Frau Doktor Doktor. "Oberstrasse was bombed. Why is this the first time I'm hearing about this adventure?"

There was a good reason why I hadn't told Ilse about the piano: I didn't want her interfering.

"I'll have my husband look into it," Frau Doktor Doktor said. "A piano, out in the middle of the street—"

"It's *not* in the middle of the street," I interrupted.

She waved away my objections. "The piano must be moved indoors."

And they had the space for it.

"Anyway." Ilse rattled the catalog papers. "I'd like to offer you *young ladies* a choice of dresses." She smiled in a greasy way that meant everyone was now supposed to believe Frau Doktor Doktor was young again. "That way you can decide which style suits you best."

I waited for a knowing glance from her, a silent thank-you-Katja-for-your-good-idea, but Ilse had no interest in giving me any credit. "This one." She pointed. "Or"—she flipped to another page— "I thought this one would show off your slim figure. And for your daughter . . ."

Hilde hung back, even though I was certain she was dying to point out her favorites—but Frau Doktor Doktor barely glanced at the pictures. "No, no. Those are completely unsuitable. The pleats are all wrong, and I'm not fond of those large pockets. They're far too functional to be stylish." She whisked the catalogs off the table, oblivious to the fallen look on Ilse's face. "Let me take them home. I'll let you know which ones we like." She gave me a *you can leave the room now* look, which I was more than happy to do.

"Street shoes, Katarina," Ilse called after me, sweetening her reproach for the company.

Frau Doktor Doktor made no move to take hers off. I went to the front door and slipped off my shoes, then led the way to our bedroom, Hilde dragging her feet behind me.

She shut the door, took the cookie from her pocket, and broke it in half—in other words, I got the smaller piece.

"Isn't she something?" she said.

I wanted to throw my piece of cookie at her, but then she would eat it and I would have none. "How could you do that to me?"

"Do what?" She nibbled at her half.

"Tell about the piano. That was our secret."

"It's your type of secret, then. Half the town knows about it already."

I bristled, thinking of the car.

Hilde twisted a red scarf around her neck, posing like the very Norse princess she claimed to have been named after. "She's so elegant. Wouldn't you love to wear some color on your face?"

"Where'd you get that scarf?" I stuffed the entire piece of cookie into my mouth and sucked on it.

"Oskar brought it for me." Hilde angled the shard of mirror to admire her reflection. "What do you think?"

"Who cares?" I said. "Who's going to see it?" She couldn't prance around town dressed in a fancy scarf with all those Soviet soldiers around. "Pass me that." I put out my hand for the mirror. It had been months since I'd seen my reflection. I almost didn't recognize the skinny creature looking back at me. "My God, why didn't you tell me?"

"Tell you what?"

"Everything." But it wasn't just my face. There were my ragged fingernails, the scuffed shoes I'd just taken off, my brown dress that did show stains because I counted three and those were only the ones in the front.

Why did an ungrateful snot like Carlotta get to wear such beautiful clothes? I remembered how light and soft Ilse's striped dress had felt. Imagine, blue on my eyelids. A red scarf. Stockings—real ones. These thoughts were strangers, though. They'd wandered into the wrong head. *Hilde is over there,* I whispered to them, but they wouldn't leave.

"You've never cared about your looks before," Hilde said. "Who are you trying to impress?"

"No one." *No one.*

Hilde took a dainty bite of her cookie. "Oskar heard they might open the dance hall."

What would it be like to dance with a boy? To hold his hand, and feel his arm around your waist? To be so close you could smell his skin?

"Maybe Carlotta and I will go together," she said.

Are you that blind? Carlotta wouldn't want to be seen within ten meters of girls like us at a dance. Besides which, she was vile.

"Fine, then I'll go with Liesel," I said.

That girl is trouble.

But Hilde was wrong about her. She was my friend. We trusted each other, confided in each other.

They plan to hang the guilty person.

It was only a rumor.

Nevertheless, I wished, just a tiny bit, that I hadn't told her about the car—or about Mutti.

CHAPTER THIRTY-FOUR

THE BOLSHEVIK VIRTUE
OF HARDNESS

Within two days, the weather changed. The sky had a black eye, the wind was up, and there was that rich, earthy smell in the air that made the whole world open its mouth in anticipation. I was filling the water troughs in the secret part of the barn. A small basket of eggs sat outside the door—eggs that would not go to the Soviets. Frau Weber would keep some, and Oskar would trade the rest for things they needed—like coffee, or bullets.

Outside the barn, Oskar was setting up the plow and Hilde was helping Frau Weber repair the damage to the vegetable garden. As I worked, I thought through the opening of the third movement of the *Moonlight* Sonata, trying to recall the changes Herr Goldstein had made to the score—even though Oskar still hadn't brought me any sheet music. It felt like one of those never-never plans you make on a warm summer evening with a full stomach, but it was nice to make those plans all the same.

Beethoven changed the whole nature of music," Herr Goldstein had told me. *He made it personal.* After he went deaf, he never had the chance to adjust what he'd written to suit the musical tastes of the world. He couldn't. What we got was the music he heard in his head.

Somewhere in the background of the morning came the rumble and backfire of a vehicle on the road. During the first days of working in the secret barn, those noises had panicked me, but after a few weeks I'd grown used to them. It was the business-like hum of Occupation.

Then, nearby, the noises stopped. All of a sudden, Frau Weber's illegal chickens sounded like raucous old women disrupting a church service. I set down my bucket and hurried out of the hidden stalls, sliding the door shut behind me with a bang. I was positioning the hay bales to cover the door when I realized the basket of eggs still sat in plain view.

Footsteps crunched across gravel, then a shadow darkened the barn entrance. There was Arkady, looking first at me, then at the eggs. Pinpricks of fear erupted across my face. If he found the animals Frau Weber hadn't declared, he and his father would confiscate them and then raise the quota of food she had to produce for the soldiers. It would mean much less food for her, and for us—all because of my carelessness.

I leaned against the hay bales, trying to convince myself he couldn't see the outline of the door. But I knew he could. Surely he would say something—now.

Where did those eggs come from?

Or now.

What are you hiding behind the hay bales?

But all he did was beckon for me to follow him. I left the eggs behind and walked toward him in my clunky wooden work clogs, wondering what I looked like: Dirty? Guilty?

"What are you doing here?" I asked.

He didn't answer. He didn't have to. Outside the barn, his cement-faced commandant father stood at attention in front of Frau Weber. Beside him were three soldiers, their hands bound in front of them, heads down.

Hilde hovered near the vegetable garden, and I crossed the yard to be next to her.

The commandant didn't merely stand in the yard. He had a way of filling the space that made everything in it his. I could have fit into his pocket like a forgotten handkerchief.

Arkady nodded toward the three soldiers. "Are these the men?"

Frau Weber's lip wasn't swollen anymore, but the bruise on her cheek had turned the pale yellow of grease. Her man-sized hands were dirty from working in the garden, her face a mixture of rage and fear. Even though she wasn't holding her gun at that moment, it seemed like she was pointing it right at them. "Yes. Those are them. But—" She opened and closed her mouth, looking first at Hilde, then at me. I wanted to take the credit for having resolved this, but I was beginning to feel nervous. I never expected Arkady to bring the men here. *Your attackers are in prison* was the news I'd hoped to deliver to Frau Weber, the whole thing happening at a distance. But here were the men, standing right in front of us, one of them crying. For some reason I'd expected them to be older, but these soldiers were so young. All three sets of legs trembled.

Maybe I should have consulted Frau Weber before telling Arkady. Or maybe I should never have told him at all. Mutti had warned me countless times not to make someone else's business my own, and this was something so humiliating and private I had no right to share it.

I was working out how to explain what had happened when the commandant drew his gun. The bruised sky went gray; the green leaves turned brown.

The commandant tucked in his chin and frowned, the way men with important jobs always did—like someone had to do it, whatever it was. He handed the gun to Arkady. Arkady held it flat in his hand like a dinner plate.

His father said, "Yes. Now. You do it." I had picked up enough Russian to understand the simple words—and his sharp tone was unmistakable. If Arkady's voice was perfect for singing opera, his father's was more suited to giving orders.

No, I wanted to shout, but every part of me was frozen in horror.

Arkady said something to the bound men in Russian, and they all began talking at once, their voices swelling with emotion. Anyone could tell they were begging for their lives. They spoke first to him, then to Frau Weber. One of them fell to his knees. She stared at them and didn't say a word.

Arkady led the men around the side of the barn where we couldn't see them. Maybe he would negotiate with them in private. I gripped Hilde's arm. She stood straight and motionless, as though she was made of wood. Maybe he . . . One shot—it was so loud I jumped, and then I started shaking and couldn't stop. Somewhere in the field the horse whinnied. Oskar—where was Oskar? I hoped he hadn't witnessed it. The air smelled of gunpowder and reverberated with sound.

I tried to prepare myself for the second shot, but it didn't come. The commandant's face rippled with anger as he marched behind the barn. We could hear him shouting in Russian, Arkady's replies calm but forceful. Back and forth it went, until two shots rang out in quick succession. The commandant strode around the corner holding the gun, Arkady following with his head bowed.

"I teach my son the Bolshevik virtue of *tverdost*," the commandant said to us in German as he holstered his gun. "Tell them," he barked at Arkady. "Tell them what *tverdost* means."

Arkady shrank back. "It means hardness." He stared at the ground.

Hardness. The word hung in the silence. "I apologize for those men," the commandant said to Frau Weber. "I don't tolerate—" He hesitated. "Mischief." Shook his head. "Bad behavior. We maintain order."

Order? That was supposed to mean forced labor, not execution.

Splotches of red had broken out across Frau Weber's face. "It's what they deserved," she muttered. But her hands shook violently.

Arkady wouldn't meet my eye. Maybe he hadn't expected to shoot anyone either—even though he was the one who'd reported the men. Because of me. I hated that his father had made him do that, and I had the feeling it wasn't the first time. It seemed like his father was making a point—not just with us, but with him.

I brushed hair away from my eyes that wasn't in my eyes. More soldiers arrived, and the commandant directed them behind the barn in a whoosh of Russian that ended in *"Something-some-thing-something* Pavlukhin."

"Who?" I blurted. Pavlukhin was Dmitri's last name.

But as far as the commandant was concerned, I was a fly. He waited for the soldiers to emerge, carrying the dead men out of the yard by their arms and legs.

"Don't look," Hilde said. It was what Mutti would have said too.

But I had to. Three broken bodies appeared, bloody and limp. At the sight of them, Frau Weber let out a cry and Hilde ran to her. I'd expected her to feel gratified. These men had probably raped other women; she'd gotten rare justice—but executing them was just more violence, more death, and it solved nothing.

Was one of those men Dmitri? I racked my memory for an image of the man I'd seen by the freight train that day when Liesel and I had stolen the coal, but he'd been wearing a cap and I hadn't gotten a good look at him.

Maybe Private Pavlukhin was one of the men carrying the dead soldiers. But those men were all much older.

Maybe it's a popular name, Pavlukhin. Like Schneider, or Schmidt.

It couldn't have been Liesel's Dmitri who had raped Frau Weber. The way she spoke about him, he was a decent man, educated, a gentleman. He was going to marry her. He couldn't have—

But he might have.

No. He couldn't have. Because if he had—

The commandant glanced toward the pasture. "Those cows should go to Soviet Union."

"Those cows provide milk for the soldiers in your garrison,"

Frau Weber said, her voice lacking its usual strength. "If you send them east, your men will suffer."

The commandant frowned at his son, pointed to the barn, and spoke in Russian.

I braced myself. Would Arkady mention the basket of eggs, or direct his father to the door behind the hay bales?

But he responded in German: "I already inspected the barn. Everything is in order."

"Very well." The commandant turned to Frau Weber and, with a slight bow, said, "Good day." Then he marched off with Arkady following.

The men drove away, leaving the yard in uneasy silence—not the silence of anticipation but of aftermath. None of the noises knew where to settle.

"Girls," Frau Weber said. "How did they know about this? Did you report the attack?"

"Of course not," Hilde said. "We would never speak of something so private without your permission."

I couldn't even nod in agreement. The trick of not blaming myself for the thing I had done had lost its magic long ago. My actions had brought three men here, and then my words had killed them. And one of them might have been—

Behind the barn there would be blood on the ground. "I'll clean up." It seemed only fitting. I took my bucket to the water pump.

Oskar came around the corner wielding a hammer and looking fierce.

I thought of how sensitive he'd been about the rabbit. "Thank God you didn't see."

"I was in the field. I saw. Don't feel bad for them, Katja. You weren't there. They were merciless with her."

I didn't know how to feel. They deserved what they'd gotten. And Arkady hadn't wanted to shoot all three of them. I was quite certain he'd only shot the first one. But—his father had ordered him to kill someone, and he'd done it. The man with the beautiful voice had ended a life.

As I pumped water into the bucket, all I could hear were the gunshots. I couldn't stop hearing them, couldn't help but think of Mutti in the field that day, how casually a life could be taken. The blood on the ground was thick, and the water turned it into a murky pink pool. The rain hadn't started yet. I needed another bucket, and another, and still the ground was stained pink, and the air thundered with *how did they know about this,* plus three gunshots, plus all the gunshots it had heard in six years of war. It couldn't possibly hold all that sound.

Three families would receive the news that their sons would not be coming home. Or they would hear nothing: the silence of an empty chair at the supper table; the hollow sound of no more letters home.

And Liesel? Who would give her the news?

It wasn't Dmitri. It couldn't have been.

Frau Weber stomped over to the puddle of blood and water and spat into it.

Did you know Schumann used to tie weights to his fingers when he practiced? Herr Goldstein had told me Schumann wanted to improve as quickly as possible and thought weights were the best way. Instead, the weights damaged his fingers so badly he was never able to play again.

Later I overheard Hilde and Oskar arguing. "You had no right to tell anyone," she said.

No matter how much he denied it, she wouldn't believe him.

CHAPTER THIRTY-FIVE

LITTLE MUSHROOM

It rained all day, filling the air with the dependable smell of wet soil.

Frau Weber tackled jobs on the farm that involved hammers, nails, and force, the rain running into her eyes. The blood behind the barn soaked into the ground and disappeared (or did it?). The piano would be ruined, but it wasn't the piano that was on my mind.

As soon as the workday was done, I practically ran to the square.

"Slow down, *Scheisskopf*," Hilde called from behind me, but I didn't.

I had to find Liesel—and find out if . . . I couldn't even finish the thought. All day long I'd been telling myself there was more than one Private Pavlukhin. There had to be. But if it was him? I had no idea what I would say. Did she know her boyfriend was capable of such a thing? How would I apologize?

We entered the square, where the trees cried inky tears for missing family members. Even though the rain had let up, the cobblestones were slippery and my shoes were wet through.

Right away, we noticed there were more Soviet soldiers than usual. It seemed like even the trees and lampposts wore uniforms. These soldiers weren't lolling around singing or riding bicycles. Two of them appeared in front of us, badgering us with questions in Russian.

"Forgive us, but we don't understand," Hilde said.

That just made them ask louder. Two more soldiers joined them, and one pulled out a pistol.

My head reeled. We needed someone who could speak German. "Captain Voronov," I said to the men. "Please. He can help."

Hilde grabbed me by the arm. "Shut up, for once. Can you?"

The men spoke among themselves, and one of them rushed off.

"Who is Captain Voronov?" Hilde said. "I swear, if you've done something dumb—"

One soldier kept his gun trained on us as we stood there, and stood there. A breeze picked up, chilling me on the outside the way the waiting froze my insides.

Finally, Arkady appeared in his pressed uniform, serious eyebrows knit together until he was close enough to recognize us.

"Are you crazy?" Hilde whispered. "That's the officer who shot those men at Frau Weber's." Realization spread across her face like falling darkness. "You told him about Frau Weber. You're the one."

I had no time to confirm or deny it.

"Katarina," Arkady said. "How nice to see you again."

Heat burst onto my face, no matter how hard I fought it.

"And your sister," he added.

Hilde held out her hand and tipped her head to the side with a careful smile.

Here we go. Next would come the well-placed laughter or the witty comment, and I would evaporate. She didn't even do it on purpose. That was why I'd never learned how to speak to boys in a way that made them want to walk me home—in the rain, in a blizzard, in the dark. What was the point? I couldn't compete with a Norse princess.

Arkady took her hand, and then let it go. He didn't stare at her the way Oskar did, with that goofy look on his face like he'd just met a film star. Instead he turned back to me.

What?

"My men were simply asking where you girls were on the afternoon my father's car was vandalized."

I wanted to look Arkady in the eye, but I knew I wasn't capable of that. Instead I focused my attention on his scar, which:

- he'd gotten in a knife fight, at a beer hall;

- no, not a beer hall; his father had done it—

- because Arkady had spent his life defying him, trying against all odds to be honorable. He wasn't one of them at all.

"We heard something about that," Hilde said. "What happened?"

"A slashed tire, and a vicious scratch on the passenger door," Arkady said. "It was the work of a vindictive coward."

I shrank three sizes and wished I could climb into a hole.

Did you know Schubert was so short his friends called him Little Mushroom?

"But justice will be done," he added. "My father insists on it."

I'd seen how Arkady's father handled justice. It was all about hardness—whereas mercy required the opposite quality. But softness was not a Bolshevik virtue.

"When did it happen?" Hilde asked.

"Last week." He waited for me to say something. The Soviet soldiers who'd been questioning us stood off to the side, following the conversation as if it were a card game for which they didn't know the rules.

"We must have been at work. Or playing piano," I said. "Right, Hilde?"

"Where else would we have been?" Pretend-sweet Hilde—my most ardent fan.

"We're on our way to Oberstrasse right now," I added, "if you'd like to come listen. I could play Tchaikovsky."

Hilde gave me a look.

So did Arkady. "I thought you didn't know any Tchaikovsky." A smile played at his mouth. "You're full of surprises. But sadly, no, today my father insists I get to the bottom of this situation."

I toed the cobbles with the tip of my shoe. Things at the bottom of a situation weren't usually very nice:

- sludge

- the insects and creepy-crawlies that lived beneath rocks

- the burnt bits of stew that used to go uneaten (not anymore)

- me

"Another time, then," I said.

"Definitely." The smile won over his face and, despite every-thing—everything being, *Arkady is Soviet and this is wrong*—the ground tipped and I nearly lost my balance.

"This shouldn't take long," he added. "The weapon has been turned in. All that remains is to find out who it belongs to and then the matter will be resolved."

The scissors.

Arkady said something to his men and they saluted him.

The scissors.

I wanted to hold on to Hilde, but if I did she would know something was wrong. So I held on to myself, standing with every muscle tensed.

Hilde waited until the men had left. "What the hell was that about?"

"What?" Did she know about the car? Had she figured it out?

"Don't be such a goat." Out came the basket. This time she got me on the shoulder. I rubbed it to take the pain away.

"So this was why you wanted to know what you looked like," she said. "For what's-his-name."

"Arkady." It felt like a small explosion in my body to say his name out loud.

"You're on a Christian-name basis with him?" Hilde looked like she wanted to hit me again. "Mutti always said if you want to dine with the devil, make sure you have a long spoon."

"It's nothing," I said.

"It better be nothing. He's the enemy, or have you forgotten? Not the best choice of boyfriend."

I searched for a way to justify him, but all I could come up with was, "At least no one will ever bother Frau Weber again." I thought of Liesel and Dmitri, and then wished I hadn't. Their relationship had given her the freedom to walk down the street without being afraid. Now what?

It wasn't him.

But it was. I knew it in my gut.

Hilde looked at me like I was the dumbest person on the planet. "You weren't involved in this vandalism business, were you? With that girl—the grocer's daughter?"

I pretended there was something in my shoe so I didn't have to meet her eye. "Obviously not. What do you think?"

"You won't have anything more to do with him. It's an insult to Mutti."

"Arkady's not the one who shot her," I said.

"But he could have. You saw how he shot those men on the farm."

"Only one. His father shot the others. And they were guilty of something." Why had I said that? I was guilty of something too. What would Arkady do if he found out I was the one who'd ruined his father's car?

Hilde flicked her hair. "Anyway, you're too young for him. You're not eighteen, like me."

And when I was eighteen, I wouldn't be twenty, like her. It was a game I could never win.

CHAPTER THIRTY-SIX

THINGS THAT ARE BETTER THAN CHOCOLATE

There was no little bell on the grocery shop door. Liesel's mother was not a little-bell person.

I used to love going to the grocery store: the tins and packages that promised surprises, the different-colored sweets, the powerful scents of sliced ham or meat pie. But the grocery store in Fahlhoff smelled like the bottom of an empty box. No promises; only disappointment.

Liesel's mother stood at the counter, weighing out packets of beans, her white apron splattered with brown stains. Behind her was a long line of empty hooks where salami and sausage should have hung.

I poked my head into the back room, but Liesel's mother said, "She's in bed. Not feeling well."

I followed the smell of cabbage up the dark and narrow flight of stairs to where Liesel and her mother lived. With every step I moved more slowly. The thought of losing my friend was almost more than I could stand. I knocked softly—no answer.

The door was unlocked, so I opened it and stepped inside. The apartment consisted of one room, cramped and dim, the lacy drapes at the window discolored from grease and smoke. Things in that room came only in twos: two chairs, two hooks for coats, two tiny beds. I thought of Liesel's older brother. How long had it been since they'd given up hope of needing that third chair, or hanging up the extra coat?

When Liesel saw me, she sat up in bed. I wanted to run and comfort her. I wanted to tell her how sorry I was that Dmitri was not the man she'd thought.

But before I could say a word, she shouted, "How dare you show your face here? He's dead. He's dead, and it's your fault. I would have been safe. He would have taken care of me. I would have had nice things."

There was no denying my role in this. Liesel had been with me when I'd told Arkady. "But I didn't know it was Dmitri who . . . I didn't think there was any way he . . ."

Her face went red. "He didn't. Your asshole boyfriend needed to solve the problem for his impatient asshole father, so he grabbed three men and blamed them for it."

"He didn't choose three men at random," I said.

Liesel seized her hairbrush from the nightstand and hurled it at me. It struck me on the forehead.

Rage sparked in my chest. "Your boyfriend was guilty."

"Shut up. You don't know anything. It wasn't him."

Are those the men? Frau Weber would have admitted it if they weren't. I'd seen her face.

"You're wrong," I said.

I expected Liesel to yell at me again, but instead she grew calm. "That's fine."

She was settling down, thank God. I backed away and kept silent, allowing her the time she needed.

"I don't have to do anything," she said. "Your turn will come soon enough."

"My turn?"

Liesel smoothed the thin blanket with her hands. "Vandalism is a coward's crime. You can't confront the person you want to hurt, so you destroy their property."

I held on to the wall. "What does the car have to do with this?"

She fixed me with a smile. "I know who did it, don't I?"

"You're going to tell him?" It was a careful question, like the first step onto December ice on the pond.

"Why shouldn't I? You deserve it after what you did."

"But I didn't—"

"Spare me."

"What if—" My mind reeled at the thought of facing the commandant's justice. "What if I give you a reason not to tell?"

"My boyfriend is dead and you think you can buy me off?"

"No. Of course not." *Yes. Exactly.*

"That's offensive." She stared at the far wall. "Why should I take anything from you? They're offering a reward."

"I'll bring you something better."

Right away I regretted saying it. Something that was better than chocolate? I listed off the options in my head.

- Nothing. Nothing was better than chocolate. I could practically taste its rich sweetness, feel it melting on my tongue.

Everything felt heavy—my legs, her words, the air in that room. I cleared my throat. "I could ask you, from friend to friend, to forget what I told you about the car. We're all in this together, aren't we?"

"Maybe. If we were friends. But friends don't turn on each other the way you turned on me. Miss Celebrity."

She was jealous. The realization stunned me. "I didn't turn on you. I was trying to help Frau Weber. How was I supposed to know Dmitri was involved?"

"He wasn't!" Liesel shouted so loudly that her mother thumped the ceiling.

She pinched her thin lips tight. "Fine, then. Bring me something to change my mind. Otherwise I'll go straight to the authorities, and you can hang for all I care."

The way she spoke shocked me. Where was the generous girl who risked her own safety to help strangers? Where was the girl who'd been my friend? I left the room and trudged back down the stairs. All the moments I'd imagined sharing with Liesel—the cigarettes, the conversations at the park about boyfriends—were over, done, slammed shut. But even worse than that: she would take revenge.

Bring her something. Sure. My one pair of shoes. My brown farm dress. My pockets full of nothing.

She's bluffing. She won't really tell.

Right. And Ilse's boys would come home, and Mutti wasn't

dead, and we'd be on the train tomorrow back to our farm in Pomerania.

Let her tell, then. I'd deny it.

I'd run away. *Where?* And by myself? I wouldn't survive.

If Liesel wanted to inform on me, there was nothing I could do about it.

CHAPTER THIRTY-SEVEN

THE HARD ANSWER, AND THE HARD ANSWER

The next morning after we'd milked the cows, mucked out the stalls, and collected and washed the eggs, I sought out the person who reminded me most of Mutti: Frau Weber. She was in the kitchen churning cream in a large earthenware pot to make butter. The kitchen was warm. Mutti always said a warm kitchen was essential for making butter. In the winter she'd done the churning by the fire.

I hadn't seen butter in a long time. When I was little, I used to sneak small chunks of it from the cellar at night when Mutti thought I was asleep. I would sit in my nightgown in the dark hallway and let it melt in my mouth—until Hilde told me the men with knives got leg cramps from being under the bed for so long and sometimes crawled out to have a look around.

"All this butter is supposed to go to the Soviets," Frau Weber said as she worked the wooden plunger up and down. "But Oskar and I will make sure some of it gets into the hands of our countrymen."

I wished the vandalism of the car had at least helped someone. I plunked myself down at the kitchen table. "What do you do if someone has the power to hurt you? How do you keep them from doing it?"

"You buy a gun."

Mutti wouldn't have said that. But Frau Weber might not have said it either until a few days ago. She pulled out the plunger to see if the cream had thickened enough. It hadn't, so she kept working.

"I don't mean hurt physically," I said. "More like if someone knows something about you." I couldn't help but think of her knowing Mutti was dead.

"Ah. And you have to buy their silence."

I nodded.

"That's a dangerous game. You know there will be more than one transaction, right? The price for silence will keep going up, and eventually you won't be able to pay it anymore."

"I can't even pay it now."

"That's probably a lucky thing." Her strong hands kept moving.

I shifted on my chair. "It doesn't feel lucky." Mutti said not to be defeatist, but how could I help it?

"Well." Her gaze wandered to a corner of the room. "I don't have any easy answers for you. You want the hard answer, or the hard one?"

I fought the feeling of dread that was building inside me. "The hard one, I guess."

"Everyone has a weakness. Find theirs, and use it against them. But that could get ugly. It sounds like they already know yours."

"What's the other hard answer?"

"Do nothing. Call their bluff. In my experience, most people who talk tough won't follow through. Problem is, the odd one will. It's a risk. Both options are risky."

She stopped again and removed a large scoop of butter, which she placed in a bowl to work by hand. "I'll send you and Hilde home with some."

Do nothing. Sure, it was easy to say.

During a lull in the afternoon, I crossed the field and went back to the shady spot near the creek where I'd left my three stones. The rain had let up and the summer sun was warm.

The music of the forest reminded me of the afternoon Herr Goldstein had played *The Moldau* for me on his gramophone. It was music that sounded like a river. Or was it the other way around? The composer, Smetana, had been inspired to write it by the walks he took along the Moldau River. Herr Goldstein thought the sound of the water might have eased the terrible headaches the composer suffered from. He played the record for me while I sat on a wooden chair with my eyes closed for almost fifteen minutes, listening. When I opened them, Jacob sat across the cellar from me. The music had conjured him out of thin air— almost the way he and his family disappeared later that year.

Afterward, I tried to explain the music to Mutti, but it didn't translate well into words. Music spoke a quieter language: wind, creek, the chatter of birds. I wished she were here now so I could ask for her advice. She would be disappointed in me at first. She would make that face. But then she'd have ideas about what to do.

I would pretend to ignore them, because what did mothers know? But there would be a good idea in amongst the old-fashioned ones, there always was, and I would mull it over until I was convinced I'd thought of it myself.

Would the Soviets figure out who the scissors belonged to? Surely not. They could belong to anyone. If they'd been marked with the store's name, someone would have already shown up at Daschner's Damen und Herrenmode. I winced at the thought.

I went back to the creek and found three more stones. When I returned, Oskar stood at the fence waving some papers above his head. The world grew brighter. Even from a distance I could see it was sheet music.

"I saw you walking across the field." He climbed over the fence to join me.

The three stones had grown warm in my hand. I hadn't intended to tell anyone about Mutti's memorial, except maybe Hilde. "Is that Beethoven?"

"Yes. The third movement of the *Moonlight* Sonata—as requested." The edges were ragged. The pages had been torn out of a book.

I took them from him and flipped to the end to hear the final thunderous chords in my head—but they weren't there. "Where's the rest of it?"

"This was all I could get."

Even so, it was an unexpected feast. I couldn't wait to sit down at the piano and work on it. When I hugged Oskar, he turned into an awkward stack of arms and legs.

"What are you doing out here?" he asked.

I showed him the stones in my hand. "I'm making a memorial

for my mother." I set one stone down next to the three that were already there. "This is for the time I stole money from her to buy a chocolate heart on a red ribbon."

"That doesn't sound like a good memory," Oskar said.

"It wasn't, at first. She caught me and I had to do extra chores for a whole month. But that year at Christmas, guess what we had?"

Oskar smiled. It made him seem calmer.

"This one is for the time I spilled ink all over one of her lace doilies."

"Wasn't she angry with you?" Oskar asked.

"Yes. But then she taught me how to crochet so I could make her a new one."

I placed the third stone on the moss. "This one is for bedsheets— the worst chore ever. It took us three days to wash and dry them, and by the end of it our hands were sore and our arms were exhausted."

"I don't get the point of what you're doing," Oskar said.

"It was three days we all spent together working and singing and laughing. Mutti was always so busy, but during those three days we were busy together."

I stood back and evaluated the placement of the stones. I had no idea what the finished product was supposed to look like. Finished meant I didn't feel guilty anymore. It would never be finished.

CHAPTER THIRTY-EIGHT

THIS BENCH IS TAKEN

I saw them before they saw me. Liesel and Arkady sat on the bench by the thousand-year oak, the one where she and I used to sit. Both of them were smoking. Liesel appeared to be doing all the talking.

The black Mercedes was parked down the road. Someone had polished it so that it gleamed in the sunlight, which made the scratch in the door look even worse. The tire had been repaired.

I hid in the park and watched. *She's telling him. Right now.*

I should have known. Frau Weber had been talking about normal people, people who weren't particularly brave, who didn't follow through. But Liesel wasn't like that. She didn't talk tough. She was tough.

The thousand-year oak was full of crows. They always made me think of thieves dressed for a night of banditry. Arkady looked thoughtfully at them, taking another puff of his cigarette, which was now burned to his fingertips. He flicked it to the ground, stood, and straightened his tunic. One short nod and he walked back to the car and drove away.

I felt like a blind person who didn't quite know how to read Braille. The nod might have meant *Yes, I knew she was the one who did it; I'm going to tell my father right now. The execution will be tomorrow.* Or it meant *Thanks for the cigarette, have a nice day.*

I waited until the car had turned the corner before I approached the bench.

"Did you tell him?" I hadn't intended to blurt that out. It meant I'd been spying. It meant I was desperate—and afraid.

She tossed her half-finished cigarette away, daring me to scavenge it. "Wouldn't you like to know?"

I went to sit down beside her but she put out her arm to block me. "This bench is taken."

"Fine," I said. "If that's the way you want to be." Standing made it easier to walk away.

She pulled a peppermint stick out of her pocket and unwrapped the cellophane. On another day, before Dmitri had been executed, she would have given me half and we would have sat on the bench together in the sun to eat them. But she kept the whole thing for herself, put one end in her mouth and sucked on it.

"Arkady tells me his father is very impatient. He wants every problem solved five minutes ago."

That sounded accurate. "So?"

And why was she calling Arkady by his Christian name? *To unnerve you. That's all.* I refused to let it show.

"Bad for the men's morale if someone doesn't get punished soon for that car," she said.

Maybe she hadn't told Arkady.

She pointed at the thousand-year oak with the end of her peppermint stick. "Right there. That's where they'll hang the guilty person."

The branches stretched out like sturdy arms.

"Have you ever seen a hanging body?" she asked.

I didn't answer. I remembered the German boy who'd been forced to fight, the one with the sign around his neck. *This is what happens to cowards.* I could still hear the rope creaking as it swayed in the breeze.

"Do you know, the commandant doesn't even have the patience to catch a fish? Arkady told me he throws hand grenades into the lake and then sends soldiers out with nets to gather the dead ones."

I took out the small package of butter Frau Weber had given me and handed it to her. "I know this doesn't make up for how you're feeling, but—"

She unwrapped it and tasted some with her finger. "It's good." She put the package in her pocket.

I let out my breath.

"But chocolate's better."

Liesel bit off the end of her peppermint stick and crunched it with her teeth.

The church bells struck the hour.

I forgot all the manners Mutti had taught me and walked off without saying goodbye.

"I'll expect something more tomorrow," she called after me.

So. Frau Weber was right. This was only the beginning. I should never have given her anything.

I couldn't bear to face Ilse who, I now realized, would be

expecting butter from me because Hilde had brought some home. The only thing that would make me feel better was to work on the third movement of the *Moonlight* Sonata, so I crossed the foot-bridge and headed to Oberstrasse.

All that rain. Would the piano be ruined? I quickened my pace.

Families had moved into the bombed-out houses, creating shelters out of blankets, scraps of metal, and the walls that were still standing. A fire burned in a trash can in the middle of the road, a young boy roasting a pigeon he had skewered on a stick. The air tasted of cooked meat.

I passed ruined sitting rooms and dusty piles of rubble. I loved the moment when the piano came into view. First there'd be the stalwart chimney—yes, there it was. Then I would see the bathtub. And then the piano would be there. I looked and looked—but it wasn't.

I felt as though I'd been kicked in the chest. Frau Doktor Doktor and her heinous *musical* daughter had gotten there first.

I sat on the curb with my head in my hands, fighting tears. The sun was hot on my back. I was sweaty from working on the farm, and a pungent odor came from my underarms. I reached into my empty pocket, wishing I still had the doily Mutti had made a lifetime ago. The thing about doilies was, you had to have a proper place to put them. They weren't like washrags or hand-kerchiefs. They were beautiful but useless, precious only because they reminded you that the world still had room for loveliness.

On top of a piano: that was the proper place for a doily.

I remembered the evenings Mutti would stay up late knitting socks or scarves while Hilde and I were already in bed. We would leave our door open to catch the tiny bit of lamplight she used. I would lie there and listen to her knitting needles clicking in the next room: *knit, purl, knit, purl.* Sometimes there was the low hum of the radio.

If only Hilde were with me now—I would have smashed my basket against her head. This was her fault. She'd wanted to impress Carlotta so badly she couldn't keep her big mouth shut.

CHAPTER THIRTY-NINE

SCRATCH A GERMAN

"And where is your butter?" Ilse asked.

I slipped off my street shoes as slowly as I could, all the while thinking. Where was my butter?

- I ate it.

- I lost it. (Right. That was like losing salami, or a winter coat.)

- It melted.

"A soldier took it away from me," I said at last.

Otto emerged from the sitting room looking more rumpled than usual, his tuft of gray hair standing straight up on his head. "Didn't you hide it like I showed you?"

"I forgot."

He took off his crooked glasses and cleaned them on his shirt, as if pretending he didn't see right through my story.

Hilde gave me the polite face for strangers, the one that meant she was calling me a *Scheisskopf* in her head. Fine. I'd call her one to her face as soon as we were alone.

"I don't know," Ilse said. "I just don't know." She set down a piece of pinned fabric on the kitchen table. "What do you think of the checkers? Won't they suit Carlotta's coloring?"

For a second, I thought she was asking me. But Hilde bustled over as though the question was on fire, holding the red-and-black fabric at arm's length and saying, "Yes, yes, it's pretty."

She'll hate it. The girl who wanted to make up someone to blame for the vandalism just so she could get her hands on some chocolate—as if she didn't have enough stuff already. And now she had my piano.

I followed Otto back to the sitting room where he knelt in front of a radio, working the knob. He must have brought it up from the secret room beneath the stairs.

I sat on the lumpy armchair. "Are you looking for news?"

"Ach, who wants news these days? I want to find that Lale Andersen, 'My Lili of the Lamplight.'"

When he turned another knob, the room erupted in static. Radio fascinated me. The music that escaped from it—polkas, marches—and the voices that rose in a frenzy with speeches and special reports about this or that battle. I used to struggle to match the voices to the people they belonged to, especially Hitler's. On the radio he sounded strong and full of energy, but in newspaper photographs he looked like a pudgy old man who needed more sun. Someone who might go door-to-door selling shoe brushes. How had a man like that turned the entire world upside down?

Tchaikovsky came on. *No, no, no.* I would not think about Arkady or his blue eyes. I would definitely not think about how it felt to play Schumann with him singing beside me, and how all of that would be over the moment Liesel told him the truth. They would hang me. I thought of the blackened tongue protruding from that young soldier's teeth, and the way his clenched hands had turned a deep red. It was such a terrible vision, my mind refused to linger there.

And if I told Arkady first?

Look what had happened at Frau Weber's barn. Arkady had refused to shoot the other two soldiers, so the commandant had done the job himself.

Otto waved his arms in frustration. "Listen to this music. The Soviets are edging their way in, I'm telling you. This will be the end of Germany, *schnipp, schnipp,* off the map."

"You don't mean that," I said.

But by the way he frowned I could see he did. "They're making me apply for a permit to reopen my own shop."

"Surely they'll give you one," I said. "Why wouldn't they?"

"There's no guarantee." His pockets fell open as he leaned forward. "If they decide I'm a fascist, they'll confiscate the whole business and I'll go to a camp. Don't you see? By applying for a permit, I'm putting myself in their crosshairs."

"But you're not a fascist." I now knew it was the Nazis who had been fascists.

He shrugged. "Their theory is that our shop couldn't have been so successful during the war unless we were collaborators."

Scratch a German and we're all colored brown. People had said that on the road. It meant we were all Nazis. But that wasn't true.

Our family hadn't supported the Nazis. Papi hadn't wanted to go to war, and Mutti had never voted for *that man*, as she'd called him. We'd only greeted people with a *Heil Hitler* because you got into trouble if you didn't.

A man on the radio talked about the upcoming conference in Potsdam. Everything was still war, war, war, even though it was over.

"At least the boys will come home soon," Otto said.

I studied my fingernails. Otto hadn't been on the roads. He hadn't seen the German soldiers hanging from trees, or heard stories about the prisoner camps in the east, where the men died of typhus or starvation. I didn't dare say any of it out loud. If hope was a bird, I wouldn't be the one to break its wings.

Naturally I wanted their boys to come home—but not quite yet. Because as soon as they got here, we would be sent on our way.

"We'll have a celebration when they return," Otto continued. "A real party. Maybe you can catch us a rabbit."

"Maybe." I waited for him to ask me about the butter. I almost wanted to tell him, to practice hearing what the whole awful story sounded like. But I couldn't make myself say it, especially not to him.

"Hopefully your mother will be out of hospital before too long."

Mutti. Never mind that Frau Weber knew. I'd told Liesel about Mutti. I held the sides of the armchair, but it didn't keep the room from swimming.

CHAPTER FORTY

THE WORLD OF IMPOSSIBLE THINGS

That night I lay awake listening to my sister breathe beside me. The apartment was silent, and I was restless. I wandered into the sitting room and opened the curtains. Outside, the streets were quiet because of the curfew. Dmitri's execution must have sent the message the commandant had hoped for, because there were no more drunken soldiers staggering around the town. Only one person walked past: Herr Johannsen, probably looking for his Isabella. Didn't he understand what curfew meant? Or maybe the Soviets had decided to ignore him.

The moon was high and nearly full. If Ilse had had a grandfather clock like Frau Doktor Doktor, it would be ticking in the dark. There would be a whirring noise before the chimes rang, and then the bells would echo in the silent apartment.

What would I do about Liesel? I'd have to give her something else to keep her quiet. Where would I get anything else, though? I didn't want to give away more food. I wished there were a door that could open beneath me and drop me out of my life, into some other place and time where I could have actual girl problems: deciding which dress to wear, or which boy I wanted to impress. Like the door beneath the stairs. If only it would open onto the world of impossible things.

But it did.

I crept over to the kitchen and lit the kerosene lantern we used whenever the electricity went out. Then I unlocked the apartment door and went down the stairs, holding my breath with each footstep. I waited to make sure the rooms above me were still silent. Then, ever so slowly, I leaned against the stairwell wall.

I expected a click. There wasn't one. I tried pushing lower down—nothing. Then I reached up and tried it at Otto's shoulder level, and the door clicked open beneath my hand.

The room was small and cold, and had a musty smell, but the ceiling was high enough for me to stand. I held up the lamp, almost breathless with anticipation. Surprise did not begin to describe what I felt. The room was full of more things than I could ever have imagined: a fur coat, framed photographs, tins and jars of food. There was no grandfather clock, but a cuckoo clock cast a long, expensive shadow. There were tools, knitting needles, a tall blue vase for flowers. And there were dresses, a whole row of them in different patterns of fabric, some with bows or lace, some long-sleeved, some short.

Above me the floor creaked. Our farmhouse used to creak and settle all the time. Hilde would tell me it was the men with knives, stretching their legs. But—what if someone was awake? I turned down the lamp and stuffed a handful of silverware into my pocket.

Immediately I felt a pang. Could I really steal from Otto and Ilse? Even though Ilse was a broom nearly all the time, she and Otto had taken us in and shared what they had with us. Or some of what they had. Apparently they had a lot more than I'd realized.

But I had to steal to keep Liesel quiet. If I wanted to stay alive, I had no choice.

The apartment was silent again. I knew Liesel well enough: silverware wouldn't make her happy, so I began searching— behind the linens, behind the cans of peaches and pears. I found candlesticks, a teapot—and I found a box. I hauled it out; it seemed as likely a place as any for storing treasure. Except the box was marked *Partei*.

My spirit sank. *We all have things in life we regret,* Liesel had said. I could just put the box back, pretend I hadn't seen it.

I opened it. Mostly it was papers: as in, Otto's real papers. So much for Herr Hartmann. *World, meet the real Herr Otto Daschner.*

On top of the papers was a Nazi Party badge. I picked it up. It didn't have a gold wreath around it, so at least he hadn't been an early joiner—a true believer. I riffled through his papers but I wasn't really looking at them. The Party badge felt cold and sharp in my hand. I squeezed it until it hurt.

When a shadow of tufted hair appeared in front of me I nearly screamed.

"What are you doing down here?" Otto asked.

Nothing I could say would explain or excuse the situation, so I said nothing.

He stared at the open box. "You understand, they pressured us to join. They would have closed our shop."

I put the badge back. "When you said you couldn't have been successful unless you were collaborators, I didn't think—"

"We weren't collaborators. We just wanted to survive." He circled the tiny room, straightened a row of cans. "You don't know what it was like, Katja. You were too young. The pressure, the threats. The way everyone watched each other for the slightest signs of disloyalty. Half the country walked with its head down to avoid being noticed." Even now, the way Otto stooped beneath the low ceiling made him look like he was hiding something. "Then again . . ." He let out a long breath. "We let it happen. Even those of us who weren't hundred-percenters. We're all responsible. Any Germans who survived that war will drag it behind them forever."

The word *Partei* practically glowed in the dark. "Let what happen? What do you mean?"

"We let the Nazis take power. We let them pass and enforce laws that were worse than unjust. And now there are rumors, such terrible rumors."

The death camps.

Could the Nazis have been stopped, once they were elected? Wasn't it more like a runaway train than a series of scheduled routes?

Once I'd been in the grocery store in our town when Frau Goldstein had been told to leave. I followed her out, asked what she needed, and returned to buy it for her, but the grocer must have seen me. He always seemed like a nice man, handing out sweets to the children. But when I tried to buy apples, he knew they were for her and refused to sell them to me.

Could the Nazis have been stopped? It would have meant stopping all the little people too: the grocers and other shopkeepers who wouldn't sell to Jews; the waiters in restaurants who wouldn't wait on them; the people on the street who walked right past someone who needed help.

Otto stuffed the box back into its dark corner. I could almost believe the whole secret room existed for the sole purpose of housing that box.

"So the Soviets *are* looking for you," I said.

"Not really, not for people like me. They want the bigger fish."

"Surely there aren't any hiding in Fahlhoff. I've never seen them."

Otto rubbed his nose beneath his crooked glasses. "They don't walk around with black marks on their foreheads, you know. But they're here. You think the Soviets can put together a German civil administration without any Nazis in it? They'd like to, but it's not possible. And they're not blockheads. Sure, lock up all the Nazis—there go the doctors, there go the engineers."

"You know who they are?" I asked.

"I have my suspicions." Otto patted down his fluff of hair. "I don't have proof, but people talk."

We stood in awkward silence in the dim light of the kerosene lamp. Otto picked up a photograph of himself with his sons and held it the way one might hold a kitten. It was another hunting photograph, possibly from the same trip. He pointed to the smaller boy, who looked uneasy about the boar at his feet, even though it was dead. "That's Franz. He wasn't so keen on hunting. I brought him out there to toughen him up."

I flinched. It was the Bolshevik virtue of hardness all over again. "Did it work?"

"I hope not. I regret it now." He pointed to the other boy.

"Helmut is the older one. Now, he has a shot. Steadiest hand I've ever seen."

"The boys look like you," I said. They didn't, really, but Mutti had always liked it when someone said we took after her. "Does Ilse know I'm down here?"

"*Nee, nee*, she sleeps like a tank. But do me a favor next time. If you have questions, or if there's something you need—come to me and ask." He put out his hand for the lantern and extinguished the flame. "Now, get back to bed and don't come down here again. If Ilse catches you, I won't be able to stop her from throwing you out."

My legs were heavy as I climbed the stairs, one hand in my pocket to keep the silverware from clinking.

CHAPTER FORTY-ONE

FIVE GIANT STEPS

"Forks?" Liesel said, when I showed them to her the next day in the back room of the grocery store.

"They're real silver." I had no idea if that was true. "You can trade them on the black market. They're worth a lot."

"They're basically useless." Though she didn't give them back.

I stood there, knees locked, mind whirring.

I'd trap another rabbit. *Frau Weber will think I'm a coward if she finds out why.*

The cuckoo clock. Wouldn't Liesel stop blackmailing me for a cuckoo clock? How about the fur coat?

She crossed her arms. "You live with the dress hag. Get me a dress." *Or else* perched on the edge of the sentence like a precious jug of milk, just waiting for Liesel to push it down. "Or else I go to your fancy boyfriend and tell him the truth about the car."

One dress. That was all. *Ilse won't miss just one.* But if Liesel wore it around town; if Ilse ran into her—then what?

"Why are you still here?" Liesel said. "Go."

I pushed the curtain aside to re-enter the grocery store—and ran straight into Hilde, her basket on one arm and an expression of horror on her face. She hauled me outside toward the park.

"You did it," she said under her breath. "All this time I thought it was her, but no, it was you."

There was no point denying it. She'd heard everything.

We walked between the trees, Hilde looking around to make sure no one was near.

"The commandant's car? What's the matter with you?"

"I didn't think—" I caught my toe on a root and tripped, catching myself in time.

"No, you didn't. That's the problem—you never do. This is just like when we were younger. You haven't changed. Do you remember playing How Far May I Go?"

I nodded. *How far may I go? You may take three medium-sized steps.*

"And you always cheated when my back was turned, and I always caught you. Why? Because you'd go too far. One small step? I wouldn't have noticed. But you? You take five giant ones, and then it's too obvious."

It was just like Liesel had said. If I'd only flattened the tire, no one would have assumed foul play. But the scratch? That small decision had changed everything.

We sat down on a bench at the edge of the park. The messages on the trees seemed so hopeless. No one ever took them down, so I didn't know if any of those people had been reunited. The note I had left about the Goldsteins was still there, but the writing had faded and the paper was stiff from having been damp and then dried. The names were barely visible.

Hilde kept her basket on her lap. "You tell me what's going on with the grocery girl, and you tell me right now."

How far could I go? Nowhere. I was at the end of the road with my sister. *Wait till she finds out Liesel knows about Mutti.* "You remember what happened to Frau Weber?"

"No, *Scheisskopf,* don't change the subject. I asked about—"

A gunshot exploded. Then came shouting in Russian.

Hilde leapt up. "We need to get indoors. Now." We ran across the square to the pharmacy. Several others had already sought shelter there and were gathered by the window.

Outside, six Germans were lined up in front of Arkady and his father. When people lined up on their own, it was always for something good, like food. But when they were forced to line up, it was bound to be bad.

"They keep repeating something," I said.

"Ten," a woman said.

"Ten what?" Hilde asked.

But the question answered itself when an older woman came out of the church. Arkady's father pointed his long right arm at her, and her face changed in an instant from thoughtfulness to disbelief. She was number seven.

"What's going on?" I asked.

"It's collective punishment," the woman beside us said. "I heard the Soviets plan to take ten people every day until the guilty person comes forward."

Number eight was an old man chasing his cat.

"The guilty person?" I could have stepped outside. Right then,

I could have put an end to it. I wanted to. Arkady's father was picking people off like pigeons. But my legs wouldn't move.

"The car," the woman said. "That black Mercedes. I guess no one's claimed the chocolate reward, and they're getting fed up."

Number nine was a girl my age. Wasn't she too young? Where was her mother? Cement Face didn't seem to care.

Herr Johannsen sauntered past, but the commandant didn't even look at him. He pointed to another man instead, and that was number ten. The number sank right through my stomach and down to my feet.

Soldiers marched the row of people past the pharmacy, their arms raised in surrender. Hilde wouldn't look at me. She was not-looking at me so hard it would soon start a fire. The Soviets must not have traced the owner of the scissors. I wanted to feel relieved—but this? I couldn't feel relieved about this.

The road outside the pharmacy was empty now. "What's going to happen to those people?" Hilde asked.

"Forced labor," the woman said. "Maybe to Berlin to move rubble."

Or maybe Siberia. A hundred wings flapped inside my stomach. Ten people's lives were about to be ruined—because of me.

CHAPTER FORTY-TWO

LISTEN TO ME THIS
ONE TIME, *SCHEISSKOPF*

The town was so quiet it seemed like a plague had swept through it.

"She's blackmailing me," I said.

Hilde walked as though she was balancing a coffee set on her head. "Didn't I warn you she was trouble? I thought you two were friends. What happened?"

I told her about Dmitri. "I didn't know he was involved in the attack on Frau Weber. How could I have?"

"You gave her your share of the butter."

I nodded.

"What else have you given her?"

"Silverware," I said.

"Where the hell did you get silverware?"

I let out a long breath. "From the secret room under the stairs."

"Number one, stop it. I asked a real question. And number two, don't be stupid."

"That's the real answer. Ilse and Otto have a secret room in the stairwell. It's full of stuff. If you don't believe me, I'll show you."

Hilde stopped walking. "You stole from Ilse? Are you crazy? If she finds out, she'll send us away for sure." Out came the basket with a crash, and this time it had potatoes in it. "Why did you wait so long to tell me?"

I rubbed the side of my head. "Why do you think?"

We walked for a minute in silence. "What else is in that room?" Hilde asked.

I thought of Otto's papers and the Nazi Party badge. "A cuckoo clock. A bunch of clothes."

Hilde pulled me into a passageway between two buildings that was so narrow there was barely enough room for us to face each other. It smelled like a hundred people had peed in there. "Listen to me. You need to give her something that will keep her mouth shut—for good. And not a dress. Ilse will notice."

"That's the only thing she wants," I said glumly. "Nothing else will do."

Hilde dug into the bottom of her basket. When her hand came out, Mutti's locket was in it, so shiny it looked like a handful of fire. "This will stop her."

I wanted to put it on. I wanted to pretend Mutti had given it to me with a message, a secret about how to live. "Liesel will not have Mutti's necklace. And anyway"—I cocked my head toward the sound of boots—"shutting her up won't solve anything. If no one comes forward, they'll keep sending people away."

Someone needed to speak out. That someone was me. But if I

did, they would hang me.

I waved away a swarm of flies. They'd multiplied with the heat, and the dead bodies, and the people who'd been walking for days, weeks, months. Sometimes I wondered if the people would ever stop. Maybe they'd walk right to the ocean and into the water and keep on walking until they fell over the edge of the horizon. I wouldn't have minded joining them.

"I wish we could run away," I said to Hilde. "Ilse wouldn't care. She doesn't want us here anyway." Maybe Ilse wouldn't, but what about Otto? What about Arkady?

"And go where?"

"Why can't we just go home?"

All along I'd been expecting it, the moment when someone would come up to us and say, *Okay, the game is over, you can go back now*, and it would all still be there: our bedroom, our clothes. Even the chickens that the Soviet soldiers had set free would have found their way home by now. The jars in our cellar would be lined up and labeled in Mutti's spindly handwriting. Papi would be saddling the old mare for my first riding lesson. The spotted kitten would have grown so big. And Mutti would be there, sitting by the fire and crocheting a new doily, apples wrapped in dough baking in the oven. There was her hair in its careful bun; there was the slight curve to her back.

"You know what we'd come home to," Hilde said.

I did. The homes we'd hidden in on our way down here had been stripped bare. Every spoon and sock, every tool and can of food; even the doorknobs had been taken off some of the doors. Would I really want to see my home like that—like a corpse left beside the road?

Home had become a fairy tale, and no trail of breadcrumbs would ever lead us back to what we'd left behind. Anyway, running wouldn't solve the problem: every day ten more people would be sent away for something I had done.

"I didn't mean for this to happen," I said. But wasn't that always the problem? Who ever meant it? Who ever wanted the true consequences of their thoughtless mistakes?

When we reached Ilse's road, I handed Hilde my basket.

"What are you doing?" she said.

"I'm going to find Arkady and tell him the truth." I set off at a fast pace back toward the square, hoping fear wouldn't catch up to my feet and stop them. Already the rest of me was shaking.

"Wait, what?" Hilde called.

"You're not talking me out of this," I said.

Hilde caught me and took me by both shoulders. "Yes, I am. Maybe he likes you"—she said this in the tone of *I don't really know why*—"but you saw how he was with his father."

The father who was too impatient to fish, so he blew up the pond instead. The father who'd sentenced ten people to hard labor today, and tomorrow ten more. How many more orders could Arkady refuse to obey? Even if he wanted to save me, he couldn't.

"So what should I do?" I said.

"You'll listen to me this one time, *Scheisskopf,* and keep your mouth shut the way Mutti always told us to."

"That won't stop the Soviets from sending people away."

"Ten strangers are not your problem."

But they were. "I can't live with that."

"I won't let you die for it. You're my sister. You're the only family I have left."

"What, then? They won't stop until they've arrested someone."

Hilde looked off into the distance. "Then you'll give them someone. Remember what Carlotta said about making something up to get the chocolate?"

"You mean blame someone else?" A feeling of horror shot straight through me. And besides, it wouldn't work. "Liesel knows the truth. She'll just keep blackmailing me, or else she'll tell Arkady."

Hilde gave me the frown of disappointment perfected by older sisters everywhere. "I didn't say blame someone random, did I?"

She wants me to blame Liesel. My mouth hung open, but no words fell out.

"It's the easiest way to solve the problem," Hilde said.

Yes, it was. It would solve everything. I didn't want to admit it, but a small part of me brightened with relief. This was the answer. But, "I can't."

"You can, and you will. You made this mess, and you're going to clean it up." She took her hairbrush out of her basket.

"Do you carry that thing everywhere?" I asked.

"Stand still. You can't talk to him looking like a ruffled goose."

I braced myself. Hilde was an aggressive hair-brusher, and today was even worse than usual.

"If you pull it all out, it won't look nice."

"Quiet. I know what I'm doing." She took the yellow ribbon out of her pocket and wove it into a braid, tugging and tsking and waving away the flies. At the water pump, she wet her sleeve and rubbed at my face, which I was sure was not as dirty as she made it out to be.

"I don't see why all this fussing is necessary," I said.

"Insurance. If he's in love with you, Liesel can say anything she wants and he won't listen." She stood back and appraised me. "There. Nectar for the bee." The way she said it made me realize: she was complimenting me.

The number of times my sister had admired the way I looked? Zero. A big fat zero. I was always the one with crooked braids and drooping knee socks.

I wanted to run back to Ilse and Otto's apartment and hide under my blankets, but Hilde tugged me by the arm and said, "Let's go."

CHAPTER FORTY-THREE

BEING HILDE

On the backstreets where no one could see, Hilde made me practice moving my hips when I walked, like the sort of Berlin woman Mutti scorned: one who wore see-through stockings, and lipstick, and showed too much leg.

I smiled until my cheeks hurt. Being Hilde was harder than it looked.

"I didn't need to do these things before," I said. It all seemed so silly. I'd never been one of those girls.

"You didn't know you needed to do them. Show me the face you'll make when you see him."

I tilted my head and made my eyes bigger.

"Tone it down, or you'll look like an idiot. Tell me the first thing you're going to say."

"I'll talk about the weather. Mutti always said—"

Out came the *God-you're-dumb* sigh. "You will talk about him, about something that interests him."

Hilde knew how to talk to men. But me? "I can't. I'm no good at this." *You mustn't be defeatist,* Mutti was practically shouting in my ear. But I'd never felt more beaten in my life.

"Don't talk about Mutti being dead," she said, "or anything depressing, like hunger or the flies."

"Can I tell him about Joseph Haydn? When he was a boy, he cut off the pigtails of—"

"Don't even." She brushed the dirt off my dress. "Now. How will you tell him about Liesel?"

The day felt sticky. I wanted to peel it off and throw it away. "I don't know. Am I supposed to work out everything in advance?"

"Yes. How do you think you get your way?"

Good question. I never did. It explained a lot.

Hilde stepped closer to me. "You'll say you were there. You warned her not to do it. She refused to listen."

I eyed the road home. "This is a terrible idea."

"It's the only idea," she said.

Somewhere in the distance a truck backfired. "Ilse will want to know why I'm late."

"I'll tell her you went to the grocery store because there was a rumor about sugar."

The grocery store. My skin broke out in prickles. How could I do this to Liesel? "Don't tell her sugar. It will only get her hopes up. Tell her lentils."

Without saying anything, we both slowed down. By the time we reached the square, some of my hair had slipped out of the braid, and I chewed the ends of it.

"Stop that." Hilde pushed the hair away from my face. "Go into the *Kommandatura* and ask for him. If he isn't there, someone will know where he is. Do it now, before you lose your nerve."

The Soviet hammer and sickle fluttered in the breeze. The hours of curfew were posted on a bulletin board near the door, as well as an order stating that all Germans must turn in weapons, ammunitions, explosives, and radio transmitters.

The wings were back, fluttering in my stomach. "Come with me. Please."

"I can't. You have to do this yourself or it will look like we've concocted the story together. Come straight home afterward. I'll be waiting."

She turned the corner and I stared at the spot where she had disappeared, wishing I could run after her, and keep on running, right out of my life.

CHAPTER FORTY-FOUR

ROBERT SCHUMANN AND HIS BELOVED CLARA

Arkady was not at the *Kommandatura*. One of the soldiers suggested he might be at the barracks, where the schoolhouse had once been.

I wished the walk would last forever, but it only took ten minutes to get there. The building was an anthill of busyness. There were Soviet soldiers everywhere, and when they saw me they hooted and whistled until someone shouted at them to stop.

A guard stood at the entrance. I told him Arkady's name and he sent someone into the building to fetch him, and then I stood there with him and his rifle. My arms felt long and awkward, my feet hot in their shoes.

The sound of gunshots made me jump. The noise rippled in my head, drawing other sounds to it from days, weeks, months ago. At the far end of the schoolyard I saw what looked like naked bodies. But . . . there was something wrong with them. They looked frozen. *No.* They were mannequins. A man and a woman. The Soviets were using them for target practice.

Arkady appeared in his uniform, those bright blue eyes fixed on me. All the advice Hilde had given me disappeared.

"My goodness," he said. "You look very pretty."

"Thank you." I smoothed down my dress. *You're staying on.*

"Every man here wishes he was me right now."

"I'm sure that's not true."

"You don't see their faces. But—what's the special occasion? Why have you come to see me?"

Special occasion? *Did you know when Joseph Haydn was a boy—* I touched my braid to make sure it was still attached to my head. "Do those men really have to shoot at the mannequins?"

Arkady didn't understand the word, so I pointed. "They belong to my uncle."

He shielded his eyes with one hand and stared out into the yard. "Wait here."

He yelled at the men to stop firing and marched over, rescuing the mannequins one under each arm like stiff dead bodies. It was hard to imagine them anymore in the display window wearing Ilse's beautiful creations. The male mannequin was missing a hand, and half his head had been blown off. The female had several holes in her chest.

Arkady returned, balancing the mannequins on their feet. It felt like we were at a party and he'd brought friends to introduce to me. I wished they weren't naked.

"Is this why you've come?" he asked.

"Actually, no." I couldn't tell him right here. But then I remembered something I could say. "The piano is gone."

"Ah." He smiled. "That was going to be a surprise, but since you're here . . ."

He set the mannequins down next to the guard, speaking to him in Russian. "Don't worry," he said to me. "They'll be well taken care of."

He put out his arm and we walked into the schoolhouse together. He was much taller than I was, and walked too fast; but when he realized it, he slowed his pace to match mine.

We reached the end of the hallway and entered a classroom— or what used to be a classroom. Some of the children's artwork and compositions were still posted on the walls. There were also maps covered in circles and arrows, and a framed photograph of Stalin. The teacher's desk was strewn with papers, and on top of them sat Otto's scissors. *Don't look at them.* But I couldn't help myself. I wanted to pocket them so badly my hand itched.

School desks were positioned at random in the room, the kind I remembered from my town, where two students sat together. In the far corner, two small beds were impeccably made. Next to one, on the windowsill, were books, the titles on their spines in both German and Russian. Against the side wall—there was my piano.

I forgot about the scissors. I forgot about Liesel. I nearly forgot to breathe.

"It needs repair," Arkady said.

I was already walking toward it and pulling out the chair.

Arkady stood by the piano while I played scales and arpeggios. I felt self-conscious having him so close, but it wasn't long before the music took over.

I knew about eight of Schumann's *Lieder.* Arkady's voice

was deep and smooth. I thought of Robert Schumann, waiting in a café for hours just to catch a glimpse of his beloved Clara after a concert she'd given. I thought of his year of song, a long outpouring of love and despair and uncertainty over his future with the woman he loved. The way Arkady sang, he seemed to understand all of this.

Arkady was . . . The only word I could think of was an old-fashioned one. He was dashing. That scar on his face. The way he took charge of things. His voice—so deep you could sink a ship in it. *Dashing* was the right word.

Here was another word: *Soviet.*

And another: *enemy.*

For every heartbeat, my brain supplied a reason why my heart should not beat for him.

There were a few songs he didn't know, so I wrote out the words and taught him the tune—which I did by playing it on the piano, not by singing, because I didn't want him to laugh at me the way Hilde used to.

We were in the middle of the last piece, Arkady bent over my shoulder, when a deep voice said something in Russian. It was the commandant. His dark hair was oiled back, his nose just the right length for looking down at me.

Arkady straightened to attention, his face reddening.

The commandant turned to me. "Stay away from my son. You are a distraction, and I don't want him to catch disease. You Germans are all dirty, disorganized. Lazy."

I shrank back. Apparently his vocabulary was improving.

He left without waiting for a response. The sound of his heels clipping along the hallway floor seemed to go on forever.

"Forgive him," Arkady said. "He doesn't actually think that."

On the contrary; I was quite sure he thought exactly that.

"I have to go," Arkady said.

I turned in the chair to face him. "Why? Because your father told you to?" I couldn't let him leave before telling him about Liesel.

Arkady took a step back. "My father is an important man in the Soviet military administration. It sends the wrong message if I don't obey him."

"Like when he tells you to shoot people?"

That was unfair. I had no idea if I would have been bold enough to disobey my father. Papi had been gone from my life for several years now. I'd been much younger when I had to listen to him. It had never bothered me when he told us to take off our dirty clogs at the door, even though he was allowed to forget about his and we were not allowed to point it out. He had never ordered me to do anything terrible.

"I don't expect you to understand," Arkady said, "but my father has hopes for me. He wants me to have a real military career."

What must it have been like to grow up with a man like the commandant? Did Arkady have to salute him at home? I pictured polished belt buckles and tightly made beds, silent suppers and bedtime stories that involved guns.

"And that's what you've always dreamed of doing?" I asked him. "Being in the military?"

He brushed dirt from a high F-sharp. "What we dream of doing, and what we know we're going to do, can be very different things."

I couldn't lift my eyes from the pedals. Compared to him, I'd spent most of my life in a gingerbread village. My parents had never challenged my dream of being a concert pianist, even though it was so unlikely: a farm girl playing in Berlin concert halls. The only thing that had come between dreaming and doing for me was a war.

He stepped away from the piano. "I'm wanted on army business."

When I looked out the window, I was surprised to see the light had changed. How long had I been here? And I still hadn't done what I'd come to do.

"Do you remember Liesel?" I asked him. "The girl who works in the grocery store?" Mutti's disappointed face flashed in front of me. *How can you do this?*

"Sure," Arkady said. "She's your friend."

Is she?

I took a deep breath. "Please don't send anyone else away."

Arkady straightened his tunic. "My father insists on justice being done."

"But the tire has been fixed. And you can repaint the car, surely."

"That misses the point. The guilty party has been asked to come forward. They have not done so. We must do what we've said we would do, or we lose respect."

I held the sides of the chair. "What if I knew who did it?"

He searched my face. "Do you?"

"I'm just saying, what if I did?"

"Katarina, this is not a game. If you know, you must speak up."

Tell him the truth. It was me. *Just say it.*

I stood up. "I don't know." I couldn't blame Liesel, but nor would my own confession creep out of its hole. Where did courage hide, anyway? In a pocket? Under the bed with the men with knives? I glanced at the scissors on the desk. If only I could take them and throw them into the river.

The way he tilted his head, he knew I wasn't telling the truth. But he offered his arm and said, "Come, I'll walk you out."

The hall felt like an escape route. "I'm so glad the piano is here," I said as we walked, "instead of at that broom's house."

"Who?" Arkady's eyebrows rose.

Why had I brought up Frau Doktor Doktor? "No one. An awful woman, the wife of a very important man in town." I made *very important* stick out like a nose. I didn't mind talking about him; it was a relief to be off the subject of that car. "Herr Doktor Doktor. A doctor of spiders and something else, I don't know what. I'm surprised you haven't heard of him. He and his wife are the only people in this town who seem untouched by the war."

"Is that so?"

Our footsteps echoed down the empty hall.

"That was very nice, this afternoon," Arkady said. "When will you come again?"

"But . . . your father—I mean, is it all right?"

"I'll speak to him. I'll make sure there won't be any trouble."

"Tomorrow, then." Tomorrow I would tell him.

One more day means ten more people. But not if I told him early. This was definitely a problem for Tomorrow-Katja to handle. Today-Katja was a little too frightened, and also a little too enthralled with the way Arkady's arm felt on mine. There was a scent about him I hadn't noticed before: leather, and maybe diesel fuel, and tobacco. We'd never been indoors together. I could have breathed it in for hours.

"Under other circumstances I would walk you home, but my father needs me. Would you like one of my men to see you back? They can carry the stiff people for you. They're not heavy, but they're a bit awkward."

The stiff people. "No, I'll manage."

He touched my face. Warmth rushed through me. I wanted to trace his scar with my fingertips, or lose my way in his blue eyes. His face was so close to mine, I wondered if he would kiss me.

"I'll see you tomorrow, then." He sounded out of breath.

When I saw the Mercedes idling near the gate, with his father at the wheel, I felt a pang of unease. Arkady got into the car, and they drove away.

I tucked a mannequin under each arm and set off for home. I could practically feel curtains opening and people staring as I walked down the road carrying two bodies.

Arkady's eyes. The way he looked at me while he sang Schumann's love songs—as if he was singing them to me. His voice. *The car.*

The male mannequin slipped, and I had to stop and readjust my grip.

I hadn't told him about Liesel. I couldn't.

Tomorrow I would. *Would I?*

As soon as I did, I wouldn't be the same person. Nothing would feel the same, not even playing Schumann together or walking arm in arm with him. It would all be based on a lie.

I rounded a corner and almost ran straight into Herr Johannsen.

His eyes widened. "Who are those people you're carrying?" He grabbed the woman by the shoulders, as if checking to make sure it wasn't Isabella. But as soon as he touched the hard body he let it go, an expression of horror on his face. "What's the matter with her?"

"They're mannequins," I explained. "From the clothing shop. It's okay."

"But what are you going to do?" He looked right into my face. "What are you going to do?"

The question unnerved me. "I don't know."

When I reached the shop, I clattered up the stairs with the mannequins. First their heads banged against the walls, then their feet.

The door opened and Ilse cried, "What on earth?"

The male mannequin crashed into the doorframe and fell to the floor. I pushed him forward with my foot and stumbled in after him with the female under my arm.

"Uncle Otto, look what I found."

"Such foolishness," Ilse said. "They're no good anymore. Look at the man's head."

But Otto's grand mustache rose into a smile. He took off his glasses and rubbed his eyes. Then he stood the man on his feet. "Good afternoon, Herr Mucky-Muck. You're not looking so good today. Have you been ill?"

"He's got a bit of a headache," I said.

Otto burst out laughing. "Nothing that a hat won't fix."

"So," Ilse said. "Were there any beans at the grocery store?"

Hilde looked at me with a thousand questions in her eyes, but all I said was, "No," and headed to our room.

CHAPTER FORTY-FIVE

THE STIFF PEOPLE

I lay on my stomach on our pile of blankets. Hilde came into the bedroom and shut the door, towering over me like the giant shadow of a church spire. "What happened? You were gone forever. Did you do it the way we practiced? Did you do the thing with your eyes?"

I didn't answer.

"You told him. Didn't you?"

I let out a long breath. "I tried."

"You tried?" Her voice was wound around her baby finger. "Either you told him or you didn't."

"I couldn't."

"Take the pillow out of your mouth. What do you mean, you couldn't?"

I turned my head so I didn't have to look at my sister. "It's wrong. She didn't do it."

"Well."

I felt certain Hilde was pursing her lips.

"You can't tell him it was you. So, do you mind telling me what your plan is?"

I didn't say anything.

"Liesel has it coming," she said. "I feel sorry for her, I do. But life isn't a pony ranch. Someone has to take the blame, and she's always doing things she shouldn't. So, it's caught up to her. It was only a matter of time." Hilde plunked herself down beside me. "What's the matter with you, anyway? You seem— Wait. Did you guys . . . did he . . . did you have sex with him?"

"No." My face flushed at the thought.

I told her about the piano, and about playing Schumann, which now felt disloyal to Mutti, who had loved that music so much. I'd played *her* music with a Soviet officer. And yet—my whole body tingled at the memory.

Hilde poked me, and I turned over. "What?"

"Did you hear a single word I just said?" She crossed her arms and stuck out her chin. "I know that look. You're in love with him, aren't you? I can't believe you'd do that."

"I'm not," I said. "I haven't done anything."

"Don't you remember who killed Mutti?" There was another bucket of ice-cold water on the afternoon. "You have to go back. Tomorrow. You have to fix this."

It seemed Tomorrow-Katja would have a busy day.

Hilde stood up. "Anyway, supper is almost ready."

"I'm not hungry." That was a sentence I hadn't uttered in months.

"You should eat. Who knows what there'll be tomorrow?"

It was an unspoken rule: you ate when there was food.

But I couldn't eat. I couldn't get up. The thought of innocent people sentenced to hard labor because of what I'd done made me feel sick. I stayed in my room and imagined the sky darkening, and then the walls, and then my heart. *Mein Herz ist schwer,* Schumann had written. My heart is heavy.

* * * *

Later that evening, while Hilde helped Ilse with Carlotta's ugly dress, Otto popped his head into the room. "The mannequins are waiting. Which one would you like to dress? The man or the woman?"

I sat up. "Really?"

"You rescued them. You get to choose."

"The woman," I said. "With something pretty."

"I know just the thing."

I waited in the sitting room while Otto went downstairs. The mannequins were propped against the wall. When he returned, he had a suit over one arm for the man. He handed me a dress that was robin's-egg blue, with tiny yellow flowers on it and a tie at the waist, and a neckline so low it made me blush.

"Aunt Ilse made this?" It was so soft and light that if a person put it on, there was every possibility they would disappear.

I held it to my nose, imagining the flowers on the dress would smell like real ones. But it had been in the stuffy room beneath the stairs for too long. It smelled like it was afraid of sunlight.

Otto smiled. "Would you like to try it on?"

I rushed into our tiny bedroom before Ilse could come out of the kitchen and forbid it. It had been such a long time since I'd seen anything lovely. I took off my brown farm dress and slipped on the cool, soft fabric. Its heart beat against me—pretty, pretty, pretty.

When I came out, Otto said, "My. It suits you."

I tugged on the neckline. "Mutti would crap her knickers if she saw me in this."

This dress had only one job: to impress a man. It was exactly the sort of thing she would never have let me wear.

"Turn around." He tied the strap into a bow behind me.

I twirled. The way the skirt flared made me feel like a film star. Then I spied my ugly brown shoes sitting by the door.

"My shoes would ruin it." They were so scuffed and dirty, they looked like they'd lost a fight with the road.

"Ah, you see," Otto said, "that's why we don't bother with shoes on the mannequins. Shoes are the shoemaker's headache, not ours."

I'd only ever had one nice dress, the recital dress Mutti had bought for me. And it had been fancy, not sexy. This was quite different. I changed back into my regular clothes, and then slipped the flowered dress over the female mannequin's head. It didn't quite cover her broken heart.

Otto chatted as he dressed the male mannequin. When the two were ready, he called to Ilse. "Come see, darling. Come see our fashionable friends."

Ilse put a hand to her mouth. On her face was an expression that mirrored my heart: the wish for things to go back to the way they once were.

Otto took her in his arms. "The shop will be open again soon," he said. "I'm applying for the permit. These stylish people will be back downstairs in no time."

He glanced at the boys' bedroom door, which was ajar. "You know, the bedroom sits there empty. It's such a waste. The boys aren't home yet, and we have two girls."

Ilse stiffened. "We don't *have* two girls."

"Give me this chance. Please."

A chance to do something good. The hair on the back of my neck stood up. What had Otto done in the past that needed to be balanced out? My mind went to Jacob and his family, to the piano lessons I no longer had, the kisses I'd never experienced, the sweet poppy seed cookies I no longer ate.

We let it happen, Otto had said. I had never been fond of the marching and boots and guns, but during those early years of the war when Germany had stretched its muscles, I'd felt taller. Neighbors used to compliment my blond hair like it was something I'd done to be proud of. Aryan blood, they'd said.

I hadn't known about death camps. But I'd known about the Goldsteins' cat. I'd known Herr Goldstein wasn't allowed to teach me piano for the sole reason that he was Jewish. I'd known those things, and I had done nothing about them.

Ilse stomped her that-way foot. "I'm at my limit, do you understand?"

But Otto was the man of the house. His feet were bigger. Eventually Ilse sank into his arms as Otto told us to gather our things.

I stepped into the room that reminded me so much of a forest and laid Mutti's green sweater across one of the boys' pillows. A bed. I sat on it. My bed—at least for now. The lump in my throat caught me by surprise and made me realize how much I'd been longing to feel more than temporary.

When it was time for bed I lay down, certain I would fall asleep immediately. But my thoughts turned over and over like tilled soil. *Give me a chance to do something good.* I couldn't get my mind off the Goldsteins. Mutti had had a plan for surviving the war: *don't speak out, don't touch anything, make yourself invisible.* Too bad I hadn't listened to any of her advice. But did it even work? Hadn't the Goldsteins tried that?

And was it good advice? The Goldsteins had suffered precisely because no one had spoken out. We'd all been paralyzed by the fear of those men in their long leather coats and big black cars.

"Hilde?" I said into the darkness.

"God, what now?"

"Do you think all of us Germans were responsible for what happened during the war?"

"Not us. What did we do? Nothing."

I thought of Jacob's eyes, worn out from studying, and the way Herr Goldstein's glasses shone in the lamplight. I thought of the sweet-smelling lavender that used to grow in Frau Goldstein's garden, and the cat with black and white patches on the roof of its mouth, and the metronome on top of the piano that kept my fingers from running wild.

"That's the point," I said. "We did nothing."

Liesel's neighbors had hidden three Jews. Someone had hidden Herr Johannsen, and he was still alive.

Hilde sat up. "What are you saying? What should we have done?"

"I'm not sure. But if we'd known something bad was coming, couldn't we at least have warned them?"

"Warned who? What are you talking about? Are you accusing me of something?" Her voice rose in the dark room.

"Quiet. You'll wake Ilse and Otto." Was I accusing her? And if so, of what?

I curled into a ball and lay there listening to my sister toss and turn, and then breathe and breathe. And the church clock chimed twelve, and tomorrow became today. I had to tell Arkady the truth. I could do something good, and stop the Soviets from punishing innocent people for what I had done.

CHAPTER FORTY-SIX

MAKE YOURSELF BRAVE

"You're quiet this morning," Frau Weber said to me. She was washing eggs in the kitchen while I churned the butter.

I didn't bother answering.

Frau Weber's pots hung in a neat row above the stove, and empty canning jars lined the counter (the full ones were still buried in the garden). There was order in her kitchen, as there had been in Mutti's. It made me feel like a mess.

"Look at this." She held up what Mutti used to call a fairy egg. It was smaller than the others, and greenish-white instead of brown. It probably didn't even have a yolk. "In our family we always said it was good luck when a hen laid an egg like this. Gather some sticks and we'll draw to see who gets it for lunch."

Oskar got the fairy egg.

I felt so ill I finally asked Frau Weber if I could go home.

Hilde watched as I left the barn. I went into the house to change my shoes, but as soon as I came out again she was waiting for me.

"You'll tell him," she said quietly. "Today. Right now."

"Yes." I would tell him—but not about Liesel.

I walked into town thinking of ways to soften my confession.

Maybe I could tell him the vandalism was an accident.

How can you slash a person's tire by accident?

I hadn't meant to do it. I was upset about Mutti. I wasn't thinking.

I remembered the day we had left our farmhouse for the last time. "Make yourself brave," Mutti had urged me, her own voice cracking. I could almost hear her saying it now.

Arkady was not at the *Kommandatura*. Nor was he at the barracks. No one seemed to know where he was.

Bravery leaked out of me like the air from the slashed tire. I walked back to the clothing shop. I would have to try again later— no matter how hard it was. No matter if I didn't want to, or didn't think I could. I trudged up the stairs and let myself in.

Ilse wasn't home. Otto sat at the kitchen table, an accounting book open in front of him and a pencil in his hand. "What are you doing home so early?" he asked.

"Not feeling well," I mumbled, and went to lie on my bed. Funny, I already thought of it as mine. As soon as even one boy showed up, we'd be back in the storeroom or out on the street.

Conversations passed beneath me along Rosenstrasse. Otto banged around in the kitchen. The day continued without me, while I lay in the dark turning Herr Johannsen's question over and over in my head. *What are you going to do?*

And then there was a knock on the door downstairs—the kind of knock that stopped the heart.

"Open!" someone shouted.

I came out of the bedroom and peered into the kitchen. Otto was pale. *Fascist, fascist.* Was that what this was about?

"They'll break the door in if you don't answer it," I said.

"I know." Otto pulled on his cardigan, even though it was too warm to wear it.

"Do you want me to come with you?" I asked.

He shook his head and went down the stairs, while I watched from the door.

"Are you the owner of these scissors?" a man asked in accented German.

Every muscle in my body went slack. *Say* no. *You've never seen them. You have no idea who they—*

"Why, yes, I am. Where ever did you find them?"

"You'll have to come with us," said the stranger.

My stomach lurched. I ran down the stairs crying, "No! He didn't do anything. It was me."

Otto was already out the door by the time I reached the bottom of the stairs. His eyes widened in surprise. "Katja. What are you talking about?"

I was startled to see not one man on the sidewalk with Otto but three: the man who had spoken, plus Arkady, plus his father.

Arkady's face fell when he saw me. He stepped into the entryway and held me by both arms. "You need to stay inside. This is not your business."

I shook my head. "It was me. Don't take my uncle. I'm the one who did it."

"Shh." He led me toward the staircase. "You can't pretend to have done something just to spare him."

"You don't understand." I peered around him, trying to see Otto outside. "I scratched the car. I slashed the tire."

"Let us do our job," Arkady said. "Stay home. I'll talk to you about this tomorrow."

I felt like I would burst. Why wouldn't he listen to me? "Please, Arkady, I—"

He marched back to where his father stood with Otto. I tried to run out after them but the third soldier blocked my way. All I could see from where I stood was Otto's tuft of hair blowing in the breeze as the commandant led him away. He hadn't had the chance to put on his hat.

CHAPTER FORTY-SEVEN

A FAMILIAR ROAD

I spent the afternoon sitting in the park with all the wilted, faded messages to people who were lost. *He was a member of the Nazi Party.* But that could mean a hundred different things. I'd gone to League meetings—but not because I'd wanted to. *It was the Nazis who took the Goldsteins.* Yes, the Nazis. Not Otto. That was like saying Arkady had shot Mutti.

Anyway, what did I even mean? They'd arrested Otto for the scissors. Was I trying to tell myself he deserved it?

Arkady had said we would talk tomorrow. Good. Tomorrow I would tell him the truth. *You tried that. He wouldn't listen.* Then I would tell him again, and again—as many times as it took, until he believed me. And then they would have to release Otto.

When I arrived back at the apartment, Ilse was sitting at the kitchen table sewing Carlotta's ugly checkered dress by hand. The female mannequin stood in the corner wearing a portion of it.

Ilse must have taken the flowered dress back to the secret room. Or she'd sold it.

"Where's your sister?" she asked. "Why are you home before her?" She put down her sewing and studied my face. "What is it? What happened?"

I could barely get the words out. "Uncle Otto. I tried to stop them, but they—"

"What?" She stood so quickly the chair screeched across the floor. "They who?"

"The commandant. They took him. They—"

Ilse's face fell apart. I was surprised when she reached for me. "Stupid, stupid. I told him not to apply for that permit. I knew it would call too much attention to him."

I held her and we both cried, but in the back of my mind I was putting things together. She must have been referring to Otto's Nazi past—which I wasn't supposed to know about. She wasn't blaming me for his arrest. She didn't know it had anything to do with the car.

Then keep your mouth shut this one time, came my sister's voice in my head.

"How will I manage without him?" Ilse said.

"Hilde and I will help you. We'll bring food from the farm. We'll take some of the clothes to sell on our way home."

"What if he never comes back? And my boys. My God, can a person lose everyone?"

It didn't seem like it should be allowed to happen, but I knew from Frau Weber that it could. I thought of the Goldsteins: an entire family, more than likely erased from existence.

Grief was becoming a familiar road, but it wasn't the type of grieving you could ease into. There was too much of it. We had to rush past it and continue with our lives, or else be swept into the ditch.

When Hilde got home, Ilse told her about Otto's arrest. Told, and didn't tell.

Arrested for what?

We're not sure. The box marked *Partei* was a secret Ilse had no intention of revealing.

Hilde glanced at me, but I wouldn't meet her eye.

As soon as we were alone in our bedroom, she cornered me. "This was your way of fixing things?"

"No. I didn't mean—"

"You never do." She let out a long breath of frustration. "This wouldn't have happened if you'd done what I said. It's not too late. Go tomorrow. I'll tell Frau Weber you're still sick. Tell him, Katja, or things will only get worse."

It was hard to imagine how that was possible.

CHAPTER FORTY-EIGHT

THE ROSE, THE LILY,
THE DOVE, THE SUN

The next morning I went straight to the barracks. This time
Arkady hurried to the gate and took my hand, his eyes fixed on
mine.

"Hi," he said in a rush.

No, no, no. "We need to talk."

He pulled me through the school doors and down the hall.
"This first. I found something for you," he said. "For us."

Such a small shift, from *you* to *us*, yet the ground shifted with it.

"I asked my men to keep an eye out for piano music, and look
what they found."

We'd reached the classroom with the piano. It didn't smell like
a classroom anymore—that chalky, floor-waxy smell I remembered from when I was younger. It smelled like leather and
tobacco. I wondered what the schoolhouse thought of all these

giant children living in its rooms—eating kasha and comparing stolen wristwatches. Talking about the number of people they'd killed or the houses they'd burned down, while they played dominoes and drank schnapps.

Arkady passed me a volume of Schumann's *Lieder*. I hadn't held a book like this since the day Mutti had been—

I opened it, turning each page carefully as though the notes might fall out onto the floor. *The rose, the lily, the dove, the sun.* It was one of Schumann's songs, a simple list of beautiful things. Put together like that, they formed a world that no longer existed. I hummed the tune to myself, then another, and—

I closed the book. "Whose was it?"

Arkady's brow furrowed. "I have no idea. Does it matter?"

"You took it from someone's home." Right, wrong: once again, the meaning of things slid sideways. "I can't keep it." I told him about my own book of *Lieder* (Herr Goldstein's book), torn to shreds by soldiers on a day that seemed so long ago—but felt like yesterday.

His hands closed over mine, around the book. "Not every soldier is like those men."

"So this is okay because you took the book but didn't rip it up?"

He touched my cheek, turning my face to his. "Please accept my gift. It will make me so happy to learn these pieces with you. Don't you think the person, whoever it is, would be gratified to know the music was being played somewhere?"

Was that why Herr Goldstein had given his book to me? If he had known what was coming—*How? Who had known? How could people have known and not done anything?*—if he had known, maybe he wanted the music to go on through me.

I pulled away from Arkady and set the book on one of the school desks. "I need to speak to you about my uncle."

"Ah." Arkady brushed at his tunic sleeves. "He's being held in the basement of the *Kommandatura*. I've made sure he is comfortable. I can probably arrange for you to visit him, if you—"

"I don't want to visit him. I want you to let him go."

"Let him go?" *Would you also like me to grow wings?*

"I need to tell you something." My heart beat in my throat. The worst thing of all was being on the edge of a moment that you knew would change everything, and knowing you couldn't back away. You had to say the terrible thing.

"This isn't about the car, is it?" he said.

"Yes." I could feel red patches burning on my cheeks. "You mustn't punish my uncle for this crime."

Arkady looked at his boots. "My father—I told you before, it's not possible."

"You need to understand." I took him by both shoulders. "I'm the one who vandalized the car."

He stroked my hair. "I refuse to believe that."

I pushed his hand away. "I was angry with you. You'd taken my rabbit. And that car, it reminded me of the Nazis. And my mother: on our way here, Soviet soldiers—" I swallowed hard. I couldn't tell him about Mutti.

I didn't know how his lips found their way to mine, but when he kissed me, the room melted at my feet. Or maybe it was me who melted. His hands were in my hair, mine were at his collar, touching his neck. I hadn't expected him to be so soft. His neck was warm, and his skin smelled of something so different and foreign to anything I'd ever known. It was the smell of a man.

This is wrong, a voice said in my head. *He's Soviet. You shouldn't.*

And then I remembered something else and pulled away. "Liesel told me you were engaged to be married. To a girl in Moscow."

Arkady laughed. "That's an excellent story. Tell it to my father. You'll make him happy."

"It isn't true?" I said.

Instead of answering, he kissed me again, and again, and all the voices warning me to stop got smaller, and finally faded away.

"Listen to me," he said when we pulled away from each other. "Your uncle has claimed ownership of the scissors that were found at the scene of the crime. My father is convinced he's guilty, and when he gets a thing like this in his head, it's difficult to change his mind. Was it really you? Tell me the truth."

I forced myself to look him in the eye. "It was."

I could see on his face that he didn't want to believe me.

"Let him go," I said. "If you have to punish someone, it should be me."

"You know I won't do that. Someone must be held responsible, but it won't be you."

"Who, then?"

He glanced at the papers strewn across the teacher's desk. "Maybe I could find someone else to blame for this."

One of the big fish, as Otto called the higher-ranked Nazis. Someone who deserved it. But who deserved it more than I did? "I can't let you do that."

He laughed. "Are you going to stop me?"

There's nothing you can do about it, Today-Katja said. Whoever got punished, it wasn't my idea.

Oh, but this was getting tiring. How long could I go on

pretending none of this was my fault?

Nearby came the laughter of men who were off duty. Someone played the accordion and the men sang.

"What's going to happen to this person?" I asked.

"That's my father's decision." Then Arkady said, "Wait here a moment. There's something I'd like you to have."

A few minutes later he returned with several small packages wrapped in clear plastic: the chocolate.

"I can't accept that," I said.

He tipped my chin to kiss me. "Yes, you can. To make up for the rabbit." He placed the packages in a canvas bag and pressed it into my hands. It felt like he was handing me a bomb that I would somehow have to dispose of.

CHAPTER FORTY-NINE

FELLOW TRAVELER

Arkady hoisted his gun onto one shoulder and led me toward the back door so there was less chance of running into his father. "Let me drive you home."

As we walked down the hallway, my lips felt swollen. The thought of how he'd kissed me made the bottom of my stomach drop. All the things Hilde had spoken of when we'd sat side by side on her bed finally made sense—about her boyfriend, Paul, and about boys in general. Love was the best-kept secret in the world. You couldn't really know, until you knew.

The Mercedes was parked behind the barracks. Arkady opened the scratched passenger door for me and I climbed in warily. I had never been in a motorcar before. The leather seat was soft, and warm from the sun. The interior of the car smelled like a fancy home library, where members of the Prussian nobility might have drunk whiskey and discussed politics. I could have sat there all day, just breathing.

A whiff of diesel filled the air as he started the car. He took a different route home than the one I would have walked, crossing the river and circling back onto the road that led out of Fahlhoff. It was still so busy with people walking. I could hardly look at them. I knew how they felt. I knew how they smelled, how sore their feet were, and how hungry they were. I knew the desperate feeling they had of not knowing where they would end up.

The way they looked at the car as it passed made me feel sick. No one had forgotten that these cars had once been driven by Nazis. No one could shake the automatic fear that came with seeing a black Mercedes in your neighborhood. And now it was the Soviets, with their lists of fascists or their demands for jewelry, clocks, women. *Reparatsii*. Reparations.

And there I sat in the passenger seat, a *Mitläufer*—a fellow traveler. It was one of the categories being used by the Allies to define different levels of collaboration with the Nazis. Category four: the follower, someone who'd joined the Party out of convenience.

I shifted in the warm leather seat. *I didn't do anything.* But wasn't that the definition of a fellow traveler? Someone who went along for the ride. It wasn't as bad as being the driver, no. But I was still in the car. It wasn't being driven by Nazis anymore, but what did that matter? They were still soldiers. Same boots, different mustache.

I thought of Herr Goldstein, bent over the third movement of Beethoven's *Moonlight Sonata*, adjusting the fingering for me. I imagined Jacob, hovering just outside the cellar door, trying to listen. I thought of the first time I'd seen them on the street with yellow stars sewn onto their coats in fine, even stitches. *Look away*, Mutti had said.

"Let me out."

"Don't be silly," Arkady said. "I'll take you home."

"I can't be in this car. Let me out." I opened the door while the car was moving, but when I saw the ground speeding past me I slammed it shut. My breathing went shallow. I looked out the side window, then out the back.

He glanced at me. "What's the matter with you?"

"Just, please. Stop the car."

Arkady pulled over. "Did I say something to upset you?"

"No."

"The problem with the vandalism is solved, I promise you. I'll have them release your uncle. No one will know it was you. I'll find someone to take your place."

Someone to take my place. Who? Who would it be all right to punish in place of me?

"I have to go." I got out of the car, shut the door, and hurried across the square. I didn't look back when I heard the car move, and I didn't look at Arkady when he passed me on the road.

I should have felt better. It was over. I was free. Arkady would get Otto released from prison, and this whole ugly mess would be behind me. But instead, I felt worse. Something dark had opened up inside me, and if I leaned too close I was afraid I would fall in.

Liesel stood by the oak tree, a cigarette in her hand. "So, he's your boyfriend now." She must have seen me get out of the car.

"No." I hugged the canvas sack against my chest and swore I could feel it ticking. If she found out I had the chocolate, she would know I'd pinned the crime on someone else.

"How many more innocent people are going to suffer because of you?" she said.

Only one, now.

People on the street turned to look at us.

"He won't save you, you know," she said.

He already has.

"Even if he says he can. His father is the one in charge."

His father. What if the commandant refused to release Otto? What if Arkady's whole plan fell apart? I willed my face to keep still, but my eyelid twitched.

Liesel took a slow pull of her cigarette. "Bring me a dress or I'll tell that hag aunt of yours where your mother is, and you and your sister will be out on the street."

"Can't you just leave it?" I said. "It's not your business."

"Dmitri wasn't yours."

I walked away with short, quick steps. Flies circled my head and buzzed at my ears, drawn by the sweat. Or maybe they just knew when a part of you had died.

You know there will be more than one transaction, right? Frau Weber's words echoed in my memory as I made my way down Rosenstrasse to the clothing shop. *The price for silence will keep going up.*

I opened the street-level door and stood in the entryway in front of the secret room. *Do nothing.* But Liesel wasn't afraid to carry out her threat. Whatever might happen to me, I couldn't let any of this touch Hilde. I popped open the stairwell door and took down the blue dress with yellow flowers, stuffing it into the sack.

When I walked into the apartment, Ilse was sitting at the kitchen table, picking up pieces of fabric and setting them down again as if she wasn't sure how they'd gotten there. I felt so terrible;

I had to say something.

"I heard some news," I said carefully. The fewer details, the better.

Ilse rose. "What did you hear? What happened?"

"They're going to release Uncle Otto."

"When?" She crumpled the fabric in her hands.

"Soon. Everything's going to be fine."

I opened the sack, pushing the dress to the bottom and taking out the packages of chocolate. I hadn't intended to give them to her. I'd planned to take them to Oskar, the one person I could think of who wouldn't ask questions. But the run-in with Liesel had me panicked. "These will be good for trading."

Hilde walked in, eyes wide, mouth shut. If Ilse understood where the chocolate had come from, she didn't say anything. She simply nodded and set the packages onto the counter.

As soon as Ilse left the room, Hilde rushed over to me. "What happened? You told him? You did it?"

"Yes." It was all I could manage to say.

"I guess it's done, then," she said quietly. "Liesel won't be a problem anymore." But she wouldn't look at me when she said it.

Hilde and I made supper, and afterward Hilde did some of the sewing for Carlotta's hideous dress. Frau Doktor Doktor and her daughter were set to come over the next day.

I still had Mutti's crochet needles, and Frau Weber had given me some yarn in exchange for another pot of rabbit stew. While Hilde sewed, I went into the sitting room. If Otto had been home, he would have found something nice to listen to on the radio. Even though it hurt more than anything, I took his place, sorting through the static until I found some Rachmaninoff. Then I sat on the armchair and began crocheting Ilse a doily.

On a list of things you need when your husband has been arrested, a doily wouldn't be at the top. It wouldn't even make the top one hundred. But I still believed beauty could be a remedy for almost anything.

When Ilse walked in and saw me, she said, "Where did you learn to do that?"

"Mutti taught me." I cringed at the mention of Mutti's name. It was an invitation for unwanted questions—but the questions didn't come.

I still ached every time I thought of Mutti's face, or that sweet clove scent on her skin. I remembered the shape of her finger-nails. I remembered how she pursed her lips whenever she wrote anything, and how skeptical she was about gadgets. Most things that were foreign to her she considered as gadgets: wristwatches, ballpoint pens. The radio had been a gadget until the first time she'd heard Schumann on it. Then it had become an essential part of our sitting room.

How could the world go on without her in it?

The male mannequin stood in the corner, his hat sitting at a jaunty angle that didn't quite cover his blown-apart head. The mannequin didn't seem right without Otto there fussing over him. The violin lay silent in its case, and there was the place on the sofa where Otto would have sat with his bushy mustache, crooked glasses, and disheveled hair. The room hadn't changed, yet it was so much emptier.

CHAPTER FIFTY

NOT WHAT I WANTED

On the way home from work I stopped at the grocery store and gave Liesel the dress. She didn't say a word, not even a *thank you,* and I didn't have the energy to act like the insulted sausage with her.

I rushed home, expecting to see Otto's shoes by the door. They weren't there. I smelled chicory and perfume, and held back a groan. Frau Doktor Doktor and her daughter were still over. I had hoped to miss them. Hilde had stayed home from the farm to help Ilse with the dress, and when I peered into the sitting room the female mannequin wore it. She stood propped against the wall as if waiting for someone to ask her to dance.

Ilse sat in the armchair across from the two women, Frau Doktor Doktor patting her arm with a manicured hand. "He'll come home. They'll straighten it all out. You'll see."

"But he's not home." Ilse shot me an accusatory glance. "I know how these things go. If they think he's guilty of something? They won't even bother with a trial."

I picked at the wooden doorframe. What if Arkady couldn't do what he'd promised? What if his father refused?

Hilde buzzed around pouring the pretend-coffee. A glint of light caught something at her neck. She was wearing Mutti's locket. I narrowed my eyes at her from the doorway, but she wouldn't look at me. She kept touching it, probably hoping Carlotta would notice.

"War is a difficult time," Frau Doktor Doktor said. "It's best placed behind us." When she said *War* like that, with a capital *W*, it sounded more like something that had happened, like an accident, rather than something people had done. "No cookies today?"

Ilse rose. "I almost forgot." She bustled into the kitchen and came out with a flowered plate, which she set onto the small table. On it were several pieces of chocolate.

I wanted to look anywhere other than at that plate of chocolate, but my eyes refused to leave it.

"My, my," said Frau Doktor Doktor. "How ever did you come by this?"

"Katarina brought it home yesterday," Ilse said.

Carlotta fixed me with a resentful look as she stuffed a handful into her mouth.

Ilse stood beside the mannequin, pulling the dress straight and adjusting pins. "It's almost finished. If Carlotta would like to try it on, we can adjust the hemline."

Frau Doktor Doktor studied the checkered dress, arms crossed at her chest. "The garment is well made, anyone can see that."

"You can wear it to the dance hall," Hilde said. *With me,* her whole body said.

Carlotta frowned. "Mummy. It's not what I wanted."

"I can change the buttons," Ilse said. "I can redo the—"

"I want something pretty," Carlotta said. "Something with flowers on it."

Ilse clasped her hands. "I have just the dress for you."

She hurried out of the room and her footsteps clattered down the stairs. A heaviness settled in the pit of my stomach.

"It's ugly," Carlotta said. Hilde looked at the floor. "What if the flowered dress is ugly too?"

"Then we won't take it," Frau Doktor Doktor said. "There's no harm in speaking your mind."

"Though you might try not to hurt anyone's feelings," I said.

Ilse stomped up the stairs, and the front door flew open. "Well. Someone owes me an explanation." She looked at me. "Where is it?"

"Where is what?" Heat gathered on my face. Hilde glared at me.

"The dress is gone," Ilse said.

"Otto must have sold it," I said.

"Did he, now? Do you think I'm stupid? Where did the chocolate come from?"

"It's the reward," Carlotta piped up. "For the vandalized car."

"Hush," said Frau Doktor Doktor.

Ilse seemed confused. She turned on Hilde. "And your necklace? Where did you get that, I wonder?"

There was a subtle pinch around Hilde's eyes, as though Ilse had stepped on her toe and she didn't want anyone to know it.

"It looks like something two girls could trade a pretty dress for," Ilse said.

It was my turn to glare at my sister. *Let's see you talk yourself out of this one.*

"Mutti gave it to me," Hilde said.

"Your invisible mother," Ilse said. "*She* gave you that necklace. At such a dangerous time. I find that highly unlikely." She looked like she wanted to stick Hilde with one of her pins.

"I like the locket," Carlotta said.

Hilde covered it with one hand. "It's not for sale."

"Oh, I think it is," Ilse said. "That's my dress, hanging around your neck."

Frau Doktor Doktor took one sip of her pretend-coffee, then clanked her cup back onto the saucer. "You have a family issue to settle. We don't want to intrude. Come, Carlotta. The dress shop in Leipzig has a much better selection."

Carlotta looked like she wanted to ask for more chocolate, but her mother insisted with one sharp nod. They left without even shaking Ilse's hand. As they went down the stairs I heard a murmur of laughter between them. I wanted to trip Frau Doktor Doktor so she ripped a hole in her still-stretchy stockings. They weren't even silk. They were old-timer stockings, the kind I wouldn't wear unless I had gray hair and moles on my chin. I wanted to knock out one of Carlotta's big front teeth, or break the long golden arm off their grandfather clock.

"So." Ilse stomped her this-way foot at us. "Explain yourselves."

"We didn't trade your dress for this necklace," Hilde said. "Our photograph is inside the locket." Behind her eyes I saw the glimmer of jagged thoughts waiting for when we were alone.

"So you got the necklace and put the photograph in," Ilse said.

"We didn't."

"Something isn't right, and the two of you are in on it together, as usual. You're quite the pair. One sister farts and the other is already headed to the *Klo*."

I gaped. Mutti would have been livid at the toilet talk.

Ilse wagged a finger at us. "I'll get to the bottom of this soon enough, and when I do, you will sell that locket to Frau Doktor Doktor at a fair price and reimburse me for the dress you stole. In the meantime, you girls stay out of my sight."

I followed Hilde into the boys' room and we stood across the beds from each other. "Good thinking, *Scheisskopf*," I said.

"I could say the same to you," she hissed. "You gave that dress to the grocery girl, didn't you? What the hell is going on? You were supposed to tell your Soviet boyfriend about her. I thought that was how you got the chocolate."

I hung my head. "I couldn't."

"You didn't tell him?"

"Not about her," I said. "They're arresting someone else."

"I don't believe that. Who?"

"I don't know. Someone. Arkady's taking care of it." I didn't want to think about what that meant. The whole business made me nervous. Where was Otto? Why wasn't he here?

Hilde marched around the room. "You confessed, didn't you?"

"No." But *yes* was smeared across my face.

"She'll make trouble, that Liesel. She's that type. You should have done what I said. And now we'll have to give Ilse Mutti's locket, because you stole the dress."

"She wouldn't know about the locket if you hadn't worn it in the first place," I said.

"Why didn't you discuss this with me first?" Hilde said. "We could have worked out a plan. Instead you have to fly off half-cocked and do things without thinking. You're so damned impulsive. You always have to get involved. That's why—" It was as if she'd come to the edge of a cliff.

"That's why what?"

"Nothing," Hilde said.

"No. It's something. Tell me."

But she sat on the bed with her back to me and started brushing her hair.

I picked up Mutti's green sweater and held it against my chest. How could she not be here anymore? And not just her. So many people who'd been in the world were suddenly gone, as if half the stars in the sky had blinked and gone dark. A small group of crazy men had turned the world on its head—but they couldn't have done it without the rest of us standing by, following orders . . . or doing nothing.

You always have to get involved. But was that true? Had I spoken up when the Goldsteins had to give away their cat? Had I said anything to anyone about the yellow stars? Could I have? "Hilde."

"What now?"

"I rode in a motorcar yesterday."

There was a moment of silence, and in that moment I knew she was jealous. "Good for you."

"It made me think."

"Well now, don't go doing that. It never leads anywhere good."

I ignored the insult. "What did you know—about the Goldsteins? Did you know they were going to a death camp?"

She turned to look at me. "How do you get from a motorcar to the Goldsteins?"

"It was the Nazi car. The black Mercedes. I was a passenger." A fellow traveler.

"You mean the car you vandalized." She put down the brush. "What are you suggesting?"

"I'm not suggesting anything. I'm asking you a question. Did you know where they were going?"

"Not exactly. But I knew it wasn't good. Everyone did."

"I didn't."

"Yes, you did," Hilde said. "You're lying to yourself if you say you didn't. We all knew something terrible was happening. Even the Goldsteins did. We just didn't know what it was."

"Herr Goldstein told me they were moving to Poland." I remembered that day so well. It was the last day I ever saw him, when he'd given me his book of Schumann's *Lieder*. Everything in their home had been holding its breath, waiting for the next awful thing to happen. It was impossible to have lived in Germany during the war and not have known things were bad for the Jews. I knew. But also I didn't.

"He only said that so you wouldn't be frightened," Hilde said. "He didn't want to tell you the truth."

"But you knew the truth."

Now she was on her feet. "What do you mean, exactly?"

I crushed Mutti's sweater against me. "Didn't you? I think you did. That day I came home and told you Frau Goldstein wanted to talk to Mutti."

"I don't know what you're talking about," Hilde said, her tone clipped.

The very next day after Herr Goldstein had given me the book, I saw Frau Goldstein leave our house. I was on my way home from school. I remembered the way she walked—slowly, uncertainly— as if every footstep was laced with mines. "Mutti spoke to her. What did she want?"

Hilde flattened her skirt with both hands. "That was three years ago. How am I supposed to remember?"

"But you must. You and Mutti were talking, right afterward. And you stopped talking as soon as I walked in. You didn't want me to know. What was it?"

Hilde didn't answer.

"I think Frau Goldstein asked for help. And you told Mutti to say *no.*"

"Of course I told her to say *no,*" she shouted. "Would you rather have been sent away with them?"

"Shh," I said. "Ilse will hear."

Hilde didn't seem to care. "It was bad enough that you had to take lessons from him when it was forbidden. You had no sense of the danger. That's why we never told you anything. You would have insisted on getting involved. You would have hidden them, just like the Gestapo suspected."

I felt as though the floor had opened and swallowed me whole. "They wanted us to hide them?" How had I not guessed? I could have offered, without Hilde and Mutti even knowing. I thought of Herr Johannsen. Someone had hidden him and here he was, wandering around Fahlhoff—alive.

I picked at the blankets. "We could have helped them."

"I know that's what you think. But the Gestapo would have found them. They searched our entire house, and the barn. They found out about the piano lessons."

"What? How?" I'd been so careful. No one ever followed me.

The cellar was soundproof.

"That's what I'm trying to tell you. You think people didn't notice how often you went there? You think no one talks? Where would you have hidden a whole family? Under the bed? In the hayloft? We'd all be dead."

"We could have found a way for them to escape."

"They wouldn't have gotten far. Paul told me. The SS went into the countryside with dogs and shot the people they found. Is that what you would have wanted for your Herr Goldstein?"

I imagined escape to a foreign country, with wigs and glasses, false identities—the stuff of storybooks, I realized with a heavy heart. That was what I would have wanted, but that was not what would have happened.

Look away, Mutti had said so often to us. And we had.

I felt sick.

I couldn't help but see Mutti's face in my head. Not her smiling face. *That* face, the one made of vinegar and disappointment. The face she used to make before launching into the Every Bad Thing speech. Would she have said *no* if Hilde hadn't talked her out of it? The woman who hadn't let a single refugee go hungry when they'd knocked at our door—she must have carried so much guilt in her heart about this.

The Goldsteins' lives had been in our hands and I hadn't realized it. It was like trying to hold water, watching it slip through the cracks in your fingers no matter how hard you pressed them together. In the end your hands were wet, but empty.

"I wish you'd involved me in the decision," I said.

"Sure. And you would have put the whole family in danger. That's exactly why we didn't tell you. Because we knew you would have done something reckless."

Reckless? Or brave. Maybe it amounted to the same thing.

The thought of Jacob's dark eyes made it hard for me to breathe. "Doesn't it bother you? That we did nothing?"

"It wasn't our fault." Hilde's voice rose again. "We weren't Nazis. We weren't the ones who wanted to get rid of the Jews. What were we supposed to do?"

"Help them." That was what we were supposed to do. And we didn't.

For a long time Hilde sat on the edge of her bed staring at the rug. Then she looked up at me. "You did. You took them food nearly every day."

I was startled. "How did you—"

"Mutti told me. I think she was proud of you. You were braver than I was—than any of us."

"It wasn't enough," I said. "And in the end, what difference did it make? I didn't save them."

I felt a desperate need to be forgiven, but who could give that to me? The silence in the room was stifling.

"It haunts me, what happened with the Goldsteins," Hilde said softly. "I think about it every day. But it's a lot easier to imagine hiding them now. At the time, it was different. I was so scared. Everyone was."

The clip of tall black boots on the cobblestones, middle-of-the-night arrests, someone banging on the door so loudly it echoed through the neighborhood—I remembered.

I came over and sat beside her. "That day in the field when Mutti was . . . when they took that girl, and the soldier hit her. I didn't mean to say anything. It just happened. I was scared. And all Mutti did was look up."

She moved in closer and put her arm around me. "I know."

CHAPTER FIFTY-ONE

WHAT HAPPENS
TO COWARDS

"Where do you think you're going?" Ilse said when I came out of the boys' bedroom.

"To sort something out." Too many things haunted me already. I had to stop Arkady from following through on his plan. I slipped on my shoes and went outside. I hoped I wasn't too late.

As I approached the square, several people were congregated by the thousand-year oak. I broke into a run. They weren't really going to—they wouldn't. But yes—there was a bench beneath the tree, and a rope, and soldiers standing with a man I recognized right away.

It wasn't Otto.

It was Herr Johannsen.

"Have you seen my Isabella?" he asked the soldiers, a tremor in his voice. "I must get a message to her."

A sign around his neck read *Guilty of vandalism*. Arkady stood some distance away, observing the event. This was who he'd found to take my place? I couldn't think of anyone who deserved it less. The summer air wrapped itself around my face until I felt like I would suffocate. Arkady had warned me the man's fate was in his father's hands. I should have known this was how it would end.

I remembered another hanging body, another sign: *This is what happens to cowards*. But the sign was wrong. What happened to cowards was they ended up alive, looking on as other people got punished for the things they had done.

Herr Johannsen's hands and feet were bound with rope; his black shoes were scuffed and missing their heels. His trousers were worn at the knees, and someone had tied them so they wouldn't slip down. It was hot, and there were swarms of flies, and I couldn't look at him without feeling like that dark place inside me might swallow me up.

That would have been me up there. I was ashamed, yes. Horrified. But beneath it all there was an undeniable feeling of relief. I was off the hook. *Did you really just think that?* What was happening to me? Was this the person I'd become?

Be hard: the Bolshevik virtue of *tverdost*. A hardened heart couldn't break.

A breeze picked up, easing the heat for a moment. The messages on the trees rattled and flapped, desperate to fly to the people they were meant for.

Look away. Was that what Mutti would say now?

A heavy silence hung in the air, the kind with labored breathing and its own heartbeat. I felt dirty, and not only from the day's work at the farm. Out of the corner of my eye I saw Hilde running toward me. *Not now.* She arrived by my side breathless, and pulled me away from the crowd.

"Don't you dare," she said under her breath. "I know what you're going to do—and then you'll be the one hanging from that tree. And for what?"

"Because it's the right thing to do." Every inch of my skin felt it. My fingernails, my eyelashes; there was no part of me that could live with this man dying because of something I'd done. "Do I need another reason?"

"No," Hilde said. "Except—" Her shoulders curved as if with an impossibly heavy weight. "He's a stranger. He's no one to us. You're my sister. Please don't leave me alone in the world."

When the soldiers slipped the noose around Herr Johannsen's neck, my legs threatened to give way. I held on to Hilde's arm.

"Stop!" I shouted. "Please. He's not right in the head. You can't do this to him." *It was me.*

"For God's sake, keep your mouth shut this one time," Hilde said.

Arkady approached.

"Tell them to stop," I said to him.

"That's right," came another voice. "They must stop."

Hilde whispered, "*Scheisse.*"

Liesel strode toward the tree, shouting at the soldiers and pointing at me. "She did it. She's the one. But she's arranged for Herr Johannsen to be punished in her place."

Herr Johannsen blinked repeatedly.

"What does she mean?" someone in the crowd said.

"Nothing," Hilde said. "She has a big mouth."

"That's right, I do," Liesel said. "Especially when someone won't admit the truth about what they've done."

Arkady was about three meters away from the tree, and several more away from me. The soldiers turned to him, waiting to be told what to do. I watched his face, praying that this time he would be strong enough to defy his father completely. Take a stand. Execute no one. But could he? Liesel had publicly exposed me.

He raised his hand. One of the soldiers removed the noose. I tried to catch his eye. Did he mean to pardon me? Or—?

"Justice!" Liesel cried.

"Please," Hilde said. "She's my sister."

But I realized he wasn't listening to any of us. I followed his line of sight. I should have guessed. There was his father, walking toward the square with another man who wore even more medals than he did. No, not walking. They were marching. These were men who slept in their uniforms. I counted four stars on the other man's shoulder boards—one more than the commandant. He was a general, no doubt visiting from Moscow.

The general gestured toward the gallows, shouting in Russian, his voice rising with questions.

Liesel pointed at me. Whatever she was saying, it was clearly an accusation.

Cement Face spoke to the general in a tone I'd never heard from him before: apologetic. I picked out two words I knew only too well: *vandalism* and *automobile*.

The general was still shouting. His face went red. At first I could hardly breathe; then I realized his anger was directed at the commandant.

Arkady spoke quickly to the soldiers, who unfastened the

ropes from Herr Johannsen's arms and legs.

Liesel was still trying to get the general's attention, but he didn't even acknowledge her. He drew the commandant away in the direction of the *Kommandatura* and motioned for Arkady to follow them.

In an instant, I understood. Arkady hadn't had mercy on Herr Johannsen. He'd seen the general coming. He must have gauged the look on his face and known whose orders to follow. What would he have done if the general had sided with Liesel? Would he have stood up for me?

Before Arkady left I met his eye. I wanted to look at him the way I once had over the piano, but I knew in that moment things would never be the same between us.

"This isn't over," Liesel said to me.

Hilde was pulling at me to leave, but I ran over to the tree and held on to Herr Johannsen. His whole body was trembling.

"Will you help me find Isabella?"

"Yes," I said. "I'll help you. I promise."

I broke away from him. "I need to go home," I whispered to Hilde. Though it wouldn't be our home for much longer; Liesel would make sure of that.

Hilde took my arm and helped me back to the apartment where I went straight to bed. There were potatoes for supper, but I couldn't eat.

Why hadn't they released Otto yet? Had his Nazi past been worse than what he'd admitted to me? I couldn't think about it. I couldn't even say his name.

CHAPTER FIFTY-TWO

THE SOUND OF
A CLOSED MOUTH

The splash of milk hitting the bucket in Frau Weber's barn didn't calm me. Nor did the creek, or Mutti's stones.

Did you know a violin is made from more than seventy separate pieces of wood? Papi taught me that. I wondered if Otto knew. Did he know Mozart started his musical training on the violin? There were so many things I hadn't told him yet.

On the way home from the farm Hilde and I went to the *Kommandatura* to inquire about Otto. The man at the desk told us he wasn't there. Did that mean he'd been released?

I raced to the shop, my sister barely keeping up, thumped up the stairs, and crashed through the apartment door. "Aunt Ilse, I think Uncle Otto is—"

"My goodness, you'd swear the devil himself was chasing her with his pitchfork."

Ilse sat in the kitchen changing the buttons on the checkered dress. Beside her stood Otto, looking even thinner than before. But there was his bushy mustache and empty pockets. There were his crooked glasses and poof of hair. I ran across the room and threw myself into his arms.

"I'm sorry. I'm so sorry."

"*Na, na*," he said, the way Papi used to shush the horses. "I'm home now. It's okay." I could feel the air getting smoother as he spoke.

"But it was my fault. I'm the one who—"

"You're the one who got me released." He patted my shoulder. "That's what matters."

We were all in the kitchen when a voice from the road called, "Frau Daschner." It was so loud there was no missing it. Hilde and I exchanged a look.

"What is all that hollering?" Ilse said.

"It's nothing." Hilde straightened her back. "Just some crazy girl who—"

"Their mother is dead," Liesel shouted from outside. "Katja told me so herself. And she is the vandal. She's the reason your husband was arrested."

Ilse put down the dress. "Is this true?"

I took a deep breath. "Yes. I'm the one who vandalized the Mercedes." I turned to Otto. "With those scissors I was supposed to take to the shoemaker."

Ilse looked like she wanted to say something—probably a lot of somethings. I kept speaking. "I tried to stop them from taking Uncle Otto, but they wouldn't listen to me." The words came easily. In fact, it was a relief to stop pretending. "I shouldn't have done it," I said. "But the Soviets killed our mother."

"I knew it," Ilse muttered. "I knew she wasn't coming."

Otto put a hand on her shoulder.

"It happened right in front of us," I continued. "We watched her die, and we couldn't save her."

I remembered the sound of the gunshot. I saw her fall to the ground all over again, and not get up, and still not get up. The moment stretched itself out so that I could see every part of it: how quickly someone could decide to end a life. How I'd known what would happen one second before it did. Mutti must have known it too.

Ilse's face was twisted in anguish, as though she could see right into my head.

Otto said, "Why didn't you tell us this right away?"

"Because you wouldn't have kept us," I said. "You would have sent us away."

"That's not true," he said, but only with half a heart. We all knew it was.

"I had a piano teacher," I continued. "His name was Solomon Goldstein." I glanced at Hilde. Her head was down, but she didn't stop me.

I heard the door shut downstairs. In my haste I'd forgotten to lock it. Liesel would be on her way up.

"He moved his piano into the cellar and taught me, even though it was against the law. He had a wife who baked poppy seed cookies," I said, "and a son named Jacob who wanted to be a doctor and used to listen to me play every Sunday. The SS came through our town in their black Mercedes, and then my piano teacher and his family were sent away." Savages. My own people.

"We could have helped them. Maybe we could have hidden them. But we didn't. I never saw them again. I'm quite sure they're all dead."

Ilse and Otto were silent. Footsteps sounded up the stairs.

I took a breath. "That's why I vandalized the car. I had to do it."

The door burst open and Liesel stood there in the flowered dress. It looked stunning on her. I remembered how I'd worried about shoes for that dress, but no one looked at your feet when you wore something that pretty.

I braced myself for the coming storm.

"Isn't it lovely?" Liesel said.

Ilse's face went red. "What is the meaning of this?"

Hilde strode right over to Liesel and said, "It looks nice on you. I'm so glad you decided on it."

Liesel ignored her. "Katja gave me this dress so I would keep my mouth shut about the car—and about her mother. She's too much of a coward to admit the truth." She raised her hand as if she wanted to slap me. "My boyfriend is dead because of you."

"Your boyfriend is dead because he raped Frau Weber," I said. "You don't want to believe it was him, but it was."

"Katja gave you the dress to keep you quiet?" Ilse stood. "And yet, this isn't the sound of a closed mouth. Do you mean to tell me you blackmailed one of my girls?"

"Do you know what she did? That bitch—"

"That is pigpen language," Ilse said, "and I won't have it in my house."

Liesel backed away.

"Blackmail doesn't seem very brave," Otto said.

"I would thank you to return the dress," Ilse said, "or else pay for it properly."

Liesel stared at them. Then she stormed out, slamming the door and thundering down the stairs. The room reverberated with the noise. For a moment, nobody moved.

"I'm sorry about the dress," I said.

Ilse put water on the stove, her hand shaking as she set the kettle down. "I'm very sad to hear about your mother. She was—" Her voice caught.

I stood beside her and she put her arm around my shoulder.

When the blue dress appeared at the apartment door a few days later in a crumpled heap, Ilse held it against her chest like a lost child.

CHAPTER FIFTY-THREE

LOST AND FOUND

Things with Ilse shifted. She knew Mutti wasn't coming back, but she didn't throw us out. Nor did she mention anymore what would happen if the boys came home. In the meantime, we brought her more salami from Frau Weber's farm, as well as a rabbit for stew. I spent my evenings listening to Otto play the violin while Hilde and Ilse sewed a dress from a set of old curtains.

"Didn't your mother have photographs?" Ilse asked. "I should like to see them."

When Hilde brought out the handfuls of photograph pieces, Ilse's mouth dropped. "That won't do at all."

She helped us arrange the pieces on the kitchen table, painstakingly lining them up and repairing them with sticky tape.

After we'd hung them on the bedroom wall, she brought out a magazine and sat on Hilde's bed. "Come, sit."

Hilde went. The magazines were her thing. But I hung back until she said, "You too," patting the bed.

I sat on her other side as she flipped through the pages.

"It seems all right for women to wear trousers now," Hilde said.

"Yes," Ilse said. "It's an interesting development. And thank God Dirndl are finally going out of style. I never could stand them."

She sat with us for half an hour, then got up in a fluster, saying, "I mustn't neglect Otto," with a small smile on her face. I wondered if he had sat in here years ago with the boys, discussing hunting, while Ilse had been the one left on the sofa by herself.

"We're indispensable," I whispered to my sister.

One afternoon when we came home from the farm, Otto was waiting on the road for us, beside himself with excitement. "Come see," he said, pulling me up the stairs. "You won't believe it."

The black Steinway from Oberstrasse was in the sitting room. I had to touch it to make sure it was real.

"A group of them hauled it up the stairs," he said. "You should have seen them. They handled it like it was nothing."

"I can't keep it," I said quietly.

Hilde put her hands on her hips. "You can, and you will. This is your whole life. I've heard too many stupid composer stories for you not to become a concert pianist."

"But—"

"Herr Goldstein would never forgive you," she said. "Neither would Mutti."

That evening Otto made me play every piece I knew. He insisted on seeing the score for the third movement of the *Moonlight* Sonata and I promised to learn it for him.

"There's a music academy in Leipzig," he said. "I used to pass it every time I went to the city. When it reopens, I think you should audition there."

Me. At a music academy. I could scarcely think of it without feeling dizzy. "Is that even possible?"

"Why shouldn't it be?" Otto said. "Isn't that what you want?"

"Yes, but—"

"I know what you're thinking," Otto said. "You think you don't deserve it."

"I don't," I said quietly.

"Nonsense," Otto said. "Imagine how proud your mother would be. And your piano teacher. You'll become a concert pianist, and you'll perform all over the country, and they'll be listening to every single note."

"But they're not here." I swallowed hard. "Because of me."

He held me by both shoulders. "They're not here because there was a war. You're here. Do it in their memory. It's the good you can do."

Three times that following week I saw Arkady at the wheel of the black Mercedes. The third time, he pulled over, got out, and followed me.

"Katja, please. Speak to me."

I turned. "Thank you for the piano."

Arkady smiled. "Who should have it but you? I would like to come over and sing Schumann with you. Surely your aunt and uncle would enjoy—"

"No."

"I don't understand what I did."

I thought of Herr Johannsen blinking in the sunlight. Arkady had chosen him to hang in my place. And then he'd pardoned him, but not because of me. But the fault was ultimately mine. It was too much for a relationship to bear.

When I found out he and his father were going back to Moscow, I was sad, but also relieved. Maybe Arkady and I had been a version of Schumann and Clara after all. Schumann's story didn't end well either. After trying to kill himself, he'd asked to be placed in an asylum, where he spent the last two years of his life battling a serious mental disorder. But at least he'd had Clara. It was hard for me to listen to his *Lieder* on the radio without feeling desperately sad.

Even without the *Lieder* I was sad. I couldn't seem to get to the other side of that dark place inside me.

* * * *

After work one day I stopped in the square and found Herr Johannsen sitting in the dry fountain. I sat down next to him and said, "Tell me about Isabella. Who is she? Is she your sister? Your wife?"

"She's Isabella."

I smiled. "When did you last see her?"

"Before."

I understood that. Before everything in the world had tipped sideways. "Did she write to you? Do you have anything from her?"

Herr Johannsen reached into a pocket of his worn jacket and pulled out an envelope. The return address was faded but I could make out the street name, and the city: Halle. Where Händel was born. *Did you know that if Händel had had a better doctor, his blindness might have been corrected?* It was possible Isabella didn't live there any longer, but Halle was only an hour away by train. It was worth checking. Life was cruel and unfair, but for once, maybe someone would get what they wanted.

I didn't want to take Herr Johannsen with me, in case I didn't find her or I got bad news. Otto didn't like the idea of my wandering around Halle alone, so he accompanied me on my mission. We walked up and down the long street knocking on doors. "Do you know Isabella?" we asked over and over, sounding like Herr Johannsen. *Her name might be Isabella Johannsen. She lived here before the war.*

Finally we knocked on a door that was opened by a tall woman with the same sad brown eyes as Herr Johannsen.

"Isabella?" I said. She was his sister. When we told her Herr Johannsen was still alive, she almost didn't believe us.

"He disappeared," she said. "I was sure they'd taken him to one of their hospitals and . . ." She couldn't finish the sentence.

We arranged for her to travel to Fahlhoff the following day.

"Should we tell him she's coming?" I asked Otto.

"Maybe not," he said. "What if she doesn't show up?"

Even though I was certain she would, I was so used to things not going as planned that I couldn't bear to get Herr Johannsen's hopes up.

That next day Otto and I sat in the square with Herr Johannsen, talking about birds and the warm weather as if we were just killing time. He sat calmly with his hands in his lap. I fidgeted; stood, then sat, then stood again, until Otto finally said, "Katja. Take a breath."

When we spied a tall woman approaching the fountain, I put a gentle hand on Herr Johannsen's shoulder and said, "Look. Look who it is."

He lifted his head. Recognition took a moment. They hadn't seen each other since before the war, Isabella had told us. When his mouth fell open, she broke into a run.

"Is it possible?" she said. "Is it really you?" She clutched him by both arms and wept.

CHAPTER FIFTY-FOUR

THE ONE THING I KNOW ABOUT COMPOSERS

Rumors of Herr Doktor Doktor's involvement with the Nazis began to spread that fall, right around the time fifty tons of Nazi Party files were discovered in Munich. One day I heard he and his family had left town, no doubt with suitcases full of fancy clothes. The grandfather clock stayed behind.

"A bribe?" I asked Otto.

He patted down his hair. He didn't want to say *yes*. But he couldn't say *no*.

That same fall, the theater reopened and the first film they showed was called *Tractor Drivers*, a Soviet saga about collective farms. The worst thing about it was that for the rest of my life, whenever anyone asked, *What was the first film you ever saw?* I had to say, Tractor Drivers.

Otto received his permit to reopen the shop.

"We'll set it all up," he said. "It will be just like before."

It wasn't. Nothing was.

The display window was still boarded up, the wounded mannequins hidden inside. Ilse and Otto had traded most of their pretty dresses for food. No one had fabric, so Ilse started making clothes from dishrags and army blankets, Hilde helping her at the kitchen table. While I practiced piano I'd hear Hilde say, "A button here would dress things up a little," and Ilse would say, "Yes, you're right. You have an eye for this."

On the day a black-bordered envelope arrived, Hilde and I were the first ones home.

"Should we hide it?" I asked, thinking to soften the news somehow.

But Hilde said, "No. It will never be the right time to tell them, and they've been waiting so long to find out."

Ilse cried. But then she held Hilde and me on either side of her and said, "This would be much harder to bear without the two of you."

That night, Otto sat on the sofa holding the hunting photograph of himself with the boys, Ilse by his side. The wild boar stared down at them with its hard, dark eyes, those yellow tusks a perfect curve for goring somebody. I wondered if Otto was remembering holding his son on his lap, maybe bouncing him on his knees to "*Hoppe, Hoppe Reiter*" the way Papi used to do with me and Hilde. At the end of the rhyme, the rider was supposed to wind up in the swamp, but Papi never let us fall.

After we'd received the letter telling us Papi was dead, Mutti had sat at the kitchen table with a small velvet sack of his pipe tobacco. She hadn't burned it or poured it out, the way I expected. She simply sat there with it, as if part of his spirit had slipped into one of his beloved objects and sitting there might bring him back—if only she waited long enough.

A few days later, the second envelope arrived. I didn't have to ask Hilde. We held on to that one for a month, allowing the first terrible news to settle like ash.

The mornings grew chilly. Soon there would be frost.

I was shoveling manure out of one of the stalls in Frau Weber's barn when Oskar said, "The fence has fallen down again."

Big surprise—he was the one who'd fixed it.

"A goat has escaped. Since you're the master goat-catcher, would you bring him back?"

I trudged across the field with a can of grain, but within a few minutes I realized Oskar and Hilde were following me.

"You don't think I can do the job myself?" I called to them. I was a little annoyed. I hadn't been out to Mutti's memorial in some time. I was hoping to be alone with her.

I reached the fence. It wasn't broken, and there was no goat. "What's going on?"

Oskar and Hilde caught up and climbed over. "Come," Hilde said.

They led me to the memorial I had started with six stones and an attitude. It wasn't six stones anymore. Oskar and Hilde had filled a circle the size of a bicycle wheel with hundreds of stones from the creek.

"We're thinking of making a plaque with her name on it," Hilde said, "and the years she lived. What do you think?"

I couldn't speak.

"There should also be flowers," Oskar said. "Next spring, we'll plant some."

"Begonias," my sister said, because she was Hilde and it couldn't just be flowers.

She took out the locket and fastened it around my neck. "Should we take turns with this? Six months you, six months me?"

I clutched it against my chest, imagining Mutti so hard it made me ache. There she was, reminding me to cover my hands when I picked nettle leaves, and to be extra careful about mushrooms and always ask Hilde, because Hilde knew better.

* * * *

That night after Hilde finished brushing her hair, I blew out the candle and we lay together on my bed.

"Did you know Tchaikovsky used to hold his chin with his left hand while he was conducting?" Hilde said. "Because he was afraid his head would fall off?"

I rolled over and stared at her. "You're making that up."

"I'm not," she said.

"How do you know anything about Tchaikovsky?"

"Oskar told me," she said. "He heard it from some Soviets."

I laughed. "I don't believe you."

"Don't believe me, then. It's the one thing I know about composers and I'm offering it to you. But if you don't want it . . ."

I leaned against her, listening to her breathe until she fell asleep beside me.

AUTHOR'S NOTE

This novel should not be read as a justification for a particular response to the Holocaust. I write, in part, to understand, and I am drawn to what I consider impossible situations because they force me to ask tough questions and face unsettling truths. There were no simple answers in Katja's situation; there were not meant to be.

I believe it is easy to read history with the benefit of hindsight and insert ourselves into the roles of hero and heroine. Easy, but not honest. I could have made Katja more heroic, but then I believe she would not have had as much to say to us.

Katja's viewpoint in this novel is necessarily colored by both how she was raised and her limited understanding of what actually happened during the war. She makes assumptions about the Soviets based on what she would have learned from Nazi propaganda, and her sister and mother make decisions that arise from both fear and the anti-Semitism that surrounded them.

Fahlhoff is a fictional German city, and it saw far less destruction than most cities in Germany would have. Also, I knowingly bent the truth by making the commandant and Arkady father and son. In fact, it was unlikely that a father and son would have worked together in such a capacity, though what was common was that officers did not always obey the new authority in place during this time of transition. As well, while summary executions for rape did occur, they were rare. Executing a vandal would also have been rare.

The months directly following the end of World War II in Europe were rife with chaos. Not only was Germany responsible for starting the war, but its soldiers had also been brutal, particularly in their attempt to annihilate the Jews and in their attacks on civilians in Eastern Europe and the Soviet Union. News of the death camps was only just coming to light. Vengeance was uppermost in many people's minds, and for good reason. The war might have been over, but violence was rampant.

Millions of people in Germany were left homeless and hungry. Most of these were women, children, and the elderly—since most adult men were either dead or had been captured as prisoners of war. It was the women, children, and elderly who would pay for the sins of the German soldiers.

This was the situation the Allied forces confronted when they entered Germany in 1945. They had their own desires for vengeance to contend with, but these had to be balanced and overcome by the need to impose order and make Germany functional—while also dismantling a powerful Nazi propaganda machine. Order, justice, food, denazification, and a need to stop people from looting, raping, and killing to satisfy their thirst for vengeance: it was not an easy assignment.

Germans had their own issues to deal with. The death camps had been a fairly well-kept secret, and while many people knew that Jews (and so many others: Roma and Sinti, homosexuals, prisoners of war, political prisoners, the mentally ill, Jehovah's Witnesses) had been sent away, their systematic extermination was not commonly known. The guilt and soul-searching did not happen overnight. For most people, survival was their first concern. A slow realization of the horrors of Nazism would follow.

Much has been written about the rape and looting that occurred during that time, mainly (though by no means exclusively) by Soviet soldiers. What is seldom mentioned is that this behavior was not representative of all Soviets.

While mass violence and destruction was the policy of the German advance onto Soviet soil, it was not the policy of the Soviet commanders entering Germany—but many soldiers had their own ideas about that, fed by Soviet propaganda and the destruction they had witnessed on their journey over. Many came from simple villages; they were stunned by Germany's wealth and could not fathom why such a rich country would need to start a war. Soviet leadership insisted on differentiating between Hitler's henchmen and the ordinary innocent German, but to little avail; in the minds of many soldiers and released prisoners of war, everyone was guilty.

To make matters worse, most Soviet soldiers resented being stuck in Germany after the war. All they wanted was to go home.

Much has also been written about the Iron Curtain that would later slam shut on half of Germany, as well as countries to its east. What is not talked about is the organizational miracle that the Soviet Military Administration accomplished in getting Germany back on its feet, while trying to control soldiers who were ignoring orders. A strange balance was struck between allowing some of the chaos to continue while punishing certain offenders; between establishing a workable system of food rationing while soldiers wandered rural areas requisitioning food and sabotaging the whole plan; between a desire to destroy and a need to reconstruct.

Ultimately reconstruction triumphed. It was not the triumph we saw in West Germany, to be sure, but the more one learns about such things as the *Einsatzgruppen* (special SS forces and police units responsible for mass killings) in Eastern Europe and the Soviet Union, the more incredible it becomes that the Soviets were able to set aside their need for vengeance and rebuild a country that killed so many of its people.

While this book is specifically about the end of World War II, it deals with issues that never leave us. How much responsibility does the ordinary citizen bear for the behavior of its government, especially if that government was elected? When resistance is necessary, and yet it doesn't happen, what is the cost of doing nothing? This is much easier to see in hindsight. At the time, Nazi Germany was a country ruled by fear, intimidation, and violence. We all like to think we would have done the right thing—but we weren't there.

The philosopher Baruch Spinoza wrote, "If you want the present to be different from the past, study the past." That is one of the reasons I write historical fiction. It is also a compelling reason to read it.

ACKNOWLEDGMENTS

This book could not have been written, and indeed would not exist, without my mother's help. She grew up in Germany during the war, and her memories and stories of that time were invaluable in enriching my research. She ended up converting to Judaism, married a Jewish man, and raised me and my brothers in the Jewish faith. To me that is a beautiful symbol of the impossible becoming possible.

This has been a long, long project. The novel went through countless revisions, and the early drafts do not even remotely resemble this one.

I would like to single out three authors without whose help I could not have made it to the end. Tanya Bellehumeur-Allatt and Nikki Vogel are my faithful critique partners who, amazingly, have not given up on me and patiently read this manuscript more times than I care to count. Their creative visions are very different, but they complement each other wonderfully. I am lucky to have them both.

When I had finally read the work so many times I couldn't see straight, I handed it over to Tara Gilboy, whose deep understanding of story inspired the final changes that brought the novel together.

My editor, Barbara Berson, knew just what the novel needed and brought a subtle vision of its arcs and relationships. The wonderful people at Annick Press have been incredibly supportive and enthusiastic about my work. It is a privilege to work with all of them.

My online writing group, the Raspberry Cordial Collective, saw things I never would have considered, and brought the work to a higher level. Thanks go to Kate Lum-Potvin, Patti Edgar, Tara Gilboy, and Tanya Bellehumeur-Allatt for their patient shepherding of this novel from synopsis to conclusion.

Authors Andrew Gray and Faye Arcand read earlier incarnations of the novel. Literary agent Hilary McMahon supplied the tough love I needed in order to abandon that earlier draft and start again. I'm especially grateful for her guidance during some difficult personal moments.

Marilyn Campeau, a University of Toronto doctoral student specializing in Russian history, and Dr. Eagle Glassheim, associate professor of history at the University of British Columbia, read the manuscript at different times for factual errors. Any errors that remain are my own. Counselor Nadine Morasse guided me with insights into Katja's character. My cousin Sabine Pogor supplied priceless books of old photographs from the small town where my mother's family lived, which informed my fictional town of Fahlhoff. Mike Hollander helped with information on anti-Jewish laws. Federica Ciancetta at the Vintage Berlin Guide put me in touch with Claus Jahnke, who explained the postwar clothing business in Germany to me.

Thanks to the support of the Canada Council for the Arts, I was able to travel to Germany to do research for this novel. My daughter, Madeleine, accompanied me and was endlessly patient with my requests to visit yet another museum. I would also like to mention the late Jean Lyons, my piano teacher, who gave me the gift of music.

Anika Scott's blog, *Postwar Germany*, was a helpful source of information, as was Hershey Felder's Google talk on Beethoven.

Online sources for the composer trivia found in the novel include: Classic FM (for bizarre and incredible musical facts); Wikipedia (for information about Robert Schumann); Listverse (for composers with extreme eccentricities); MusicTales (about Smetana's *The Moldau*); Biography (Mozart); Opera Australia (for a *Barber of Seville* cheat sheet); Interlude (for information about Handel's blindess); and TakeLessons (for interesting violin facts).

The comment "winter twelve months of the year, and summer the rest of the time" comes from "Gulag: Soviet Forced Labor Camps and the Struggle for Freedom" (http://gulaghistory.org /nps/onlineexhibit/stalin/work.php). And finally, all those sausage idioms really exist, and they come from The Local (https://www .thelocal.de/galleries/news/germans-eight-wurst-sausage-related -idioms/8).